CANVEY ISLAND

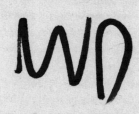

The Discovery of Chocolate

The Colour of Heaven

CANVEY ISLAND

JAMES RUNCIE

BLOOMSBURY

First published in Great Britain in 2006
This paperback edition published 2007

Copyright © 2006 by James Runcie

The moral right of the author has been asserted

Bloomsbury Publishing Plc
36 Soho Square
London W1D 3QY

www.bloomsbury.com/jamesruncie

'Gilly, Gilly Ossenfeffer' Words and music by Al Hoffman and Dick Manning © 1954
Beaver Music Publishing Corp. for the World (administered by H & B Webman & Co. Ltd)
'You're A Pink Toothbrush' Lyrics reproduced with kind permission of Dejamus Limited
© 1963 for the World
'The Bee Song' Words and music by Kenneth Blain © 1947. Reproduced by permission
of Keith Prowse Music Publishing Ltd, London WC2H 0QY
'Free of Shame/I Do What I Have To Do' Words and music by Phil Ochs © 1967
Appleseed Music Inc. and Harmony Music Ltd. Used by permission
'There But For Fortune' Words and music by Phil Ochs © 1963 Appleseed Music Inc.
and Harmony Music Ltd. Used by permission

A CIP catalogue record for this book
is available from the British Library

ISBN 9780747585831

10 9 8 7 6 5 4 3 2 1

Typeset by Hewer Text UK Ltd, Edinburgh
Printed in Great Britain by Clays Ltd, St Ives plc

All papers used by Bloomsbury Publishing are natural,
recyclable products made from wood grown in well-managed
forests. The manufacturing processes conform to the
environmental regulations of the country of origin.

For Marilyn

ONE

31st January 1953

Len

I know the fear of death is always with us but sometimes it can disappear for days. You don't think about it when your wife is coming to bed and she takes off her nightgown and you're excited by her nakedness even if you have been married for a long time. You don't think about it when your child gives you a smile that you know is meant only for you or when the sea is dead calm and you're out fishing with no one to trouble you. You don't think about death, of course you don't, it never crosses your mind, but then back it comes, far too soon, telling you not to be so cocky, don't think this is going to last, mate, this is all the happiness you're going to get and you should be grateful I didn't come before.

I should have known. I'm a fisherman. All my life I could read the sky.

I'd already decided that it would have been nasty to fish on, what with the tide rising on the full moon and a long fetch expected; but it was hard to imagine what followed. In any case everyone was in a state because of the dance. Lily was anxious and wanted to look after our boy; her sister was fossicking through her clothes wondering which dress to wear; and I was convinced we were going to be late for the bus. By the time the storm reached us we didn't have a prayer.

Violet

I don't see why I should feel guilty. My sister told me that it was all right to go to the dance without her. It wasn't as if there was going to be any hanky-panky with Len and she was never much of a party girl anyway. The little boy provided a perfect excuse to stay at home. She always said she didn't like leaving Martin alone on a Saturday night.

'Come on, girl,' I said, making a bit of an effort, 'have a drink and a dance.'

'It's all right, Vi. I've got my knitting and the wireless.'

'You need a bit of a treat, you do.'

Len came into the room, took one look at his wife and decided that there was no point trying to persuade her. 'Have you seen my cuff-links?' he said.

He liked to put them in when his shirt was laid out flat so that he didn't have to fiddle about with one hand later. But even then he kept getting them the wrong way round. He could be all thumbs, that man; which was strange given how well he could dance.

'You sure you don't mind?' I asked.

'You know what I'm like,' said Lily. 'I'd rather stay at home. Is George ready?'

'He's happy enough,' I said. 'And I've made sure he's got a blanket.'

I liked to see to my husband first so that I was free to concentrate on myself afterwards. I couldn't abide his fussing.

It was a relief when I found out that it was going to be just Len and me doing the dancing. Now Lily wasn't coming I wouldn't have to worry about getting another partner. George could sit and watch. It calmed him down, I think. It was about the only thing that did in his condition.

Afterwards people did ask if we had ever thought of staying back with Lily and the boy, but how were we to know? I'd always liked dancing and Len and I were natural partners. We waltzed with an easy sway, always moving, always light. When he led, I never had to look at my feet or worry about the steps because he gave me such confidence.

Going to the ballroom was our one chance of a bit of glamour, an escape from the cold of winter and all our anxieties about money and whether George would ever get better. I let Len take me in his arms and we floated away from everything that troubled us. Dancing can make you forget anything you like if you let it get to work. You're moving faster than the world and nothing can touch you: not war, not storm, not even death. Nothing can harm you if you keep dancing.

At least that's what I thought.

Martin

I should have said. I saw the leak in the ceiling but I knew Mum would worry if I told her. She was washing up the tea things and humming along to the wireless in the kitchen and I didn't want anything to ruin bedtime.

It was the best part of the day, the time I had my mother all to myself, when she read me a story and smiled and laughed and sang me a song. And so when I knelt at the foot of the bed, I prayed she would not notice the ceiling. I even thought that if I looked away for long enough the leak would disappear.

'What shall it be?' Mum asked when she came into the room, picking me up for a swing in her arms. 'Oh, what shall it be?' She had taken off her apron and was wearing a red cardigan, as if she had dressed up especially for me.

I tried to imagine which would be the longest song to keep her. I wanted to be snug and warm with the rain outside and my mother beside me. I wanted to fall asleep to the sound of her voice.

> *Tom, he was a piper's son,*
> *He learned to play when he was young,*
> *But all the tunes that he could play*
> *Was 'Over the hills and far away'*
> *Over the hills and a great way off,*
> *The wind shall blow my top-knot off.*

She sat down on the bed and stroked my hair. 'Close your eyes,' she said to me, 'close your eyes, my darling. Sweet dreams are coming.'

Then she kissed me on the forehead. I kept my eyes shut and felt the weight of the bed change as she rose away from me. I could hear the sound of her heels, two steps softly on the rug by the bed, and then four louder ones on the linoleum to the door. I half-opened my eyes so I could see her turn for a last look before she switched out the light. Then she gave me a little wave. I think it was her secret to keep me safe.

Perhaps if I hadn't looked then the storm wouldn't have come and we would still have been a family. Perhaps it was my fault for peeping.

Mum left the door ajar so there was still some light from the hall. She even turned the wireless down but I could hear her humming. Then I was glad I hadn't told her about the water in the ceiling. Everything changed when she was afraid.

I listened to the rain on the roof as the wind began to pick up.

When I woke up the light in the hall had gone out. Mum never turned it off because I was afraid of the dark and so I knew something must be wrong.

I tried to find my torch and put my hand down into water. At first I thought the hot-water bottle had burst or that I had wet the bed but it was too cold and there was too much of it. The floor was shining and the sea was coming in from the hall. I could hear waves outside, close against the walls and window.

I reached for my dressing gown and stood on the bed to get dressed. I had to do it one-handed because I didn't want to let go of the torch. The light made patterns on the walls, moving all the time as I tried to put on the dressing gown. Then I got down into the water and felt for my slippers. Dad never liked me coming through without them and I didn't want to make him angry.

I pointed the torch at the bedroom door and saw that it was open, blown back on its hinges. I began to wade, picking my feet up but trying to keep my slippers on. The water was almost up to my knees. I knew I had to find my parents and not be scared. Perhaps they had already left and forgotten about me. I couldn't think where I'd go, perhaps Uncle George and Auntie Vi's, but they lived miles away and we always went there by car so I didn't know how I could walk.

Then I saw Mum, dressed in her nighty, standing in the middle of the living room and staring at the water.

I shone the torch into her face. 'Mum,' I said. 'Wake up.'

She didn't seem to know who I was.

'Where's Dad?' I said.

She began to take out her curlers and let them fall into the water.

'Dancing,' she said.

I could hear the storm against the front door. 'We have to go, Mummy. We have to get out.'

She looked up at the ceiling. 'Should we go up there?'

'No, Mummy . . . the window at the back. In the kitchen.'

'I can't.'

'You must,' I said, tugging at her arm. 'We have to get out.'

I pulled her towards the window and tried to push it up but it was stuck.

'Len always meant to do something about that.'

'What are we going to do?' I said.

Mum struck at the window with the side of her arm but hit the wooden frame. 'Oh, heck . . . don't shine the torch at me, Martin . . . I need it here.'

She hit the glass with her forehead. It cracked and fell away from the centre. Then she used her elbow to push away at the edges, pulling out the bits that stuck with her fingers.

She stepped back and hit the central frame with her shoulder. The wood cracked. Mum pushed the crosspiece away so that there was enough room for us to get out. She put out her leg first, bent down and lowered herself into the water below.

'O Mary, Mother of God,' she said.

Outside everything was louder. There was wind and flood and rain; bells ringing, gates banging, police whistles, people screaming.

Mum held out her arm. 'Come on.' Blood from her forehead was trickling down into her eyes.

She had always promised that nothing bad would ever happen. 'Make it go away,' I said.

'It's all right, Martin. Shine the torch down here into the water. Get your foot out.'

'I'm frightened,' I said.

'It's only the darkness. It'll be all right.'

'I don't want to do this.'

'You must, son.' She held out her hand and helped me out of the window. 'Hold on and don't let go. The water's cold but it's not deep.'

I jumped down and the flood was up to my knees. I felt bits of wood bang into my leg. Mum took my right hand in her left and used the other to clasp to the side of the house, pushing against it for support. I could hear the creak of the outside staircase beginning to fall away.

'Into the street,' Mum shouted. 'Keep hold of the torch. The water's faster than a bus.'

I looked down and saw her hand bleeding from the broken window glass. The blood was dark, almost black, and her hands were inky blue in the torchlight.

She pulled at my arm. The water was almost up to my waist. It rushed against us, knocking us down. We were half-walking, half-swimming.

'It's no good,' Mum said, 'we must go with the tide.' We turned south towards the high street. 'O Jesus,' she said. 'O Jesus, get us out of this.'

I couldn't tell what was going to hit us next; it could be water, wood or brick. Everything was so dark.

'Get out! Get out! The flood comes,' a man was shouting. He sounded foreign.

There were green electrical flashes in the night sky. I thought I could see two dead horses. Their heads were lolling flat amidst the foam, bodies twisted away, the hair of their manes separating off in strands. I didn't know the difference between air and water but I could tell, in the sparks of light, that a bungalow across the street had been lifted from its foundations and torn away.

Then Mum's ankle gave way and she stumbled, holding on to me to save herself from going under.

'What's wrong?'

'It's all right, son, stay with me.'

She tried to move her leg but couldn't.

'Damn.'

11

She was stooping, as if she was an old woman. Then she tried to lift and turn, freeing herself from whatever lay below, but she couldn't make herself upright.

'Are you stuck?' I said.

'I don't know.'

Mum looked ahead, out into the night. 'Shine your torch into the water. Can you see anything?'

'It's too dark.'

'It must be a cattle fence.'

I put my hand down to my mother's leg. There was barbed wire. I felt it cut into my hand.

'Careful,' she said, losing her footing again. 'You'll have us over.'

Again, she tried to shake herself free. 'It's no good. We'll have to wait for help.'

'I can do it, Mum.'

I pulled at her nightgown but she overbalanced, falling sideways towards me, pushing me down so that I felt us both go under. The water bubbled up into my face.

I thought I was drowning. I knew I had to surface as quickly as I could but the current was taking me away. As I came back up I heard my mother calling, but she was no longer close. I realised I had dropped the torch.

'Get help, Martin, get help.'

I had to keep my head and body high, I had to try to let the water support me, and I swam towards the lights in the distance. Everything was noise. There were children shouting and distant sirens, but I couldn't tell where any of the sounds came from. I was going in circles through the darkness, calling my mother's name, alone in the rising flood.

I thought I heard her voice – 'Martin, where are you?' – but I couldn't trust anything I felt or heard. All I wanted was light and dryness and for everything to stop and right itself and for the world to be still again.

A piece of driftwood bumped against my shoulder. If I could half-stride, half-swim then I could survive, but I found myself underwater and out of my depth.

A group of coffins floated towards me and I wondered if I was dreaming my own funeral. I prayed in my head, *O Jesus, save me,* and heard the prayer echo back in my mother's voice. Then I heard something else, not my mother, a man shouting through the darkness, urging me to take hold, telling me to use the wood as a float that would carry me to the end of the floodwater. I found an edge and a lid, and held a coffin sideways to my chest.

The wind cut into my lips. I could feel them cracking. I thought perhaps I could rest for a while against the wood. I stopped trying to swim and held on, not knowing whether I was heading out to sea or back towards the marshes and the railway line. The nearest objects were hidden by spray, and everything was covered in the smoke of fog, foam and water. I closed my eyes and thought of fields, horses and daylight.

I tried to imagine summer: on Dad's shoulders, Mum taking our photograph.

I pushed the coffin forwards, fending off everything around me: glass and doors from porches and garden sheds, old tyres, bits of wood and metal. I thought I could see an 'Old Bill' carnival head bouncing on the water by a stone rum jar. Nearby, a pig was shrieking, caught in a mass of debris. I let go of the coffin and turned on to my back, kicking hard, away from the danger, following the current. There were no lights in the buildings and the flood took me on, further inland.

I thought of my mother, still trapped, and of my father, still dancing.

My arms ached, and I wanted to sleep, but then I saw the outline of a group of houses in Point Road, and Ivy's sweet shop where Dad always bought the papers. I realised I was near Leigh Beck School. I could just make out shadowy figures moving quickly, carrying what looked like rugs, carpets and linen, even battered suitcases, as if they had a train to catch or were waiting for a ferry through the flood.

I felt my left foot scrape against the ground. The tide was on the ebb and the water had lost its force. I could make out the torches of a family in the distance: a man with a girl on his shoulders, a woman with blankets and a baby.

I lowered my arm on to the road and felt the hard wet surface. Then I tried to stand.

The man shouted, 'Come on, son. You're nearly there.'

Scattered groups of people were making their way to a shelter lit by a car headlamp. The engine had been left running to show them where to go. They slid through the mud, the men with their hats, the women holding their skirts up against their waists, following the light. By the side of the road were ridges of salt from the water and a slew of chicken carcasses. An elderly woman in a dressing gown held a dog in her arms, a white poodle with bloodshot eyes, its body smeared with mud. Her husband carried a parcel of wet blankets tied with string. I could see another dog roosting in an apple tree and a woman rowing a dinghy with a pair of crutches.

'Are you coming?' the man asked.

'My mum,' I said.

'What about her?'

'She's stuck.'

'She'll be all right. The police are out. And the fire brigade. Loads of people to help, don't you worry.'

'I have to find her.'

'You can't go back there. Come into the school.'

'Someone has to help her.'

Then the man said, 'You're Lenny Turner's boy. He can't be out in this. Where is he?'

'He went dancing.'

'And left you alone? Couldn't he tell?'

'I don't know.'

'Are you all right?' he asked.

'No,' I said.

'Come with us,' said the man's wife. 'We'll look after you.'

A woman was pulling a drowned pig down the street. I wondered if she was going to roast it.

The shelter didn't look anything like school. The playground was filled with washed-up furniture. Survivors were brought on inflated rubber rafts, tin baths, skiffs and prams. A coil of rope led from the edges of the flood to the doorway. I looked at the faces of the people coming in. They were old and afraid.

I thought of my mother and prayed that she was inside. I tried to imagine her smile and the sound of her voice: *There you are, Martin. Come here. It's all right. It's over now.*

Perhaps we would be together again after all and my father would return from the dance, his hair slicked and his shoes polished. He would take us back to a home that would be exactly as it was when he had left it, a home where no flood had ever come, and my mother would kiss me again and for ever.

The step into the school had been covered with newspaper to stop people slipping. One man sat in a corner looking through a damp photograph album with his son. It was a boy from school, Ade. We played football together. He looked up but neither of us knew what to say. I don't think anybody did. Everyone was doing things so they didn't have to talk. Another man was carrying a kettle and two mugs, uncertain where, even in the middle of the flooding, he could find clean water. The others stood drinking tea: half-ghosts, staring out into the darkness.

Then a woman with a kind voice came and told me to get out of my wet pyjamas. 'You'll catch your death,' she said and handed me a towel that made me feel as if I'd just come out of the swimming pool. Then she gave me an army blanket and a pair of plimsolls and told me to get warm by the fire while she tried to find clothes in my size.

I could see a woman leaning forward on a chair. 'My home, my home, everything I love. All that I have is there. Take me back. Please, someone, take me back.' The straps on her shoes were broken and they left raw marks where they had been buckled.

I went over to the fire but I couldn't see anyone I knew. There was no one apart from a thin girl sitting with her knees together and her feet apart. It was Linda from the sweet shop, Ivy's daughter, but we had never spoken and I didn't want to go up to her. She had a red dress and a white band in her hair. Someone had given her colouring crayons and she was drawing. When she looked up, she put her arm round the work as if she thought I was copying.

Then there was another woman standing at the far side of the room. The light was behind her and I couldn't see her face but I recognised the dark-red ball-gown and the gloves up to the elbows.

'Martin?' she asked.

It was Auntie Vi.

Violet

We were singing 'Ten Green Bottles' on the way home but the bus broke down and we all stopped. I think that's when people began to worry because it was a filthy night and we couldn't get any further than the bridge. The driver was swearing and telling us that it was our fault for taking so long to get away from the dance. Len set off home straight away because he was worried about Lily and the boy but George and I stayed by the shelter.

'No point going any further than this,' said a policeman and I agreed. I didn't want my dress getting splattered: taffeta, it was, and strapless. You don't get that in Canvey. And we were all so cold. I knew I should have worn thicker stockings, it was stupid of me not to, but I'd planned to be indoors and I never liked dancing with hot legs.

At the shelter I saw Martin. He had a towel round his waist and was shivering in a blanket. 'Where's your mother?' I said. 'And your father? He was searching for you both. Didn't he find you?'

The boy looked at me as if I was the one who was supposed to know. 'No,' he said.

A woman came and gave him some P.E. kit and an old school coat. 'Here,' she said, 'try these.'

At the far side of the room, George was already on the shakes, rocking away, shivering and stammering, muttering the names of men he had fought with. 'Oh, so cold,' he kept saying, 'can't go down there, no, no, can't go down there.'

He had been a handsome man had my husband, everyone said so, kissed the girls and made them cry, but he had lost all his confidence in the war. His cheeks had sunk and his eyes had begun to scare people. Now he looked a bit like some great daft bird, his head turning in quick movements without ever taking anything in, and he kept muttering things that I couldn't always understand: *tracer, incendiary, tracer, armour piercing.*

It was five in the morning.

'Oh, where have they gone?' I said.

'Mum,' said Martin, 'she was stuck.'

'Where?'

'Near the house. Has Dad gone to fetch her?'

'Of course he has.'

'But why is he taking so long?'

'I'm sure they'll be here soon. You get changed now.'

I gave Martin a rub with the blanket and then handed him the shirt and shorts. He could have done with a vest but there were so many people in need around us and beggars can't be choosers.

'What about you?' I asked. 'What happened to you?'

'It was dark,' he said. 'I couldn't see. Will Mum be all right?'

I ruffled his hair to try and cheer him up. 'Of course she will. Let's have a cup of tea. There's a woman with an urn. I saw her when I came in.'

'I don't like tea.'

'Well, you can fetch me one,' I said, 'there's a good boy.'

George asked me what was going on and said he wanted to go for a walk. God knows why, but I could hardly stop him.

All that waiting was getting on my nerves. Where were they all?

George

Dirty night. Had to send out an SXX. Water rising, ship listing, gangway blown to hell. No tin hat for me. I was sick with the rolling and shivering like blazes. Had to get a brew on to calm us down. Ask men to find blankets for the survivors. Requested assistance to get them off the bridge floor. Hoped for a mine-sweeper.

Hid in the wheelhouse for a bit until things got quieter. Kept away from the trouble. So cold, I started to rattle. Thought I'd better have a walk about. Assess the situation. See what was required and if I could be of assistance. Get the ship on an even keel and head for home.

But then I saw these kids. What the hell were they doing on the ship? A woman was trying to cheer them up and they were singing:

> *Oh, what a glorious thing to be*
> *A healthy grown-up busy, busy bee*
> *Whiling away the passing hours*
> *Pinching all the pollen from the cauliflow'rs.*

The children looked too tired for playtime. I told them they should get out. This was no place for a bunch of kiddies. But people said I should leave them alone. They didn't know where their parents were. Perhaps we were taking them somewhere. Evacuees. That must have been it. But what a night. Two enemies. Gerry and the weather. Could do with some whale oil. Makes you smell of fish but keeps the cold out.

Soon be home, though. Have a bit of a dance with Vi and that nice sister of hers: Lily, the shy one. I always liked her. I wondered where she'd gone.

Martin

I found their names on the blackboard. Missing. Len Turner. Lily Turner.

Women came looking for their husbands, children for their parents, but none of them were Mum or Dad. I stood by the door, checking the face of every person that came in.

A man with sweat and water on his stubble said he'd rescued a couple from the roof of their house. They had been holding on to the chimney with a sheet tied round it. The storm had dashed the husband's foot against the metal gutter until there was nothing left but bone; but still he held on to his wife.

Auntie Vi started talking to a man in an old raincoat, a dock porter who had tried to bail out his house with a two-gallon pail. He was drying out a pound note on the radiator.

'It's all I've got left, love.'

He had thick oatmeal socks but no shoes. He padded away to the nearest chair and sat down. Then he rolled a cigarette.

The woman by the urn was telling the schoolteacher: 'Hitler didn't get me in the war and Father Thames won't get me this time. I may have been bombed out but I'll never be washed out.'

Some of the other children were playing Clap Hands but I didn't want to join in.

Then I heard a voice calling to my aunt.

He wasn't wearing a jacket, just his shirt and braces, and he'd pushed up his sleeves so you could see the tattoos on his arms: the boat and the anchor, the mermaid's tail with the word 'Lily'.

His trousers were wet from the knee down. He had rolled them up to get out of the water and I could see the cuts to his white shins above the ripped socks. There was even a bruise that had begun to yellow. He looked smaller, his hair was flat and thin, and his skin was paler than I had ever seen it.

For the first time I wished he wasn't my father.

Len

At first, I didn't know what everyone was asking. There were people shuffling all around us and I couldn't understand how none of them had been told. I thought everyone would have known. Vi said things like 'Where have you been?' and 'What has happened?' Martin asked, 'Have you seen Mum?'

'Where's George?' I said. 'Is George all right?'

'Never mind about George,' said Vi.

'Where is he?' I asked.

'He went for a walk.'

'A walk?' I said. 'In this?'

'What happened, Dad?'

'Where's Lily?' Vi asked but she said it so quickly I hardly had time to think of an answer. They weren't listening to me that well.

'I found her.'

'Thank God.'

Perhaps if I said nothing I could undo it all, I could go back to when we were getting ready to go dancing, when we were a family and were happy. If I said it aloud then it would have to be true.

Vi gave me a cup of tea but I didn't know what to do with it. I only knew that I had come to the place where I had to tell my story and I didn't want to tell it.

'I think she was breathing,' I said. 'They couldn't be sure even though they felt for a pulse. I thought I heard Lily say something but it must have been the wind. The waters had gone down, and she had either fallen or she had been too tired to go further. Either way, I could see the strength had left her.

'Her clothes were torn, and she was wearing her nightdress, the one with the rose petals round the neck – you gave it to her, Vi – and there was blood on her forehead and elbow but it didn't look like blood. It was dark in the centre and yet the ridges to the wounds were almost pink and her lips were a blue I'd never seen before. And her skin was so white. You could almost see through it.

'She was so cold but the doctor who was with me swore that she might still be alive. He said, "No one is dead until warm and dead."

'So we lifted her into the ambulance and covered her with blankets. I started rubbing her arms and her legs, and then I began to pump at her heart to get it going again. The ambulance man told me to stop and give her the kiss of life. I didn't understand what to do so he showed me. I hated him touching her, his breathing into her mouth.

'She was beautiful, Vi; she was so beautiful.

'Then he let me try and I found that I was blowing into Lily's mouth, but her lips were thin and hard and cold, and it didn't feel right, I was embarrassed, people shouldn't have been looking. I wanted everyone to go away and leave me so I could help her properly. I didn't like being watched, blowing into the mouth and pressing on the chest of a woman I couldn't believe was my wife any more.

'Then the man told me to stop. "Enough," I think he said, but he was so quiet, "that's enough, Mr Turner."

'He had been feeling for her pulse. Now he leant against her chest. When he did so I took her hand. It felt a bit warmer, and I thought she must have been coming back to life, and that there was hope. But the man said, "I'm sorry, Mr Turner." That was all. He didn't say dead or anything.

'Then he said he wasn't sure if we had done the right thing in moving her. Perhaps we had made her warm too quickly. Perhaps we had tried too hard and taken it all too fast. How can you try your best and make a mistake by doing it like that? I did what he said. I did everything he said. All I wanted was for my wife to live, for us to be together. I took off my jacket and put it over her. How can I have done too much or tried too hard?

'The man from the ambulance kept on talking like it was his wife that had died, not mine. He kept babbling on, talking so much that

I wanted to punch him. He said that if we had made her warm where she was instead of moving her then we might have had a better chance. But the road was cold and wet. There were other people and there were the cars. What were we supposed to do?'

Vi began to cry, her whole body shaking, except it wasn't so much crying as something I had never heard before. She was weeping with everything: her shoulders, her chest and her legs, her whole body twitching.

But Martin didn't move. 'Go on, Dad,' he said.

I stared forward, speaking into the space ahead of me because I didn't want to see either of them listening.

'Then other men came,' I said. 'And some women. They asked me if I wanted a cup of tea. It would help, they thought. "Well," I said, "a cup of tea isn't going to make much difference."

' "Can't do any harm."

' "Haven't you done enough?" I said.

'And then I felt ashamed I'd said that. It wasn't their fault, but I wanted to be on my own with Lily, say sorry to the girl, you understand. I didn't want posh women with cups of tea telling me I'd be all right soon enough.'

Martin

Dad put his hand on my knee. 'You're just a boy.'

'Where is she?' Auntie Vi asked.

Dad didn't answer. He didn't even look at her. Then he took out a cigarette. He felt for his matches but stopped. Everything he had was wet.

'I'm sorry, son. There was nothing I could do. Nothing. It was too late; too terrible. Life is such a mess. It's one bloody bastard of a mess.'

'I want to see her,' I said.

Dad held his cigarette as if there was something wrong with it. He couldn't understand how it would not dry out or why he could not light it.

'I'm not sure if that's right,' he said.

'I don't want to be here.'

Then Auntie Vi said, 'Let him come.'

'I don't know,' said Dad. 'I don't know anything.'

We walked down towards the first-aid centre. A man was putting slates and chimney pots into a wheelbarrow. Across the fields, I could see corn and haystacks shattered. A cowman was crying. He was crouching down with dead cows all around him. For a moment, I thought the pools of water were all the tears he had shed.

A police klaxon sounded and I could see its headlamps through the fog. When we got to Jones's stores in Long Road I saw they'd put a placard on the stuffed animal outside: 'Bear up. Canvey will rise again.'

The first-aid-centre men were smoking, stamping their feet in the cold, trying not to look at us. There was a sign beside them lying in the road. *Straight On for the Sea.*

'Don't ask us,' their eyes said. 'Don't make us tell you what's happened. It's nothing to do with us.'

Auntie Vi wiped her feet on the doormat but it was covered in so much mud that it stuck to her shoes and we had to wait while she scraped both in turn on the step. I hoped she would take longer because if she did then we wouldn't have to go in. There was still time. Something might happen that would change everything. Perhaps they'd identified the wrong body. Perhaps it had been a mistake.

I could see a trolley in the centre of the room with a sheet over it.

'You ready?' Dad asked.

Auntie Vi nodded.

There was a man dressed in a green coat and I realised he was the only dry person I had seen that night. He had a sad face with wrinkles. I wanted to look at him rather than the trolley. He pulled back the sheet.

'Oh, Lily,' said Auntie Vi.

Mum was a kind of creamy yellow I'd never seen before. At first I was almost relieved, thinking that the woman in front of me could not be her. There was a smell of stale perfume that reminded me of the time she had last been ill, the Sunday Dad had ruined the dinner. I remembered being frightened that she would never get better; that she would be ill in bed for ever, or that she might die and leave me alone and there would be nothing I could do to stop it.

'It's all right, son, it's all right,' my father was saying.

I don't think I had ever seen Mum asleep. She was always up first, or it was dark, or she was propped up in bed with pillows. She didn't look real or like my mother or anyone I had ever seen before. 'Wake up, Mummy,' I said.

Auntie Vi was staring. 'There's hardly a mark.'

I touched Mum's hand. It felt cold, like metal. She was colder than the air, the coldest thing in the room.

Violet

The next day we were taken by bus to a Southend hotel that must have been glad of the business. I'd never normally have stayed in such a place but we didn't have a choice. Martin shared a twin room with his father and George and I took the double next door. We had our meals early, at five o'clock to suit the landlady, until we persuaded her to put on separate sittings for the children. Then we could send Martin off with the other kids, eat later and have a few drinks on our own. It was nice to get a break from the boy. Most times, he looked at me as if he thought I was in some way responsible for Lily's death. Perhaps he had wanted me to die instead of his mother; but then at other times he came over all soppy and I knew I had to take her place.

Len kept going on and on about money and fishing, death and the flood, and then after a few drinks he would suddenly start laughing, a great shuntering train-like laugh that he could not stop, *aha-aha-aha aha-aha-aha*, until sometimes it turned into weeping. Gallows humour, I suppose.

'I should have known, Vi,' he said. 'I've always been good with the weather. If we'd come back sooner we might have saved her. If the bus hadn't taken so long, if George hadn't needed the toilet, if we hadn't gone in the first place . . . even then I could have got to her in time.'

I wanted to say to everyone, look, she was my sister as well as your wife and your mother, but it never was my turn to grieve.

As we drank Len started to blame other people. 'It was that ambulance man. Telling me to move her and get her in the van. I

27

didn't know what was going on, Vi; nobody knew what they were doing.'

I tried to calm him down. 'It was the flood, Len, an act of God, no one could do anything about it.'

'No, Vi. God helps those who help themselves. We should have done more.'

'But what, Len, what?'

I had to judge his moods and sometimes we had to wait until I'd got George settled and asleep before we could talk properly.

'Perhaps we killed her, Vi,' he said, 'perhaps we made it worse by going out and the world stopped and it's our fault and I've got to live with this and I'm not sure I ever will.'

'I'll look after you,' I said. 'I'm here.'

The only way I could manage was to think my sister was still alive and that none of this had ever happened.

Martin

I said my prayers in the hotel as Mum would have wanted but I couldn't see the point when she wasn't with us.

> *Now I lay me down to sleep*
> *I pray the Lord my soul to keep . . .*

I tried to imagine Mum singing, kissing me on the forehead and walking backwards out of the room. Six steps: two on the rug and four on the lino. Then the last look and the wave. I could still see her through half-closed eyes, keeping the door slightly ajar, leaving the light on in the hall.

> *And if I die before I wake*
> *I pray the Lord my soul to take.*

I could hear people in the corridors, talking about how the flood had happened and wondering why no one had been warned. If they knew in Norfolk and in Suffolk that a storm would rip through their lives in a few hours, then why had there been no mention of it in Canvey?

> *At least in the war we knew the enemy . . . you heard about Ivy's little*
> *girl? They thought Linda was lost and yet she was sitting there, drawing*
> *away as if it had nothing to do with her . . . what about the boy? Don't*
> *worry about him: he'll be all right . . .*

I wanted to wait until the sounds of the night had gone: the toilet flushing, doors opening and closing, the pull-cord on the bathroom light, on and off, off and on, the front door bolted, the last rattle of the pipes. I tried to identify each noise and every footstep: Uncle George's shuffle, Dad's cough, Auntie Vi's heels.

Dad came into the bedroom, pulled back the sheets and sighed as soon as he lay down. Sometimes he would nod off in his clothes. He turned away from the light and on to his side and then fell asleep without washing or cleaning his teeth. I didn't mind. I just didn't want him to snore. I didn't want there to be any noise at all, only the silence of the night when everyone had stopped. I thought that if everything was quiet then I might see Mum again. She would come and no one else would know.

In the following weeks, there were fifty-three funerals. I stood by the graveyard of St Katherine's Church and watched; counting the numbers attending, looking at the long dark cars. *Your forces come against me, wave upon wave. If he holds back the waters, there is drought; if he lets them loose they devastate the land.*

I thought my mother's funeral would be the same, but when the time came it felt odd to be sitting by my father with the hearse in front of us. I thought I'd still be by the church wall and watching.

Auntie Vi was in the vehicle behind with George and her mother, and two further cars carried my father's relatives: Roger and Doreen, Tracy, Mark and 'Mad Nan'. She had given me a small posy of snowdrops and primroses that I tried to hide because I thought it made me look like a girl.

It had started to snow. The flakes were over the windscreen and the wipers were pushing back so heavily that the car hardly moved. 'Mother Carey is plucking her goose,' said the driver.

I wore a suit that Auntie Vi had got from the charity packages sent to the island. The sleeves of the jacket were long and the trousers too short but she said I would look handsome if I made a bit of an effort. That was hard because the trousers itched and rubbed at my legs and in order to stop it I had to wear my pyjamas underneath. That helped with the scratchiness but they kept making me remember the night of the flood.

We sat in the church with the coffin right in front of us. I couldn't understand why everyone thought it was all right for us to be so close.

'Is she is there?' I asked.

'Yes, son, but it's not really her.'

'Then who is it? How can you tell?'

'Don't worry,' said Auntie Vi, but she wasn't concentrating because she was checking her face in the little mirror she always carried. 'She's in a better place.'

She muttered that the church smelt of stale linen. She said that the vestments must have been ironed while they were wet rather than damp. I looked at the holes made by the woodworm in the pew. Then I knelt down and tried to pray.

I tried to imagine Mum was not there in the coffin and that she had not died. I talked to her as I always did, sometimes out loud, because if I prayed hard enough perhaps she would come back and be with me. She would live with me in my head. I would keep her safe.

We stood up to sing 'Eternal Father, strong to save'. Then the priest said some prayers and talked about what had happened. 'The sea-sorrow of an island,' he called it. He said that it had been a tragedy but that even then there could be hope. He told us that the everlasting love of God would never let anyone down; it was a love that was always open to those who sought it and trusted in it. Then he asked us to sit down.

'We talk of dust to dust and ashes to ashes, but we are also water to water. We came from the sea and to the sea we must return. This is our life and we are at one with the sea.'

He told the story of Jonah and the whale and the choir sang an anthem: 'Many waters cannot quench love'.

I couldn't understand some of the words in the service. 'Man that is born of a woman hath but a short time to live . . .' (*Did that mean me? How long would I live for?*) '. . . and is full of misery.' *Is this life then?* I thought. *Is this what it means, that it will never get better?*

'He cometh up, and is cut down, like a flower; he fleeth as it were a shadow . . .' I remembered the rising waters '. . . and never continueth in one stay . . .' and returning to find my mother gone.

Dad stared ahead, gripping on to the pew like he might fall over if he didn't. The veins on the back of his left hand showed up as if they were rivers. I knew I wasn't supposed to cry even though Auntie Vi lifted her veil and began to sniff. Uncle George was swaying beside her. He mumbled to himself and his eyes kept tightening, blinking and squeezing in. He kept swatting away at a wasp no one else could see and Auntie Vi tried to pretend she wasn't with him. Then the priest started talking about Mum's 'vile body'.

I could still see the fear on her face, the wet hair swept back, the cheekbones sinking in, her nightdress wet. Even then she was beautiful. I tried to stop thinking about it and remember happy times, her singing to me before bedtime, *Doctor Foster went to Gloucester in a shower of rain . . .*

She bounced me up and down and we laughed and I hoped it would never stop.

He stepped in a puddle right up to his middle and never went there again.

'Again!' I shouted, and together we sang it repeatedly until Mum began to lose her voice and looked tired and said that it was time to kiss me goodnight.

Outside in the graveyard it was still snowing. Dad gave me a card and asked me to take the number-four cord with my uncle. I was scared because he was shaking already. I didn't want to do the job and look after my uncle at the same time. But the men had started to gather round and I could see that it would be embarrassing if I said no. I heard Auntie Vi say that it was only right.

I stepped forward, knelt down and took the lower part of the cord, leaving the top for Uncle George. He crowded in close beside me and put his hands over mine so tightly that I could hardly feel the cord and was frightened of letting go. I didn't want us to start dropping the coffin. Then the woods were pulled back and there was the heaviness as we took the weight. No one had given me any gloves and I felt Uncle George stumble and the rope slip. It reminded me of the barbed wire cutting through my hands on the night of the flood. The rope razed against the wound, and for a minute I thought I was going to fall down into the grave.

I leant back and the coffin wobbled.

'Hold steady,' my father shouted. He looked worried, like it was my fault, even when he must have known that it wasn't.

I didn't want to be there, I didn't want to be anywhere; I would rather have been dead with my mother in her coffin where no one could touch us.

The earth was flinty grey, still clogged with the flood. The priest said prayers and passed a bowl of earth. We took handfuls: Dad, Auntie Vi, Uncle George and me.

'Not too much, Martin,' said Auntie Vi. 'Leave enough for us.'

I couldn't see much point in gathering earth from the grave and then throwing it back down again. I didn't want it to fall on the coffin.

I thought what might have happened if I had told Mum about the water in the ceiling; if I had held on to her when we went underwater; if I had managed to swim in another direction and reached my father sooner; and then *if I had not been born.*

If I had never been born then Mum would have gone out dancing and she would still be alive and my father would be happy instead of standing in a graveyard.

Everyone stood in silence, above and around the coffin, until the first person moved to signal that it was over. I think it was Dad. He didn't want to be there any longer and his friends began to follow straight away.

But I waited for the gravedigger to pile the earth back. That was his job because our handfuls of mud hadn't done anything. I wanted to see how long it took to fill up a grave and whether I could stop the final covering. It was the last chance to get Mum out. The gravedigger was a small old man and he gave me a smile. There were just the two of us. I couldn't understand why everyone else had gone away so quickly.

Then Dad came back from the cars with an umbrella. I kept my eyes on the spade, the earth and the coffin. Dad waited by my side for a bit but then he put his arm on my shoulder and turned me round, so that I was looking the other way. I could see the inside of the umbrella, snow falling towards us, and smoke round the engine of one of the cars. One of the drivers dropped a cigarette and put it out with his foot. Dad took my hand. I couldn't remember the last time he'd done that. It had always been Mum before.

Back at the hotel Auntie Vi changed into a different dress that showed her arms and she asked me to hand round a plate of cocktail sausages. It would give me something to do, she said; it would stop me getting what she called *maudlin*.

Then the adults ate and drank and laughed with their mouths full of egg or fishpaste sandwiches. They gulped back sherry and bottles of Newcastle Brown and finished off the meal with Libby's fruit salad and Carnation milk. The room filled with smoke and chatter; the laughter of people with large mouths and food stuck to their teeth, men with crumbs on their ties and women who said they had to sit down. They were too tall and too fat, I thought, and they were too happy. They were people who had forgotten Mum already.

TWO

Violet

It took six weeks to get the island back to normal; there were flooded buildings with walls collapsed and the roofs off, farms drenched with salt water, people with nothing to wear. The Mayor of London set up a National Flood and Tempest Distress Fund. The Army and the Navy were mobilised, and the Queen Mother made a royal visit with Princess Margaret.

We helped sort through the paper parcels in the gym hall; clothes for Canvey that no one needed or wanted. I rummaged through faded utility suits from the war, scuffed ankle-strap sandals and tired perli-knit jumpers. Most of it was rubbish, of course, things nobody had wanted in the first place. Who in their right mind would send their best clothes to Canvey? But I did find a pair of women's slacks, loose-pleated at the waist and creased down the front, that I hoped might make me look like Katharine Hepburn.

I had this funny dream that we only had to go back to the house and we'd find Lily cooking in the kitchen with the wireless on just as we'd left her. But when we did return it looked like no one had ever lived there at all. The woodwork was swollen, the locks had gone and there was mould all over the walls.

Len told us he would have to start again. 'With everything.'

He had built the house himself, a bungalow with an attic and an outside staircase in the Newlands area by the Sunken Marsh. There was even a little wooden bridge crossing the dyke from the sea wall. He had bought it pre-fab at a time when the island was raising money by selling land at ten pound a plot. The house had been erected and decorated in a month, a simple family home with two bedrooms, a lounge, a kitchenette and a new tiled fireplace. Len thought that he had seen his family right.

Now he looked at the ruined wallpaper and the water-damaged furniture: the sodden settee, the warped table and chairs broken by flood. I told him he should have a good clear-out, light the fire and leave the windows open to get rid of the smell of damp.

'Such a waste of money, Vi,' he grumbled. 'You can feel the heat going out the window.'

'It's the only way,' I said.

I began to clean the house, disinfecting the surfaces with Zal.

Len folded his wife's clothes into piles on the bed. I could see that he was getting upset.

'I'll do that for you,' I said.

'She's still here. I can feel her.'

I ironed Lily's dresses and put them back in her wardrobe. Later that night I found one of her scarves under Martin's pillow. I think he wanted the smell of his mother, the soap and the talcum powder, the scent of Evening in Paris. When he thought no one was looking he carried it round and hugged it. I should have stopped him but I didn't have the heart.

I asked him to help with the meals so he'd have something to do rather than mope around the place getting in my way. I couldn't cook like Lily but I did my best. When we didn't have fish we had corned-beef croquettes, sausage pancakes and brisket roundabout.

One day I asked Martin to start mincing the leftovers from the Sunday roast for a shepherd's pie but he made a right mess of it. The mincer wasn't secure to the edge of the table and it kept slipping away and falling on to the floor. Neither of us could screw the nuts tight enough, and when the mincer came off it banged into Martin's hand and cut his knuckles.

Len was reading the paper and trying to ignore us but when it happened a third time he lost his temper.

'For God's sake. Let me do it. I never can get any peace in this house.'

Blood from Martin's knuckles was dripping on to the remaining pink of the meat. 'I can't help it, Dad . . .'

'Get your fingers away. Can't you do anything?'

'He's a child, Len, a child.'

'You're just as bad. Couldn't you see it was going to fall off?'

'Well, thank you very much,' I said. 'You can make your own dinner.'

I took off Lily's apron and went over to the sink to wash my hands.

'No, Vi, stop.'

'I know when I'm not wanted . . .'

'You are wanted, Vi. You know that . . .'

'Don't think you can sweet-talk your way out of it now. I know you, Len Turner . . .'

He came round behind me and put his arms round my waist. 'Always want you, Vi . . .'

'Stop that. Not in front of the boy.'

I could see Martin staring at us all judgemental and he didn't look away at all. I think he was waiting for us to stop and get back to the cooking.

'Go on, Martin,' I said. 'Have a play outside.'

'It's cold.'

'You always say that. You need a bit of air. Have a kick about with the football. Imagine you're at White Hart Lane.'

'You play with me, Dad.'

'I've just got in, son. Just kick it against the wall. But don't make too much noise about it . . .'

Martin stopped staring and went out into the corridor. It wasn't easy living in that house but I knew Len needed me. I just had to be patient. I would do my best and, if that wasn't enough, I'd retire gracefully and let other women do the cooking and the housework. After all, there were plenty of volunteers. I wasn't the only lady in Len's life.

Martin

The house filled with women who were not my mother. They came to boil up potatoes, fry cod in batter and bake jam roly-poly. They chopped carrots, rolled out suet and whipped up milk jellies as Dad sat down to his *Daily Express* and milky tea.

I watched the women measuring out flour on the scales, pouring it into the pale-yellow mixing bowl, asking me to pass the sifter or the egg beater, and I wished they would go away so that I could close my eyes and open them to see Mum back home again.

Ivy came from the sweet shop with her daughter Linda. She was a girl so we couldn't really play. Her mother had varicose veins that showed through her stockings. She brought a box of biscuits and a Victoria sponge. I had only ever seen her eat cake.

The sounds the women made were never the same as Mum's. They beat the eggs too slowly; they sifted the flour without singing to themselves. They lacked my mother's way with batter, dough and pastry. I sat in my room reading the *Eagle*, wondering when people would stop pretending to be kind to me.

When I did go out I went to look at the breaches in the sea wall and tried to work out how and why the flood had happened. I wanted to check if anyone could have done anything to stop it. I looked at the water surging up and hitting the cliff.

In the beach café a woman was selling sprats, crayfish tails and rollmops on the cheap. She gave me a cup of Bovril and I sat on a bit of sea wall even though it was cold and wet. She told me to look out at the rocks. If they shone, or stood up in the water, it was a sure sign of another easterly gale.

I watched a relay of soldiers pass sandbags down the line like they were barrels of beer. One of them was singing 'Gilly Gilly Ossenfeffer Katzenellen Bogen by the Sea'. The other men joined in as they worked. I couldn't understand why they were singing a children's song:

> *In a tiny house*
> IN A TINY HOUSE
> *By a tiny stream*
> BY A TINY STREAM
> *Where a lovely lass*
> WHERE A LOVELY LASS
> *Had a lovely dream*
> HAD A LOVELY DREAM.

When I closed my eyes the gulls overhead were birds of prey and the strands of seaweed were poisonous snakes wanting to sting or strangle me. A coil of abandoned rope on the beach had become a hangman's noose. And then, at the end of the dream, I could see a high wall of sea unfurling towards me, held at breaking point, as if it was waiting for me to realise that I could do nothing to escape it.

Violet

That Christmas Martin helped me with the mistletoe and the decorations while my husband sang songs to himself. Sometimes George would utter phrases that no one quite picked up. *I know what's right, all right . . . you put your right leg in, that's what you do . . . oh hokey cokey . . . all present and correct . . . . I wouldn't quite say that, my dear . . . where are the ratings?*

He had been on the Arctic convoy taking gunpowder out to the Russians at Murmansk. Convoy PQ13. He was the gunnery officer. They gave him ten pound extra: danger money, they called it. The Germans hit them first with a torpedo and then again from the air. The ship caught fire. Everyone said he must be dead.

'He's not quite the same,' they said to me when they brought him back. Well, that was a bit of an understatement. He was completely harpic.

I never could get used to it. He looked so different with his hair prematurely grey and those sunken stubbly cheeks. Before the war George had smooth flesh and he'd been proud of his shaving, you never saw any five o'clock shadow on him, but now his skin had gone thin and bluish and hairy. And then when you did try and engage him in a bit of conversation he had such a distant expression you felt almost stupid, as if you'd made a mistake and were talking to the wrong person.

I wanted to tell those Navy boys: 'Look. This isn't my husband. This isn't the man I thought was dead, the man I married and loved. This is someone pretending to be him, someone who's horrible, someone who thinks I'll be fooled.'

But I could see that it was George even if I didn't want to admit it. When he smiled or laughed, I almost thought he might get better and come out of it, but he always sank back. And his nerves kept changing. One day he couldn't concentrate on anything and the next he'd be obsessed with tiny details, washing his hands, wanting to be clean, hating any sign of mud or dirt.

On Christmas Eve Len sang sea shanties on the squeeze-box as I wrapped up presents for the stocking at the bottom of Martin's bed: a little wooden boat, Fry's Five Boys chocolate, a tin whistle, a cardboard kaleidoscope and a tangerine covered in foil at the toe. George hummed out of tune, staring into the distance, remembering the shanties called by line and shout, haul and stamp:

> Here's to the grog, boys, the jolly, jolly grog
> Here's to the rum and tobacco
> I've a-spent all my tin with the lassies drinking gin
> And to cross the briny ocean I must wander.

On Christmas morning, Len gave his son an orange kite he'd got from the Army Surplus that was also a kind of radio receiver. George and I had bought a set of Meccano because Martin was always making things.

Meccano is the key to a happy boyhood, it said on the box. Martin made models of bridges and dams and tested them in the bathroom, stopping the water reaching one side of the basin and watching it rise and tip over.

Len gave me a bottle of Shalimar. 'Give us a cuddle, love,' I said.

He told me not to be silly, which made him a bit of a spoilsport because I'm sure nobody would have minded. George wasn't in a position to care much about anything and the boy was busy with his Meccano.

Len read out the quiz from the paper: 'What did my true love send on the first day of Christmas, what did the third little pig have to eat, what did the girls do when Georgie Porgie kissed them and with what was the ship a-sailing laden? Come on, Martin, don't sulk.'

'I feel sick.'

'Well, best get it over with then,' I said. I never did like a sickly child.

At the end of the meal, I fetched the cherry brandy. Len was resting his fingers on the edge of the table; he was always eager for the next thing. Then he leant back and belched.

'*Pardonnez moi!*' he said, thinking it the funniest thing he had ever done.

I poured the brandy and Len got out a cigar but as soon as he started to light it George turned his face away and put his head in his hands, hiding from the flame.

'I should have realised . . .' Len said. 'Stupid of me. Stupid.'

'Never mind,' I said, but he was right. It was a bit silly because we all knew how George was about fire.

Len banged on the table. 'Come on then, let's have another song.'

> *Windy old weather, boys, stormy old weather*
> *When the wind blows we'll all go together . . .*

Martin had given George a box of coloured pencils for Christmas and he started to examine them. He took each one out in turn, studying the colours. Then he separated three from the rest: Chinese white, poppy red, navy blue. England expects. He stretched out his arm, waved it up and down, and snapped his fingers.

'He wants paper,' I said.

Martin fetched a pad and watched his uncle draw, shading the sky and then the sea. When he had finished, George took a black pencil and started to make small dark marks at the bottom of the page, first horizontal, then vertical, stick men and crosses piled on top of each other, hatch-marked bodies that almost ripped through the paper, lying at the bottom of the ocean.

'That's nice, dear,' I said. 'That's nice.'

Then he started to shake. What a way to spend Christmas.

I went over and found some music on the wireless. It was playing 'Someone to Watch Over Me', which only made it worse because that had been one of our favourites.

George sat in his chair by the two-bar fire and rocked slowly, weeping for the man he once was, and for me, I think, for the love that he had lost, and for the future of his life.

Martin

On my eleventh birthday, Dad said he wasn't going to go out fishing but gave me a model boat and said he would bake me a cake.

He rolled up his sleeves and set out the tools and utensils he needed on the kitchen table: the mixing bowl, the scales, the sieve and a cup to check and separate the eggs. I think he wanted to show me that he could be as good as Mum. He drew the line at wearing an apron and he had a bottle of brandy by his side to 'make it special', but apart from that there would be little difference between the two of them.

'I've never made a cake before but it can't be that hard,' he said. 'Who needs women, eh?'

He began to whisk up the egg whites while I stirred the yolks into chocolate melting in a glass bowl balanced over a saucepan. The steam escaped round the sides and scorched my hands.

Dad took a swig of the brandy, set out two tins and then began to beat the butter and sugar in a Pyrex mixing bowl.

'Pass me the oven gloves.'

He took the chocolate mixture from the stove and folded it into the egg whites. Then he added this to the butter and sugar and sifted in the flour so that there were three bowls smeared with chocolate and two tins waiting.

'Is the oven on?' he asked. I hadn't lit the gas and I was worried he was going to be angry with me.

'Never mind.' Dad struck a match and turned the oven up high. 'There we go. Now we can do the icing.'

He eased the cake mixture into the tins and placed them in the oven. He took out a pan, poured in some milk and then crumbled cocoa powder and chocolate squares into the mix. He had forgotten to add the brandy so he poured it into the icing, saying: 'You won't be able to tell the difference.'

Dad was using every bowl and utensil in the house. Already the smell of scorched flour filled the kitchen. I didn't like to point out that we had forgotten to line the cake tins – or even grease them.

Within twenty minutes, he was standing at the table with an upside-down cake tin trying to lever out its contents.

'This bloody thing. It's stuck or something.'

I opened the kitchen drawer. 'You cut round it with a knife.'

'It says in your mother's book, "Wait until cool and turn out on to a rack." Well, I have waited and it won't turn out. Give me that.'

He took the knife and shaped round the edge. Half of the cake slewed out, its burnt sides and base remaining stuck to the tin.

'Oh bugger it, never mind.'

He took another slug of brandy and smeared the sponge with raspberry jam. Then he cut round the cake from the second tin, placed it on top of the jam centre and began to plaster over the icing.

'This'll cover it all up,' he promised, 'then we need a candle.'

'It's all right, Dad.'

'We've got to have a candle.' He rummaged in the drawer and found the stump of an old night-light. This he wedged into the centre of the cake. He then took out a box of matches, lit the candle and poured himself another brandy.

'Cheers, son. Happy birthday.'

I looked at the uneven mass of chocolate in front of us.

'Don't you like it?'

'It's great, Dad.'

I remembered my mother trimming candles before re-lighting them, placing them carefully in blue plastic holders, one for each year.

Dad began to sing 'Happy Birthday'. He started quietly, like he was embarrassed, but then got louder and louder as he neared the end.

When he had finished, I blew out the candle. 'Now make a wish,' said Dad.

I thought of Mum.

'One that might actually come true. Not the impossible.'

I picked up my knife and began to cut away at the lumpy mixture. The cloyed icing had caught on the burnt crust and the centre was damp and undercooked. I cut two slices and handed my father his portion. Then I tried to find some clean teaspoons as I knew Mum would have wanted.

'It's all right, son, we'll use our fingers. No one can see us.'

We ate in silence, my father drinking brandy, me with my milk. I tried to slosh it round my mouth to take the taste away. I realised I should say something, be grateful, Mum would have liked that, but when I looked up I saw that Dad had begun to cry.

'I can't bloody do it,' he said, pouring the brandy. 'I can't bloody do anything without her.'

'It's all right, Dad . . .'

I didn't know if he was talking about my mother or Auntie Vi.

'No,' he went on. 'It's no bloody good. Nothing is.'

He was rocking backwards and forwards like Uncle George. I tried to think what Mum would have done. I got up and put my arm round his shoulder and he folded into me and started crying like he couldn't hide it any more.

'It's all right, Dad . . . it's all right.'

Violet

Of course word got round about the cake and the other lady helpers returned: Ivy from the sweet shop with the varicose veins and the thin daughter no one quite knew what to say to; Doris the butcher's wife with the ghastly wart on her chin that she'd never done anything about; and Gladys who'd been let down by some fickle man from the bingo. What a pantomime Len said that was.

They came because it was all a bit too much for me on my own. One man was fine, even if he was doolally, but looking after another was more than I could handle. The other thing was that I had been offered a position as an Avon lady. I had needed some freedom and so I thought I might as well earn a bit of money promoting the delights of Meadow Morn talc and Moonlight Dream cake mascara; tat, in all honesty, but the ladies loved it.

Len liked the way my eye shadow matched the pale-blue uniform and I still came over as often as I could. Besides, the other women were as much as he could stand.

'I like to keep you cheery, Len,' I said, 'I like to keep you sweet.'

'Aren't I sweet enough already?'

'Oh, you're always so sweet,' I said. 'Especially when you've been naughty.'

'Me? Naughty? I'm a good boy, I am.'

He always perked up when he saw me. And he liked my cooking. When I put the food on the table Len did his Sid Field impersonation: 'What a performance.' Then, after a few beers, he'd sing the 'Tennessee Wig Walk', doing all the movements as well until Martin ruined it by saying: 'You never did that with Mum.'

The boy wasn't so keen on the food, of course. Perhaps it was a bit too adult for him, but I always said that it was never too early to cultivate taste, whether it was a braised pigeon or a kipper soufflé. Whenever he left any scraps on his plate, I would scold him: 'Aren't you going to eat that?'

And Len would add: 'You're all bones, boy. If you were any skinnier people would see right through you.'

In the evenings, we liked to get him to bed early. I checked that he had flannelled his face and hands, but he wasn't that keen on me singing and reading to him so I got off lightly. Some nights Len and I would go dancing for a bit of a foxtrot or quickstep and it was like old times. Martin was old enough to be left but he stayed awake until we came home. I think he was checking up on us.

People were starting to talk, of course, but I couldn't see how it was any of their business. It really wasn't.

George

Where did Vi get to, day in, day out? that's what I wanted to know. She was never there when I needed her and we didn't go out dancing even though I told her I was ready. I had to waltz on my own in front of the mirror, imagining a girl was in my arms and it was before the war when we had all the time in the world. Perhaps I should have waited and married her younger sister like I'd always hoped. Then we wouldn't be in this mess. And where had Lily gone? that's what I wanted to know.

I was taken out for walks like I was a dog and every time I came back I wanted to go out again. Even if it was in the rain. I wanted the wind on my face like I was on deck. I didn't want to be alone by the gas fire, staring at the picture of a man in uniform who looked a bit like me.

I made models out of matchsticks and walked up and down to get a bit of exercise but it was like being in solitary. And by the evening, I wanted to dance.

But Vi never came back until it was bedtime. She said, 'I think that's enough for one day, George,' even though I wasn't tired and didn't want her cocoa.

Then she went out again. She never told me where.

She knew I was the best dancer. Everyone said so. Held myself tall. Never needed to look at my feet. Knew how to glide.

I was still handsome when she shaved me properly. Oh yes. Always one for the ladies, me. Got to keep the face nice and smooth even if I do have the twitch. That doesn't matter. I can calm that down if I need to. Have to concentrate. Shoulders back, eyes forward, back straight. I can do that. On parade.

I wasn't too sure about her uniform. Pale blue. Not much good for nursing. And she was always wearing too much lipstick if you ask me. It was as if she was wanting to attract other men even though she had someone perfectly good at home.

I had been a good catch but now it was like she'd thrown me back in the sea. Down, down to the bottom with the others.

She wasn't as frisky as she used to be either. That was another thing that had changed. Didn't get my oats when I wanted them. If she didn't watch it I'd have to find someone else.

I put the radio on. *Children's Favourites* with Uncle Mac.

Pity we never had any kiddies.

Too late now.

> *You're a pink toothbrush; I'm a blue toothbrush*
> *Have we met somewhere before?*
> *You're a pink toothbrush*
> *And I think toothbrush*
> *That we met by the bathroom door.*

All right for them.

I should find someone to talk to. A lady friend. Bit of comfort since Vi was away so often. Either that or take action. Couldn't go on like it was: stuck dancing round the house on my own. That wouldn't do at all.

Martin

Dad and Auntie Vi took Ade and me to the fair but the two of them acted like teenage sweethearts, buying candyfloss and going down the Cresta Run, bashing into us on the dodgems and laughing so much that anyone would think it was us taking them instead of the other way round. I won a goldfish on the darts but it died almost as soon as we got back home.

'I don't know what's the matter with it,' said Auntie Vi, 'I was just looking at it and it turned over and floated up to the surface.'

'That must be what they mean by drop-dead good looks,' said Dad.

It made me sick to be in the same room as them. They were always giggling and giving each other looks and they couldn't wait for me to go to bed.

One night I dreamt of my mother's coffin in a dark chapel surrounded by candles. I was alone and my bare feet were cold on the floor. When I lifted the lid, I found that the coffin did not contain my mother but me.

I couldn't get back to sleep. I got out of bed and knocked on my father's door. I was sure I could hear rustling inside, a second person: her.

Dad opened the door, but only slightly, so I couldn't see him properly. 'What do you want?'

'I'm scared.'

'Go to bed. It's all right.'

'I can't sleep.'

I thought he wanted me to go away.

'Where's Auntie Vi?' I said.

'Don't ask me. What's wrong?'

'I'm scared. I can't sleep.'

'What are you scared of? Was it a bad dream?'

'I dreamt I was dead.'

'Look, son, there's nothing I can do about your dreams. I'm sorry. We all have to live with them. They're not real. You just have to ignore them, all right?'

'All right.'

'Now go to bed. It'll have gone in the morning.'

'But, Dad . . .'

'On you go, son. Don't start fretting.'

Mum would have taken me in beside her but Dad closed the door. I tried to listen for noises, movement and conversation, but he was waiting to hear my footsteps going away. He called out, 'Go on. I've told you.'

I tried to stay awake and then I heard a door slam. 'Hopeless,' I heard Auntie Vi say.

Violet

Martin started to hide things. They were small objects that we didn't notice had gone, little bits and pieces that could easily have been mislaid, like Len's Sunday tiepin, or my butterfly brooch. At first we thought it must be our own carelessness but then they'd turn up in old jam jars or Lily's button box, places where we would never have put stuff ourselves.

'I think I can guess who's behind this,' I said. 'Someone I can touch with a very short stick.'

But Martin always looked innocent and we never caught him in the act. I think he thought it was funny, as if he was waiting to see how angry we could get when we couldn't find what we wanted. Sometimes, when he was bored or tired of our questions, he would go and get whatever it was straight away, pretending I had left my ring on the washstand or my gloves on the table in the hall.

When Len asked Martin to confess he just kept lying.

'It's not me, Dad. Honest. You're always losing things.'

Then he started to be faddy about his food.

'I do my best,' I said to Len. 'Sometimes I don't give him any vegetables at all and yet he still won't touch his meals.'

I tried everything: fried whitebait and pilchard splits, corned-beef fritters, steak and kidney pie, luncheon-meat surprise. We were strict with him and said he couldn't have a pudding if he didn't eat his main but that didn't stop him. At least it meant extra baked custards or apple turnovers for the rest of us, because I wasn't going to let anything go to waste.

The child was spoilt enough as it was. We gave him tuppence a week to spend on gobstoppers, pear drops and Spangles; anything he liked, we were that good to him. Perhaps Martin thought he could live off that alone. He worked out the combinations that he could buy from the jars in Ivy's shop – four Black Jacks or four Fruit Salads or a Bassett's sherbet fountain. Some weeks he would buy a tuppenny stick of liquorice and try and make it last for days, keeping it in his pocket, nibbling bits off the end when he was nervous. But I told him all those sweets were going to have to stop if he didn't eat his tea.

I tried to be cheerful but it was damned hard. 'Not hungry?' I would say brightly. 'Never mind.'

It was a Sunday when it all blew up. We were waiting for the pub to open and Len was grumpy because it was that bit later. It had been raining and so we'd been shut up in doors as well. Len was pacing up and down, annoyed with the both of us probably, me trying to do my best in the kitchen, Martin kicking his football against the bedroom wall. Opening time at the Haystack was still a good hour away. I should have been back looking after George but Len had asked me to stay on and give him a bit of company since Martin was being so difficult.

It started with the usual thing. Six o'clock and Martin refused his baked beans on toast. This time he did not even bother to pick up his knife and fork but stared ahead like he was simple.

'Come on, Marty,' I said. 'It's your favourite. I made it special because you've been feeling poorly. Speak to me. Tell me what's wrong.'

His father said, 'Come on, son. Eat it up. We can't go on like this.'

Martin turned and looked at his father all innocent, as if Len was the one that was mad, but he still didn't say anything.

'Come on, don't be silly.'

I could tell Martin was hungry because it was a Sunday and the sweet shop was closed. When I told people about it later, they said it was because he wanted attention. Well, he was certainly getting it now.

'This is daft, son, daft.'

The boy just stared into space. He wouldn't say anything. He wouldn't even look at his father.

'Come on . . . tell me why you won't eat. Is there something wrong?'

Soon it would come, Len's temper. I had not seen it for such a long time.

'Why are you doing this? Come on, tell me. Why won't you speak? Why won't you eat? Tell me.'

Martin must have known that he could stop it at any point. All he had to do was to speak or to eat, but he just continued to stare down at the plate of food, refusing to look at either of us.

Then Len lost his rag. 'Haven't we had enough problems in this family? Why are you doing this to us? We haven't done anything wrong. In fact, we've done everything for you. Everything, you little bastard.'

'Len . . . don't call him that,' I said.

'You're a selfish, ungrateful little bastard. Do you hear me?'

'Len . . .'

'No, Vi, don't protect him, his mother did that. I've had enough of this nonsense. After all we've done for you. Is this how you show your gratitude? Come on, tell me. Is this what you do? Perhaps I'm going deaf. Perhaps I can't hear you. But Vi can't either. Neither of us can. Because you're a wilful, selfish, ungrateful little bastard.'

'Len, he's a child . . .'

'I don't care what he is. Come here.'

He pulled the chair out backwards so that Martin fell towards him and on to the floor. Then he caught his son by the back of his jumper and dragged him towards the door.

Instead of struggling Martin tried to make himself as heavy as possible, collapsing his weight so Len would have to work harder.

'Don't try that on me.'

Martin closed his eyes like he wasn't in the room and let his body be turned on to its side and Len pulled him away out of sight.

'Come on,' he shouted. 'Don't think you can get away with all this rubbish. I've had enough and it's going to stop right now.'

Martin

My feet banged against the walls. Dad was shouting, 'I'll teach you, you little bastard. I won't put up with it any more. Do you hear me? No, of course you don't. Anyone would think you were deaf.'

And what if I was? I thought. *Then you'd be sorry.*

'I'm going to show you what happens to boys who don't know they're born. If you won't listen to reason then you'll listen to the back of my hand.'

He took me into his room and threw me on to the bed. I could tell he was reaching for some kind of weapon: a slipper or a walking stick.

'Say after me: "I will eat my food." Come on, say it.'

The first blow came down. It was a hairbrush. I could feel its spikes through my shorts.

Then he hit me again. 'This won't stop until you speak. Say after me: "I will speak when I am spoken to." '

I will not.

'I will not be rude to my elders and betters.'

My father began to speak and hit, speak and hit; the blows were like punctuation.

'I will not steal.'

There will be six, I thought. *I must not cry.*

'I will leave a clean plate.'

I will let my father exhaust himself. I will not speak.

'I will stop being a miserable little bastard and a mummy's boy.'

Soon he will be gone and I will be alone.

I felt the sixth blow.

'And one for luck; not that we've ever had any in this damned family. Now start crying and don't come down until you've stopped.'

The bedcover had crumpled under my face but I could see the dressing table in the corner and the brush my father had hit me with. I remembered my mother being given it on her birthday and smiling. *Allure brushes beauty and fragrance into your hair.* It had wisps from the last time she had used it. I sat on the edge of the bed and began to pick out the pale-gold strands, curling them round my fingers.

I heard her singing in my head:

> *I see the moon,*
> *And the moon sees me:*
> *God bless the moon,*
> *And God bless me.*

The next day I had to say sorry to Auntie Vi. She was sitting on the settee in a smart black dress but had crossed her legs in such a way that her skirt had ridden up. I could see the catch of the suspenders holding her stockings.

'Martin has something to say to you,' my father began.

Vi smiled.

'Well.' Dad pushed me forwards. 'Speak.'

Outside it had started to rain again. 'I'm sorry,' I said.

My father leant down so that he could speak directly into my left ear. His breath smelt of last night's beer. 'I don't think Vi can hear that. It needs to be a bit louder.' Then he leant back up. 'If you can manage that.'

Don't be sad for more than a day, I heard my mother's voice. *Don't let the sun go down on your anger.*

'Well?'

'I'm sorry.'

'And what are you sorry for?'

'I'm sorry . . .' I stared down at Vi's shoes. They were black leather with silver buckles. I wondered if my father had cleaned them for her.

When I looked up Vi smiled before glancing away at the

television we'd bought for the Coronation. It was showing an advertisement for a Cross Your Heart bra.

'It's all right, Len, the boy's said he's sorry.' She opened her arms. 'Give me a cuddle, son.'

I couldn't work out which was worse: to be hit again, to inhale my aunt's perfume, or to be called son.

I walked towards her, concentrating on her right shoulder, refusing to meet her eyes.

'Come to me, my darling.'

I noticed that her bosom had begun to crease with tidal marks. Even though I was in her arms, I could still see the slipping surface of her dress as I felt the pat of her hand on my back.

I returned to my room. Before the flood, my two greatest fears had been of darkness and of being left alone; now they were my only consolation.

Len

That eating business was a right bugger's muddle and I didn't want Martin getting weirder as he grew up so I took him out fishing to toughen him up. The boat was an inshore trawler, thirty-two feet in length, and we'd been fishing off Holehaven for a couple of generations, ten miles upriver towards Foulness or downriver in the Mucking. We were after sprats in the winter and sole in the spring, pulling up the nets on a winch made from old car axles, gutting the catch on board and selling half of it to housewives on the wharf before packing the rest off to Billingsgate.

We set off before dawn. I told Martin he would have to help with the nets, gut the fish and keep a watchful eye on the weather. I showed him how to navigate through the buoys, avoiding the sandbanks and the treacherous currents, always aware of our position and the direction of the wind. I asked him to work out our course from the charts and how to navigate by moon and star. He asked all sorts of questions: who had drawn up these charts, how depths could be measured, who placed the buoys and installed the lights?

I kept my hands on the wheel and told him stories: of my own old dad working the smacks, keeping the fish alive and storing them in wooden tanks in the estuary ready for market; of the boat facing a wall of water which I thought she could never mount; of the beauty of cockle banks and phosphorescence at night.

The boat had a fair old history. Dad had even got it to Dunkirk and, despite being attacked by the enemy from the air, he had still got men out: forty-three of them, and from the inner harbour no less.

I thought Martin would be interested in the war and how the soldiers had been saved but instead he asked if I'd ever taken his mother fishing and what she thought of it all.

He asked about her childhood on Canvey and what the island had been like when we were young. I told him how Lily had grown up on a farm and could remember when it was all fields and water, just as it must have been when the Dutch first came and reclaimed it from the sea. There wasn't even a bridge then, just a ferry at high tide and stepping-stones at low. I said how I'd courted her, bringing her wildflowers I'd gathered from the hedgerows: penny-cress, ragged-robin and shepherd's-purse. I even told Martin how I thought she liked George more than me.

'Uncle George?'

'He was a handsome man, old George, but she was too young for him and he couldn't wait. So I knew if I had a bit of patience I could win her over in the end.'

'Was she beautiful?'

'Of course. Carnival Queen, she was. Streets all lined with people in Dutch costumes waving and cheering. That was the year before I joined up. Long time ago now . . .'

'I wish she was here, Dad . . .'

'I don't think she'd like it very much. She never did like this boat, I'll tell you that. I think she was scared of it.'

There wasn't much of a wind, a light north-westerly, but it was getting colder and I was glad Martin had remembered his gloves. Normally his mother had to remind him about them. At least he was getting a bit more responsible now she'd gone.

I winched up the nets and the fish splayed down on to the deck.

'You can sort and gut them for me, Martin. You know how to do that, don't you?'

'Can I have bandages?'

'What?'

'Some of the women have bandages on their fingers. Then if they cut themselves it doesn't matter.'

'But you're not a woman, are you, son? If you don't have bandages then you'll learn not to cut yourself.'

Martin pulled the fish away from the netting with his gloves on but took them off for the gutting. 'It's freezing,' he said.

Cirrus clouds, a cold front approaching. Perhaps I shouldn't have taken him out. He was too young, but I wanted him to see what it meant to go out and earn money for a family. I wanted him to be proud of me and love me as much as he loved his mother even though you can't force these things.

'Do you think you'll ever marry again, Dad?'

'And why do you ask?'

'Will Uncle George ever get better?'

I could see what he was getting at. 'I'm quite happy as I am,' I said. 'It's you I should be worried about.'

'I'm all right, Dad.'

'You tired?'

'No,' he said but I knew he didn't mean it. Then he shivered. 'Why do you do this, Dad?'

'If I don't fish I get restless,' I said, trying to sound cheerful even though I didn't see why I had to justify myself. My old dad expected respect and he got it, but now it looked like I had to earn it.

'I have to go out,' I said. 'Sometimes I don't think I've got any blood. It's all just salt water.'

'Do you ever jump in and have a swim about?'

'Well, I don't know about that, Martin,' I said.

'Can you swim?'

'Your nan thought public swimming pools were dangerous . . .'

'Why?'

'Polio. She thought you could catch it bad in public places. That's why we never had any library books. Mam was frightened of the germs. Only time she took one out she put it in the oven to bake the infection away.'

'So . . .'

'No, Martin, I can't swim. But at least I get to drown quicker . . .'

We turned and headed back. I pointed out the curving sea walls of Canvey and their sand-banked breaches, the open throats of the rivers and the creeks with boats waiting to cast off. The first oil tanker of the day steamed past on its way to Coryton.

We docked by the landing jetty at Holehaven and unloaded our catch into crates of ice. Some of the women were waiting with the fish merchants, their wicker baskets at the ready. I remembered helping my own dad between the wars, putting the boxes in a barrow and pushing it right across the island to the station at Benfleet. Martin used the same barrow to earn a bit of extra money taking holidaymakers' luggage from the bus stop down to the camp at Thorney Bay – sixpence a bag, he charged.

'If I don't watch out you'll soon be earning more than me,' I said.

Once we'd tidied up the boat we went to the pub for a pint. Martin had hot Vimto and a full English to get some warmth into him. I asked him if he could imagine being a fisherman himself and taking over from me, keep his dad going in his old age.

'Is that why you brought me?'

'I only asked because I wanted to see what you thought you were going to do with your life.'

'I'm going to stop water,' he said.

'And how are you going to do that, son?'

'I don't know. But I will. I'm going to stop it all.'

Just when I thought I was getting through to him he came out with a remark like that. God knows what he meant.

Violet

It got to the stage where the pressure of looking after my husband became so difficult that it was almost impossible to carry on and so Len and I found a home that could take better care of him. We both knew that George would be happier with proper nursing and we could always take him out for day trips to give him a bit of company when he needed it.

The woman at the home was a bit off when we came to sort it out but I told her it was going to be best for all of us and once I'd paid a cash deposit she didn't take it further. I visited twice a week and George and I sat in the garden when the weather was clement. He liked it out there because it could be a bit depressing indoors. The window in his room was that bit too high so he couldn't quite see out of it but as it looked out on the back it didn't really matter.

Meanwhile Len and I got on with our lives. Neither of us was getting any younger and so I told him that it was only right that he should take care of me. There was hardly going to be anyone else at this stage of the game.

'I'll look after you anytime, old girl . . .' he said.

'Less of the old, dear,' I said.

He laughed but the joke was wearing a bit thin because it had been a while since men had stopped speaking when I walked down the street. I had to make a bit more of an effort with my appearance. It was getting to be hard work just to look decent.

Lily had the right idea, of course, having a child as soon as she could and then dying before she lost her looks. Sometimes I worried I was going to turn into one of those childless women I'd always dreaded, putting on a brave face, making the best of things with the past behind me, looking after an invalid husband and everyone giving me pitying looks. That's another reason why George had to go. I couldn't take the embarrassment.

When Len and I were out and people thought I was Martin's mother, I could almost believe that we were a family and that I'd done it after all. I could see strangers watching us and thinking, *They're all right.* Sometimes I thought it would be easier if George was gone, and then Len and me could be together, but it was terrible to think in that way. Imagine wishing your husband dead.

But whenever I tried to look smart and went out for a dance with Len we got these catty looks. At first I thought it was jealousy because not many couples could match our triple chassé round a corner in the quickstep, but it soon became apparent that it wasn't that at all. It was because people thought we were enjoying ourselves that bit too much.

Well, if they were going to talk, I thought I might as well give them something to talk about. Len and I had never got round to any of that saucy business in the past – well, not properly, because Martin was always snooping around – so we'd had all of the gossip and none of the pleasure.

So eventually I decided enough was enough. I told Len to smarten up and come round for an intimate birthday dinner at my house. It would make a change from the two of us going out for a meal in a restaurant and we could take things at our own pace. I would make sure that everything was right and then, at the end of the evening, we would be ready for each other.

The day before the meal I went to London and made a treat of it, shopping, meeting a friend for lunch and having my hair done (restyled, swept back, a hint of titian in the colouring; I wasn't going to be one of those women who dye their hair so black it looks purple). I went to Dickens & Jones and bought a new brassière, a girdle, suspenders and a couple of pairs of stockings in case I laddered one of them. I wanted underwear that looked good underneath but which could still give pleasure when the clothes came off.

The colour scheme, I decided, was going to be silver and pink. I bought a rose chiffon blouse and found the shoes and the lipstick to match. Then there was a grey pleated cashmere skirt with a zip down the side that would be easy enough for Len to locate should he so desire.

On the day itself I made sure that as much of the food as possible could be prepared in advance. I didn't want to have to change at the last minute or spend time cooking while leaving Len alone in the living room. We were going to have salmon with new potatoes and green beans, followed by summer pudding, keeping the pink theme going. I didn't want a heavy dessert like a pie or a trifle because I wanted Len to have some appetite left at the end of the meal.

I put on some music to relax as I laid out the pink candles and the silver napkins. Len was a bit late which suited me because when he arrived everything was ready. He was wearing a navy-blue blazer and had done his hair so that he smelt nice and clean, of hair oil and cologne, and I knew I'd been right to make such an effort. He was impressed with the preparations and soon we settled down and laughed and felt at home.

When we had finished the meal I asked Len to move over to the settee and he looked a bit surprised, saying that he was quite happy staying at the table.

'Come on, Len,' I said, 'let's make ourselves comfortable.' I took off my shoes and sat down next to him.

'Isn't this the time to open my present?'

I thought of joking, pretending there wasn't one. 'It's here,' I said. Even the wrapping paper was silver.

'Looks a bit thin,' he said. 'I wonder what it is.'

'You'll have to open it.' My voice had gone high, and there was a slight laugh that I didn't know I had.

'What's this then?' Len asked, tearing open the paper.

'What do you think?'

'These are empty packets of women's underwear. Suspenders and things. What would I want with all that? Are you having a laugh?'

'Haven't you guessed?' I said.

'What do you mean?'

He looked a bit scared.

'I'm your present,' I said. 'And there's a lot more unwrapping to be done.'

Martin

I couldn't stand seeing them together. Whenever they were in the house, and it wasn't dinner time, I went off on my bicycle, down Smallgains Avenue towards the sea, cycling along the esplanades and up the coast towards Leigh, thinking how much I hated them, remembering my mother, wondering what I could do to keep her memory safe.

At school, I listened hardest to the stories about water. I read about Noah's flood, and every deluge in the world that followed. I drew diagrams of the water cycle, and coloured the coastline of the maps, shading the black lines of land with a light-blue crayon, edging it as carefully as I could. I wanted to fill in the details of the sea rather than the land. Instead of London, Manchester, Glasgow and Dublin, I named tides and currents, tectonic plates, streams of air and water.

I wanted to learn as much as I could about the sea and remember my mother in everything I did. I studied the currents from the estuary and out into the North Sea, how they came together and then diverged, the water rising from below to fill the place where the streams had separated. The names of the channels were ghosts of the past: Knock John, Shivering Sands, Black Deep.

In the *National Geographic* magazines in the library, I saw pictures of the sea wearing down the coast by chiselling out and wrenching away fragments of rock. As the cliffs were undercut, huge masses fell away to be ground in the mill of the surf, becoming weapons of erosion. On the shore, I looked at the ceaseless grinding of the pebbles, the fierce thunder of the billows, the whiplash crack of the rising waters.

After school and at the weekends I rode round the island collecting fossils from salt-water pools, the brine of ancient seas hidden deep under the surface of the earth. I knew there were billions of tiny shells and skeletons, the limy or siliceous remains of all the minute creatures that once lived in the upper waters, fragments of meteorite, rock, sand and volcanic dust. This was the abandoned history of the world.

I imagined the sea expanding and contracting as I breathed, a giant presence from which I could never escape. This was what it was like to live in the shadow of ocean. It was the same as the shadow of loss. It would never rest.

THREE

Linda

I hated having to go round for tea with them but our mums had been friends and I felt sorry for Martin. His voice was late to break and he held his head to one side in a shy way; like a wounded bird. Of course, I knew about all the gossip and how everyone disapproved of Len and Vi after they'd carted her husband off to a home. The two of them went around like they were a couple but whenever anyone suggested anything she took the hump. Too good for us, she thought she was.

Martin had passed his eleven-plus and was already at Southend High School, but you could tell he was clever just by looking at him. He had one of those foreheads where all the brains are pressed close and seem as if they are about to burst through at any moment. When you talked to him, he didn't speak straight away but waited until he had something to say; he never spoke when he didn't have to. In fact I think he quite liked silence, just as I did, and so once we stopped trying to like each other for the sake of our parents we found that we got on quite naturally after all: it was that and the fact that Martin grew into his good looks and came out charming.

I loved the softness in his eyes. They were dark grey and appeared to fold around his pupils like clouds. I told Martin that his eyelashes were like pencil marks. I think he was embarrassed but I knew he was flattered to be seen with me.

I suppose he brought out the mother in me even though I've never really felt maternal. He certainly wasn't someone a girl would fancy straight away but he listened well. I didn't know anyone else who was so concerned about my stupid little hopes and fears; not since Dad left anyway.

By the time Martin hit sixteen, he was six foot tall and had decided to become a water engineer. He wanted to be the first member of his family to go to university and he went to Cambridge to talk about the qualifications he needed to get there. They told him he needed decent A levels and six months' practical experience in a machine shop.

That might have put some people off but Martin found work in a factory run by his friend Ade's dad at the Point. By the end of the six months he had made sure that he knew how every tool in the factory worked, learning how to weld and use the lathe, taking his turn on the shaping, slotting and milling machines, even if it meant staying late. Some of the lads there had already become my friends, especially after I'd shown them how I could take their jokes about power tools, hot rods and insertion rates.

The boys were all Mods and they wore classy suits with the Army Surplus parka coats to protect them when they were riding the Vespas and Lambrettas. We spent weekends drinking and then bombing along the back routes to Leigh and Westcliff. We liked to make old men stare.

I knew why I liked Martin but I was never sure why he was keen on me. Perhaps he thought I was confident. Or easy. Perhaps he even liked my painting.

I was about to go to art school and I'd done these spirit pictures, people against the night seas and the moon, making them look dreamy so that you could see through them while knowing, at the same time, that they were there, like angels except they were real people. I'd imagined they were dead already or hadn't even been born, the spirits of my friends apart from their physical bodies.

Martin had never met someone who wanted to be an artist and he talked about his mother and how he found it hard to believe in the idea of resurrection, and so what was I doing painting these dead people? Did I understand something that he did not?

I did a series of tiny paintings on pebbles and bits of sea glass. I wanted to use driftwood, plastic, rope and even seaweed, anything that had been discarded or worn away. Martin and I beachcombed together, collecting fragments of old beer and wine bottles on the shore, glass made smooth by the action of waves.

Martin gathered his own secret supply and stayed on late at work for two weeks, using the tools in the machine shop to make me a necklace. He'd graded the sea glass carefully, so that the darkest brown was at the centre to match my eyes, the stones becoming paler as they stretched round to the back of my neck, meeting in a silver clasp. When the boys first saw the necklace they were embarrassed, dismissing Martin's dedication because it was all too much. But I could tell that they wished they'd thought of it themselves. 'You'll get to go all the way for that, Marty,' I heard his friend Ade telling him.

But Martin was never pushy about sex, not to begin with at least. It was like he thought it was something other people did. The boys couldn't understand it. My friend Dave, who was going to be a pop star, even asked if Martin was a homo.

'Of course he isn't,' I said. 'He's just taking his time. Unlike some I could mention.'

'You were keen enough when we started.'

'It's over, Dave. Over. You said so yourself.'

'Doesn't mean I can't come back for more, though.'

'It does, Dave, you've had your share.'

When it started, boys, sex, all that, I had trouble keeping people like Dave off me and I wasn't sure any of it was worth the hurt when it ended so Martin came as a bit of a relief. He was serious, like he wanted to wait, and I respected him for that.

We were walking on the beach, following the strandline, looking for sea glass amidst the hornwrack and the mermaid's purse, and Martin had his arm round me when he finally asked, 'What's it like?'

'Sex?' I said.

'Kissing. With tongues.'

'Wanna try?'

'You'll let me?'

'You don't have to ask,' I said.

Martin

Linda was tall for her age – about five foot nine, I suppose – and she was thin, skinny you'd have to say, with boyishly short dark hair. She held her body askance, aware that she had a peculiar beauty which she couldn't be bothered to display, and she spoke so little that people thought she was odd, *too odd*. Even her parents had thought she was backward and wanted to have another child quickly, 'just in case'.

Her eyes were so many different kinds of brown and gold and amber, the ring of the iris a confusion of spots, wedges and spokes of colour like the kaleidoscope I'd been given as a child. If she hadn't had the height and the confidence, people might have said that her features were pixie-like, but she was too beautiful for that and she wouldn't take any lip. Her chin jutted forward, challenging all comers, and her voice had a withheld power.

What do you want with me, Martin?

She was a mixture of flirtation and aggression. When I looked at her mouth, I was surprised by her fearlessness and the darkness of her laugh.

What now, then?

Once I kissed the whole of 'God Save the Queen' on her bare feet. They were dark with sand and street, but the tips of her toes were pale pink. Linda told me to stop because it tickled so much but I'd already got to the second verse.

'What are the rules?' I asked.

'There aren't any.'

'No limits?'

'Anything you like . . .'

'Anything?'

'Well. Not below the waist, of course.'

'I'm already there. At your toes.'

She looked down and smiled. 'I mean naked.'

I'd tried to learn lessons from the readers' letters of porno-graphic magazines which Ade rented out for sixpence a night: *Hefty*, *Hi-Ball*, *Jigger* and *Jade*; *Sheer*, *Shanty*, *Sextet* and *Score*. Ade talked about the stages he'd been through on a scale of one to ten and I tried to work it out; kissing on the cheek, the lips and then with tongues were the first three, fondling with clothes on was four, breasts five, and a fumble down below was six. But what were the stages between six and ten? Ade talked about 'a full house' or a 'right royal flush' and I wondered if that was actually number seven and there were three more things I didn't yet know anything about. He and Dave then started to go on about 'relief', 'sand-wiches' and 'doing it with animals' so that I even wondered if there were ten further stages.

I went to the library to do some research and learnt the words for each bit of Linda's body. I told her I wanted to kiss every part of her like the song, the foot bone and then the ankle bone; I was going to be the first man to kiss her all over.

She was still keeping at least some of her clothes on but she never told me to stop. I turned it into a sort of horse race, doing a commentary in an Irish accent that I'd heard in the bookie's with my father – *he's coming up the arm, he's passed the wrist, he's heading towards the elbow, and now he's on the upper arm, he's reaching the armpit (a bit of hair to negotiate here even though it's been shaved quite recently) and he's on, on to the collarbone and neck, the lips, the nose, the eyelids and forehead, back down the hair, the neck towards the right shoulder, down the arm again, across to the breast, it could be hours, literally hours, before he reaches his final destination but this man shows no sign of stopping, he's kissing every part of her, he can't be stopped . . . He's going for parts no man has ever kissed before . . .*

'Steady,' she said.

It's true, every part of her body will be covered, there'll be no flesh unkissed, what a demon, what an animal, this man is . . .

She told me I had to wait, she didn't want to get too serious, but I went to the barber's for the condoms just in case. The atmosphere was heavy with soap and lubrication, Brylcreem and hair oil. It was the smell of anticipation.

I thought if I had the condoms and told her I was all prepared then Linda would have to let me go with her in the end. I tried to imagine what it would be like; the release of desire and for how long it could go on. In the magazines, they talked of lasting for hours, so I dreamt it wouldn't be messy and grubby and quick like Linda had once said it was. I wondered how far her friend Dave had gone and if there had been others but each time I asked she laughed and changed the subject.

'When are you going to let me?' I asked.

'It's no big deal,' she said. 'I don't think it's all it's cracked up to be.'

'So you know . . .'

'I might do, I might not.'

'Then why don't we do it?'

'Because,' she said.

'Because?'

'Because you're not ready.'

'When will I be ready then?'

'I'll let you know.'

Violet

I was surprised Martin should fall for such a tomboy. With her short hair and only a hint of lipstick, Linda was hardly what you might call feminine. I never knew what to say to her because she was almost as quiet as Martin. Then, when she actually spoke, she never closed her mouth when she stopped. I suppose she thought it was attractive, leaving her lips slightly parted, and she had this languid way of walking that was meant to appeal to men but I thought it made her look as if she'd had a mild dose of rickets.

'What do you think they say to each other?' I asked Len.

'Perhaps they don't talk much.'

'You don't think . . .'

'Yes, I do,' Len said. 'She's loose, that girl.'

He didn't mind too much as long as what they did took place out of the house but I knew he would have felt differently if he'd had a daughter rather than a son. I suppose he thought that if he said anything Martin might start making comments about us, and neither of us wanted that.

We decided to say nothing and try and make her part of the family; let her see what account she gave of herself. In January 1965 we even took her with us to Churchill's funeral in London.

Well, that was a mistake. Martin and Linda were almost embarrassed to be seen with us. They kept talking only to each other, the way young people do, whispering and giggling. Honestly, it was so rude of them. It wasn't as if I didn't have enough to cope with, what with George and the crowds and Len getting all sentimental about the day.

There were special trains laid on from Southend. By the time we tried to get on at Benfleet they were all packed and it was impossible to find a compartment to ourselves. I knew we should have gone first class and made a day of it but Len said that any train would get us there, no matter what class we travelled, and we'd be better off spending the money on a good lunch.

I had bought a new coat from Marshall & Snelgrove because I wanted to look decent and I'd backcombed my hair and flicked it out at the end; a task made easier after I asked Len to give me the heated rollers for Christmas. All the other women who went up from Canvey were wearing tweed coats and headscarves to keep warm: so drab. I was glad I stood out, although in all those crowds it was hard to make an impact.

I even brought the half a cigar that Churchill had discarded on the deck of the *Prince of Wales*. George had been serving on the ship and sent it home and I showed it to Martin and Linda on the train. It was what you might call a conversation piece.

'Winston kept dropping them, half-finished, to give the sailors a treat, a bit of a gasp if they wanted a break, but George varnished his and gave it to me as a souvenir. A lot of them ended up doing that.'

'Did you thank him?' Martin asked.

'What, Churchill?'

'No, Uncle George.'

'Of course I did, what do you take me for?'

'I just wanted to know if he knew you'd got it, before he was wounded . . .'

'I hope so, Martin, but I can't ask him now, can I? He doesn't know what it is any more.'

I glanced at George, rocking slowly with his blanket over his knees, looking out the window and humming to himself. I think he was singing 'Is My Baby Blue Tonight?' but it was hard to tell because the tune kept wandering. *If only people knew what it had been like for me,* I thought, *then they wouldn't be so sharp.*

After we'd got off the train we joined the crowds at Fenchurch Street, a mass of people huddled against the cold all moving slowly down towards the cathedral. It was such a bitter day, rain and freezing fog, and the cold was the kind that bites right into you so you find you're perishing before you know anything about it. Some women had gathered newspapers to protect their legs but I couldn't see how that was going to help. Others had got there early and were frying bacon and eggs on portable stoves: lucky beggars. There were people selling hot chestnuts and newspapers containing the whole order of service but Len said we should concentrate on finding a good spot. He wanted to start on Ludgate Hill and then move during the service towards Tower Pier. Then we could all watch the bearer party taking the coffin to the boat that would make its way downriver and out with the tide. Len wanted to be there at the final farewell.

We had to wait so long, stamping our feet, the breath escaping from our mouths. I stood between Len and George, and we had our arms round each other as if it was old times and Lily was alive and we were all friends again with the future to look forward to. I could see Linda and Martin smiling at us, but they didn't know anything really.

Then, at last, out of the sleet and the mist we saw a great sweeping procession of colour: the shining white helmets of the Marines leading the way, the deep blue of the Navy and the bright scarlet from the cloaks of the Household Cavalry. I felt proud all over again to be English, standing there watching the soldiers, sailors and airmen, with the horses and the pipe bands in perfect formation. I knew then that it didn't really matter who you were or where you were standing because we had all earned our right to be there. This was what we had fought for. This was who we were.

'England,' Len said. 'No country in the world does a parade like we do. How can anything be better than this?'

Martin smiled, holding Linda to him. 'The nation defines itself.'

The crowd swelled and people began adjusting their positions as others tried to get to the front by the railings. George shied away from a couple of darkies and I think they must have scared him because then he started shaking. 'We should move a bit further away,' I said.

'There's no need for that,' said Martin.

'Can't you see he's frightened?' I said.

'They've done nothing wrong.'

'It's all right, madam,' one of the men said; I think he must have been West Indian. 'We'll find another place.'

'I don't mean to be rude . . .' I said.

'You just have been,' Linda butted in. She was wearing a white mac and a beret so she looked quite French, hardly patriotic.

'But it's our day. What have they got to do with it?'

'They fought too,' said Martin. 'I bet they have British passports.'

'How do you know?' I said.

'They probably came over on the *Windrush*. They must have done their bit otherwise they wouldn't be here.'

'Not like George, though . . .'

'No, Auntie Vi. We all know that George did the most.'

'I reckon they should put them on the Isle of Wight,' Len grumbled, 'but then you'd have to change the name.'

'I suppose there'll be black policemen next,' I said to Martin. 'Your mother would turn in her grave.'

'And what's that supposed to mean?' Martin asked.

'It's just an expression.'

'But what does it mean?'

'Don't, Martin,' said Linda. 'You know it upsets you.'

'She was my sister, young lady, and so I'll say what I like. I mean she'd turn over in her grave so she wouldn't have to see them; that's what I mean. She'd be on her stomach.'

Then Len chipped in with a joke. 'I'd have thought it would be dark enough down there as it is. Even if she stayed right side up they'd have to flash their teeth so she could see them . . .'

'That's enough,' said Linda. 'We don't think like you do.'

'Easy, sweetheart,' said Len, 'easy.'

'Well,' I said, 'I'm sorry I spoke.'

Linda didn't have a clue what any of this was about; far too young to know about death and uncertainty and never being able to imagine a future. All she cared about was music, coffee bars and the latest hairstyle.

Then the service began and people listened in on their radios: 'He who would true valour see' and 'Fight the good fight', the Archbishop of Canterbury blessing us all, and the last post at the end. Afterwards there was such quiet, the silence of memory before the reveille. I don't think anyone wanted it to stop.

By the time the procession left the cathedral we had already made our way down Eastcheap and St Dunstan's Hill so we could get down to Tower Pier. Then we watched as the coffin was put on to the afterdeck of the *Havengore*. Every flag was at half-mast and the cranes above Hay's Wharf lowered their heads in tribute. We stood in silence and listened to the ninety guns firing, one for each year of Sir Winston's life; and then, afterwards and in the distance, I could hear a pipe band playing 'The Flowers of the Forest'. It reminded me of Mother. She always liked a cry over that.

Afterwards the five of us managed to warm ourselves up in a nice little cubbyhole at the Prospect of Whitby and we ordered beef and ale pies and steak and kidney pudding. I think we wanted the food to be as English as possible. People were crowding in, some having to drink by the river looking back to St Paul's, not wanting the ceremony to be over; others spilled out into the street while still trying to catch the warmth from the doorway. Martin and Linda got the drinks in. I think it was their way of snatching a quick kiss at the bar without any of us noticing.

Soon the pub steamed up with a fog of bodies, beer and cigarettes. There was a piano and some singing but it took time to get going because everyone was still thinking about the funeral. No one had the heart for the jollier tunes like 'Roll Out the Barrel' but the more romantic numbers upset us even more. The man at the piano had a cigarette in his mouth and a pint by his side, and he looked a bit like Hoagy Carmichael, but I don't think any of us were really ready for 'Sweet as a Song', 'I Got It Bad and That Ain't Good' and 'I Heard You Cried Last Night'. I think even then we all knew that we'd lost a part of ourselves; and there was nothing we could do to get it back.

Len and I wept with the emotion of the day, looking at George staring out into nothingness and at Martin and Linda together with the future all before them, and I tried to imagine what life might have been like if it had only been kinder to the two of us.

George

Vi's sister Lily came back. I was sure of it. It was the day we went out to say our last goodbye to Churchill. She sat next to me in the pub with all that steam and heat and all those bodies and yet she looked so young; as if nothing had touched her. The clothes were different, of course, and her hair was darker, but I could tell it was Lily. The boy was there but I didn't mind, even when he put his arm round her.

She'd changed her name. Called herself something different but I could see right through her. I knew her game.

'You're Lily,' I said and she smiled at me, sharing the secret. Then she patted me on the knee. 'Never mind, George.'

'I'm not minding, Lily, you know me. I'm only minding when you go away.'

We had some drinks and she gave me that smile of hers. It reminded me of old times, dancing in the war when I realised that I was with the wrong sister, and here she was, back again, thin and fragile, like a little porcelain doll. We sat close, right up against each other, and I got excited.

'I . . . I . . . I . . . I . . . like you very much,' I said, singing a bit of the song, and she gave that little laugh of hers and said: 'I like you too, George.'

I wanted to do a bit of ear tickling but she kept brushing my hand away. Perhaps she didn't want anyone else to see. It would be our private moment.

But the closer she sat to me the more I couldn't hold on any longer. I leant forward and whispered that I was a bit itchy and if she could help me out I'd be ever so grateful. She didn't understand and so I took her hand.

'Come on, Lil,' I said. 'You know what to do.' But she smiled and pulled her hand away.

Perhaps she was playing hard to get. So I asked her in a louder voice to give me a rub and I think the boy heard but I didn't mind that. I only wanted Lily.

But then it was getting bad, like I couldn't control it any more, and so I took out my John Thomas to show her what I meant.

'Come on, darling,' I said, 'you can suck it if you like.'

There was a bit of silence and then she laughed and the other woman screamed and Len told me to stop it and put it away. It was just when I was ready so I didn't know what to do and so I started rubbing it myself. It was the only way but the posh woman kept shouting, telling me to 'stop that at once', and said I was revolting. I couldn't understand what she was on about and I just kept rubbing. After all, it was their fault for looking.

They took Lily to the door, and for a moment I lost sight of her through the crowd. The man at the piano was singing 'Don't Sweetheart Me'.

'Come back, Lily,' I said, but I couldn't go after her because I was stuck behind the table. I suppose it was all right because I needed time for everything to calm down. I couldn't walk out of the pub with my John Thomas all proud. Only Lily was meant to see that.

'Don't go,' I said. She was at the edge of the bar by the door. Then she was gone.

Her sister took me home. She was angry with me. I don't know why. I get so confused these days.

Funny when you can't recall your courting properly. The woman spoke to me like I was a stranger, or she was a nurse and there was something wrong with me. She kept using words like 'shame' and 'embarrassment' and said she thought I'd 'got over all that nonsense' but I couldn't follow anything any more.

It was so much easier to remember my childhood, Dad and me playing cricket on the beach, and me catching the ball high above my head – *well done, son* – that was when he was proud of me for the first time and he had a surprised look on his face, relieved that I might make something of my life.

No one's proud of me now, though. I can tell. That's what the woman keeps saying.

But I'd tried so hard. I fought well. Always at the guns. Only when we were attacked did I go into a funk. I couldn't stand it. And I don't know who could have done. It was that hard. They were always at us. And if they weren't, there was always the imagining. I thought I was going crackers. And then the ship's doctor said to me softly, 'Now then, lad.' A kind word. The first I'd heard. That's when I went, I suppose.

I should have died with the others.

Martin

I suppose I was glad that Linda could see the funny side but it was a bit bloody ironic that George had got further in one afternoon than I had in weeks. I had to wait for three months, four days, seventeen hours and about thirty-four seconds.

We were going to spend a night fishing on a beach away from the island up the coast on the Maplin Sands, huddling for warmth in a small tent, listening out for the sound of the bells from drowned churches out at sea.

Before it was dark I dug a hole and prepared a bonfire of driftwood, ready to catch sand eels on the low tide. As night fell and the tide receded we could see the eels leap from the beach and we turned on our torches, crouching and running to catch them. Once our bucket was full I lit the bonfire while Linda cut off the heads and gutted the fish so that we could fry them and make sandwiches.

We ate by firelight. Linda told me that as a child she would collect shells of ormers, cutting the fish out of the shell before her mother cleaned them with a hard brush, beat them to make them tender, and then cooked them in a slow oven.

When we looked up at the sky she told me that, as a girl, she had imagined the clouds as animals. They could be an upturned bull, or a seahorse, or the crest of a grebe. Sometimes they could be human; detailed outlines might contain her father's nose or remind her of the sweep of her mother's hair. She would make stories out of the sky.

As she spoke I tried to make up my mind which of her eyes to look into. The one nearest to me was brightly lit and had its focus upon me but the eye further away had a darker intensity that suggested rather than spoke, containing secrets she would rather keep hidden. Every half-minute I switched my concentration from one eye to the other because each was telling me something different. The nearest told of hope; the furthest kept saying, 'I do not trust you. I cannot believe what you are saying to me. Don't hurt me as I've been hurt before.'

We talked until it was nearly morning. Then, when we were drifting off into sleep in the tent, lying side by side, Linda asked casually, 'Have you got them then?'

'Yeah.'

'Well, let's.'

'Now?'

'What are you waiting for? Come on,' she smiled. 'It's what you want, isn't it?'

I tried to avoid her eyes because I knew it would excite me too soon and so instead I looked back out of the tent at the sky beginning to lighten and at the water tower with its hard red brick and its desolate nothingness. I remembered seeing that someone had scrawled on it: *British by Birth. English by the Grace of God.* I wondered who had written it, and why, and I thought of the sea again, and of stemming the flood, stopping the surge, and I couldn't quite believe that this was how I had been conceived, and that everyone did this, everyone, Vi and Dad, that woman and her husband in the electrical shop, the postman, the teacher, the doctor, my God, everyone. I thought of people on the bus going home to make love, in bedrooms, on sofas or in the backs of cars, of illicit lovers booking cheap hotels and lying behind drawn curtains on hot summer afternoons, of people in woodland or in the hollows of cliffs, finding themselves and each other saying, 'At last, this is what I have found; this is what I have been searching for, now I can breathe again.'

I dreamt of Linda's body and of the sea, and everything we had done together. I don't know for how long we slept but the light was still pale when we woke.

'Where do unremembered dreams go?' Linda asked. 'What happens to them? Are they lost for ever?'

'Perhaps we dream them again and again until we remember them.'

The beach was deserted and Linda swam naked, pushing away fronds of seaweed, golden brown, pink and emerald green. As she swam I tried to imagine what our future might be like and how different it could be from that of our parents.

I could hear my mother's voice in my head, the sound of her singing.

> *Star light, star bright*
> *First light I see tonight*
> *I wish I may, I wish I might,*
> *Have the wish I wish tonight . . .*

I wondered if I loved Linda as much as my mother and if this love between us was more important than anything else in the world. Was it a betrayal and a forgetting, or the finding of a new life? What did it mean to love like this?

Linda came back and dried herself, her leg supported on a rock, unembarrassed by her nakedness.

She smiled. 'All right then?'

'More than all right.'

Perhaps this was what 'good luck' meant. Perhaps Linda was my reward for everything bad that had happened in my life.

In our togetherness we had separated from the world. I couldn't work out what the feeling meant, of being happy and yet somehow trapped at the same time, in a place that was ours alone. I couldn't even work out whether I liked the feeling or not but I knew I didn't want it ever to stop.

Linda

I don't suppose any family's normal but Martin's thought the way they did things was right enough. Funny that, because his dad was a moody old bugger, his aunt was a snobby cow and his uncle was stark raving bonkers.

But I stuck with him because he was quiet and serious and I felt safe. Besides, he always encouraged my painting. Everyone else thought it made me a bit weird. They couldn't understand why I didn't want to get a job as a secretary and get married but I'd seen what that had done to my mother and I didn't want history repeating itself in my own family: married at sixteen, a mother at seventeen, abandoned at twenty with no money and hardly any prospects. I wasn't going to be mucked around like that so I went to Southend College of Art where I was free to be whatever I wanted to be.

I don't think anyone at my art school was sane. They were a mixture of neurotics, misfits and exhibitionists, putting on events with situationists and surrealist musicians, making giant sculptures out of crashed metal and loops of string or creating the kind of performance art which almost always involved one of the girls taking her clothes off. Even the act of going for a walk could be considered a work of art if it was done in the right way, but it couldn't be any old walk, you had to '*dérive*', which meant getting a map of Paris and following it strictly even though you were actually walking in Southend.

I found myself working with painters who thought they were already part of the St Ives School and film-makers who wanted to be Truffaut or Antonioni. They introduced Martin and me to foreign movies – *Le Soupirant, La Jetée, L'Avventura,* anything with 'le' in the title and a whole load of voiceover – and we all took dope and drank Noilly Prat and couldn't imagine we'd ever get to thirty.

I started to mix flowers and wildlife into the paint and play around with the texture of the surface of the canvas, adding in plaster of Paris to bulk up the whites, blowtorching areas of darkness to create deep blacks. I showed Martin paintings by Joan Eardley, telling him I wanted to be able to paint like her, and we travelled up and down the coast so that he could look at the patterns of erosion as I tried to capture the light.

'One thing. I'm never going to do a job where I have to clock on or off,' I told him. 'This is my clock, the moon and the stars, what else do I need? I can tell the time by the way the sun falls and the moon rises.'

In the past, every time I looked at the sea I felt that anything was possible; there would always be a tide to take me away somewhere else, where life could be different and begin again. But now I wanted life to slow down, even stop, because I could be with Martin and we were easy with each other. I didn't have to worry about anything any more. I was loved.

Martin was still working in the machine shop, welding and cutting, preparing for university. One night he even took me round the factory and we did it with rolls of sheet metal around us. It was unusual rather than romantic but that was Martin all over. Always wanting to do daft things like kiss my knees or hold my hair up to the light or drink from the same drink with it in both our mouths at the same time.

'Why are you like this?' I asked.

'Like what?'

'Even when you're happy you look like you can't quite trust it.'

'Do I?'

'How often do you think about your mother?'

'Not so much as I did.'

'And why is that?'

'You know why,' he said.

'One day,' I said, 'you'll tire of me.'

'Never. I'll always love you. You know that.'

'That's what people say when they're getting rid of someone. "I'll always love you." It means you're dumped.'

'But I mean it. Nothing matters except this.'

'You have a life to lead, Martin. Don't ruin everything by making this count for too much too soon. It frightens me.'

'And what are you frightened of?'

'Of loving you too much. Of loving you so much that I can't get back.'

'You won't ever need to get back, Linda . . .'

'I need to protect myself.'

'Don't you trust me?' he asked.

'Of course I do,' I said. 'I just don't trust myself.'

Martin

When I wasn't at the machine shop I read everything I could about the threat of the sea. I learnt to read its lessons, studying the changes in texture of pebble, shingle, sand and rock. I looked at washed stone, studied watermarks over the grain of driftwood and the wet backs of pebbles scaled by time. I wanted to be like those smugglers who could always tell where they were by scooping up a handful of pebbles, knowing by size and feel from which beach they came.

I played with them like cherry stones:

> *Army, Navy*
> *Medicine, Law*
> *Church, Nobility,*
> *Nothing at all.*

Linda picked me up from home and together we rode round the island on her Lambretta, the smell of Manhattan perfume blowing back in my face, sweet and fresh, not cloying like Vi's or powdery like my mother's.

Like my mother's . . . The smell of Linda was my first infidelity to her; now I preferred the scent of my girlfriend to anything else. My *girlfriend.* I had never been able to imagine using such a word.

That summer she swam far out to sea; so far that I could hardly see her and I tried not to panic or show my fear that she might drown. I saw other people walking their dogs, or children running into the waves, unaware of the power of the tide. Sometimes I wanted to stop them all, or call out, 'Come back, come back!' but I knew my fear would frighten them.

And then, as Linda painted, I studied the currents and read about the moon, torn away from the outer crust of the earth billions of years ago like an orphaned child unable to return to its parent, longing to come home. Together, I decided, we would be sea people, Martin and Linda, water-creatures of the night. She told me how, in some societies, food was laid out to absorb the rays of the moon so that it would have the power to cure disease and prolong life.

'Scoop up the water,' she would say, 'the moon is in your hands.'

Together we tried to imagine what it might be like to emerge from the shadow of the world, to travel through the belt of film surrounding the earth's sphere, to see what there was beneath the clouds of Venus and walk on the moon's surface. We would wander through the desolation of buried worlds and future planets.

When we sat by the water she would recite bits of poetry that she had learnt by heart.

Flood-Tide below me! I see you face to face;
Clouds of the west – sun there half an hour high – I see you also face to face.

I told Linda I had thought of becoming an oceanographer, recording light penetration, pressure, salinity and temperature; registering the slow changes in deep waters, dropping a sounding line a thousand fathoms to find the starfish clinging to it. I would measure the flow of currents and the height of waves out at sea from trough to crest. I would work out the length of fetch, the distance the waves had run under the drive of a wind blowing in a constant direction without obstruction. The greater the fetch, the higher the waves. I knew that the fetch the night my mother died could have been as long as six hundred miles.

I didn't know if Linda would ever understand how much it haunted me. No matter how close we were, even then, when our love was at its height, I was afraid that there would always be something unspoken, a gap that could never be closed.

I could not believe how elated Linda made me and yet, at the same time, I was frightened of becoming so used to the feeling that I would not be able to live if it was ever taken away. It would be like losing my mother all over again.

Perhaps Linda was right not to trust the intensity of it all. For I knew that, however good it was, this was a love that didn't belong to everyday life. And then I realised that when I went to university I would be unable to live either with or without Linda. If we were still together, loving as we did, then I wouldn't be able to concentrate on anything else, everything would be her, and when she was away from me and I was supposed to be studying, I would be afraid of something terrible happening to her: illness, accident, even death.

I would spend all my hours fearing the loss of love, the return of absence.

Linda

I knew it couldn't last but I kept hoping I was wrong. I couldn't accept that if Martin left for university then he might also be leaving me.

First he began to dream and be moody. Then he started to criticise me. Little things at first, like the fact that I hardly ate anything and that, when I did so, I did it too slowly. He thought the way I arranged my body when I sat on a settee showed too much of my legs, that I said too little, and that my paintings were just a bit too weird. It got to the stage where nothing I could do was ever quite right. I even wondered whether he was being irritating and critical deliberately, like he was trying to put me off him, so that I might be the first to end it all and he wouldn't have to do it himself.

The night before he left we were walking on the beach and Martin stopped to pick up a pebble and throw it into the sea. I thought at first he was nervous about leaving home and that he'd be all right once we were in the Monico. Dave's band was playing, after all. But Martin said he wanted to talk. Then I could tell it was bad because he started to speak slowly and he couldn't look at me.

'I have to leave,' he said. 'I have to do more than this.'

'I know.'

'And I'll need to concentrate. I might not be able to see you as often as you want.'

'What do you mean?'

'I have to understand: the sea, floods, water . . .'

'Stopping it, I know. But it doesn't mean you can't come home, though, does it?'

'No. It doesn't,' he said. 'But I have to work.'

'Yes, but you can't work all the time. When you're not so busy then we can be together.'

The mist was rising. I wanted Martin to put his jacket over me like he always did when he knew I was cold, but now he was staring at the ground. 'I don't know. Sometimes I'm not sure that I'm right for you. Perhaps you deserve someone better.'

'What are you talking about? I don't want anyone else. I love you.'

'And I love you. But it's so hard to live with it all.'

'No, it's not,' I said. 'It's lovely. It's the only thing that matters. You said that once. Don't you remember?'

'But I'm afraid of it.'

I tried to make him look at me but he couldn't. 'Stay,' I said. 'Please. Stay here with me.'

'Do you mean I shouldn't go to university at all?'

'Sometimes I think that, yes.'

'But what would I do if I gave it up?'

He stopped and began to kick at the broken shells under his feet, scraping them from right to left and back again, first with one foot, then with the other. Among them was a piece of sea glass. We were the last people left on the beach.

'I'll come back. It's only three years.'

'You'll change,' I said.

'I won't.'

'You will. You'll get bored with me. You already have.' I could tell, even then, that I was making it worse.

'I won't get bored, Linda. I'll only get bored if you go on like this.'

'Well, what am I supposed to say?' I asked. 'You're the clever one.'

'You're clever too.'

'Yeah. But perhaps I'm just not clever enough,' I said.

We walked across sands and shoals of rock; the memory of waves along the strandline. I had such an ache.

Martin

Dad came with Vi to wave me off. They stood on the pavement stamping the October cold away. Vi put her blue leather glove to my cheek. 'God bless, Martin. We're so proud of you. You'd best get on the bus or I'll start crying.'

She leant forward and I kissed her.

My father handed me fifty pounds. 'I'd like to give you more, son, but it's all I can spare.'

'You don't have to give me anything.'

'I wanted to see you right. Have a drink on us. Remember your old dad.'

'And me,' said Vi. 'Don't forget your auntie.'

I climbed on to the coach, went past the driver and found a seat halfway down. Dad and Vi waved quickly, their hands close to their bodies, and I wondered what they would talk about when I had gone. The coach passed George's nursing home, Ivy's old shop, the school and the playing fields; all the brief certainties of my former life.

As we drove down the high street, I saw Linda. She had stopped by the side of the road. She gave me a silent stare and I remembered how when she was angry her face reddened slightly, all except for the dent in her forehead where her brother had thrown the toy truck at her when they were small. The scar remained white.

She looked at me without waving or smiling, and it seemed that she was already a stranger. I couldn't understand how quickly I could feel so detached from my own past.

Linda

I didn't give up, of course. I borrowed my mother's Ford Prefect and drove up to Cambridge to talk to him. It took me an hour and a half and we sat in a pub, the Baron of Beef I think it was called, and I listened to students talking about their holidays in France and their second homes in Switzerland. They either had Christian names like Crispin and Jasper or nicknames like Rodders and Pimple. Martin told me he had joined the Backwards Club and that once a term they ran a whole day the wrong way round. They started with a brandy and soda and worked their way back to a boiled egg and soldiers last thing at night. It was such a good laugh, apparently.

He said I couldn't stay in his rooms. It wasn't allowed and he didn't want the gyp to find out.

'What's a gyp?'

'He's a servant; a type of cleaner. It's what we have here.'

'I thought a gyp was a bit of trouble: like my mum and her varicose veins. Her legs giving her "gyp", that kind of thing.'

'He also comes in to check I haven't topped myself.'

'I don't believe you.'

'It's true. Someone did it last year.'

'I'm not surprised in a place like this,' I said. 'It's a wonder more people don't do it.'

Martin couldn't get me out fast enough. I suppose he didn't want his posh new friends to see me, even though I was at art school and he should have been proud to have such a groovy girlfriend, for God's sake. We went off to Aldeburgh for the weekend instead.

99

I could tell that he wasn't that interested in me apart from the sex and even that had a 'for old times' sake' ring to it.

We pretended to be married – Martin and Linda Turner, we certainly looked sulky enough – and we booked a guest house where the landlady asked questions that we couldn't answer and expected us to be 'up and out' by half past eight.

There were sheep walks covered with grass, fern and brake furze, and Martin wanted to see how the wind affected each piece of vegetation and how much each could protect the land behind. He pointed out that the trees had been blown back; lilac, privet, sycamore and chestnut were listing badly, the salt of the winds wearing away their easterly sides. Then, when we got to the beach, he kept stopping to find places where he could test the sand, telling me about infiltration and hydraulic conductivity like I really wanted to know. He'd only allowed me to come if I didn't get in the way of his experiments into what he called 'swash flow' and 'sediment transport'. I had to hold a cylinder that he was going to insert into the sand to see how quickly the tide drained away.

'What about us?' I wanted to say. 'Why don't you give this much attention to us?'

He connected six tubes to the cylinder, pushed it into the sand and asked me to fill it up with water. He got out his watch and we measured how long it took for the water to drain away. Whenever it fell an inch Martin recorded the time taken in his notebook.

'I want to see how compact the beach is, and how quickly contaminants can infiltrate the coastline.'

Nearby a man was lying down while his wife sat up to look out to sea. She had a pair of binoculars. Although the man's eyes were closed his hand rested on her lower back, checking that she was still there.

The clouds over the sky were suspended like a child's mobile, with low streaks of grey and darkening. Martin told me that if I was bored I could search the beach for other places where the sand varied in texture. He told me he wanted to see how the size of the particles and their compressibility might affect the speed at which the sea was absorbed.

I looked at his notebook and his instructions:

The change of the water level together with the pore water-pressure measurement gives the estimate of K, based on the Darcy Equation.

$$Q = -K\frac{dh}{dz}$$

$$q = -Ki_z$$

As the flow is one-dimensional q can be simply related to $\frac{dh_w}{dt}$ (the rate of change of the water level), i is the vertical head gradient, which can be calculated based on head reading from two piezometers.

'How long is this going to take?' I said.

'Sometimes it can be quite quick.'

'Good.'

'You don't have to be here, Linda.'

'I was only asking.'

Martin pulled out the cylinder and started to look for somewhere else to continue the experiment.

'Can I help?' I asked.

'You can make notes when I call out the measurements.'

'What if I don't understand?'

'You don't need to understand, Linda. Every time the water in the cylinder falls by one inch I'll call. You note down the time as each inch falls.'

'As the sand absorbs it . . .'

'Not the sand: the bits in between. The sand itself isn't absorbent.'

The tide was on the ebb and a group of women were exercising their horses on the edge of the sea.

'This isn't going to work, is it?' I said.

'What do you mean?'

'I'm not good enough for you. Not supportive. It matters when you say that I don't understand.'

'It's not like that.'

'It is. I can't be with someone who's ashamed of me,' I said.

'I'm not ashamed of you. Look, take the measurements when I call them out. It's going to be fast. We need to be accurate.'

101

'You're embarrassed.'

'I'm not. Don't pick a fight.'

'It's already over,' I said. 'You're not the same.'

There were gulls over the rock pools and water was rushing out through the channels in the sand. 'You don't love me,' I said. 'I should go.'

'Don't. Let's finish this and then we can talk.'

'No. It's best if we don't see each other.'

Then Martin stopped what he was doing and it all came out. I hadn't wanted him to say it out loud because I didn't want to know but now I'd pushed him into it.

'I'm sorry,' he said, 'I've tried.'

'You're not supposed to try. It's supposed to happen.'

'I know.'

'And it did . . .'

I had fallen in love and he hadn't. Or we'd fallen in love at different rates; the lover and the loved. It kept changing but we'd never managed to make it equal.

There was a baby crab at Martin's feet, white like an embryo, dying in the sand.

'I'm sorry, Linda . . . I can't do this any more.'

Now you tell me, I thought.

'You've changed,' I said. 'You think you're too good for me. You think what you want is more important than anything else when it isn't.'

'No, I don't think that,' he said.

'You made me believe you loved me,' I said. 'I gave you everything.'

'Perhaps you gave me too much.'

'But how was I to know what was enough, Martin? Why didn't you tell me to stop?'

'Don't cry.'

'Don't tell me not to cry. Don't tell me to do anything.'

'I don't know what else to say . . .'

'Then don't say anything.'

'I didn't mean to upset you.'

'Don't do it to anyone else. That's all I can say.'

'What do you mean?'

'What you've done.'

'What have I done?'

'You know what you've done,' I said. 'I've just told you. Don't ever do to another woman what you've done to me.'

FOUR

Claire

I didn't mean to fall in love with Martin. Flirtation, yes, of course, why not, I was always prepared for that, it was one of the reasons I had gone to Cambridge in the first place, but I certainly wasn't ready for any commitment. I was too young and, besides, I was still recovering from Sandro, my Italian boyfriend.

I was called 'VD' at school so some people thought I was looser than I was, but that meant 'Vicar's Daughter', and I'd had the nickname long before I knew about the disease. I could always take a joke and I think people almost wanted me to be rebellious. That's what often happens to the children of the clergy, but after Sandro there was no one, no one at all, and I led an almost embarrassingly chaste life.

I wasn't in any hurry to find someone else, and I certainly wasn't looking, so Martin came as a bit of a surprise.

I was asking people to come down to Aldermaston for the CND march in the Easter of 1968.

'Hello,' I said, 'I'm Claire Southey. I'm studying music at Girton and I'd like you to march with me for a better world.'

He paused for a moment and then smiled. 'Well, Claire Southey, my name's Martin Turner, I'm reading engineering at Churchill and I will.'

We sat next to each other on the coach down to Victoria and marched from Trafalgar Square for three days. I carried the banner and Martin brought the food. He nearly blew it when he suggested that it should be the other way round and it took me a while to realise he was joking.

He didn't say much at first but I could tell he was a bit different. He wasn't one of those men who try to make an impression and only say things hoping it might lead to a knickers-off situation. I talked to him about my childhood and my parents, of family holidays camping in church grounds throughout Europe and my mother's relentless baking and charity work. I joked about my father's homemade wine (carrot and blackberry, raspberry and juniper) and how he made so many speeches that he was known throughout the village as 'the pop-up toaster'.

I told him of the pressure I felt in being the eldest child with a musical talent everyone kept telling me not to waste. There wasn't much chance of that given the fact that I played in two orchestras and we put on a charity concert at home every summer. Dad played the cello and my mother the viola so I think one of their chief aims in having children was to produce a string quintet rather than a family.

I couldn't help noticing how intrigued Martin was by my upbringing. As soon as I talked about my brother or my twin sisters he stopped and asked more questions. I think he couldn't imagine what living with siblings could ever be like.

He spoke about his mother and his earliest memories: of her stooping down to kiss him goodnight or turning in the light of the doorway. He told me how she would open her handbag at the door and give him a penny for the church collection, money that he always resented giving away because he could have spent it on sweets. He had to make up for it by gathering up lemonade bottles left by day-trippers on the beach and collecting the deposits from the store at the corner.

He remembered his father getting ready to go to the football or going out for a pint in the evenings, putting on his coat and hat, checking for his keys and mumbling that in the past he had never had to lock a door. Sometimes, he said, he felt his father had lived for ever and his mother never at all.

He confessed, after teasing, that he had had a girlfriend but that it was over. I don't think it was that serious. Then he said he didn't like to talk about Linda too much and that, besides, we shouldn't let the past ruin the future.

Martin wasn't conventionally good-looking and, as I say, I never meant to fall in love with him. My mother had always insisted that the chief purpose of my time at Cambridge was to get me to respond to the charms of a lawyer or a doctor, someone with prospects so that I'd be set up with a clever man and a good income for life. I think she didn't want me to end up with a clergyman as she had done.

'I'm not saying you should marry for money,' she argued, 'but it can't do any harm if you go where the rich go and fall in love.'

Of course there were plenty of public-school lawyers and doctors to choose from, and I had my fair share of admirers, but I preferred Martin's shyness and his quiet certainties. As we spoke I felt I had met someone who understood that one could be ethically as well as professionally ambitious, that life wasn't only about earning a living and going to parties. When we walked side by side on the march I didn't need to make the effort that I did with other people. I didn't have to present myself as an attractive and amusing girl who was clever without being intimidating, or eccentric without being loopy. It was safe to be myself and that, at the time, was the closest thing I knew to love.

Despite the spring sunlight, magnolia trees blooming all over suburbia and the first daffodils in the parks, it was far colder on the march than I had expected. I was wearing a brown suede fringed jacket, a yellow tie-dyed T-shirt and a dark-orange mini skirt that I'd made from material I'd picked up at the market for four and six. But as soon as we were out of the sunlight and into the shade I started to shiver and wished I had brought something warmer. Already I could hear my mother's voice chastening me: 'Is that all you're wearing?'

We had tea with Quakers and slept on vicarage floors with people my father had known at theological college. There were protesters from India, Cyprus, Sweden, but the people shouting at us in the streets thought we all came from the same place.

'Piss off back to Russia. Go on. Piss off.'

My mother had written me a serious letter, saying that although she approved of peace I should be concentrating on my studies rather than walking halfway across England in a blouse that was far too thin. She also worried that I might take my violin on the march (it had belonged to my grandfather) and that it might be damaged.

Didn't I know how much her father had loved that instrument? She was anxious that I was not working for my exams. She was concerned that I was getting what she called 'too emotional'. And she fretted about where I was going to sleep. I had to be careful of men, she wrote, especially musicians and men with beards. She said they were both oversexed. I replied that we were going to be too tired for any of that and in any case we spent most of our time rubbing methylated spirits into our feet to stop them getting sore.

I think my parents resented the freedom and the independence of youth without war. Every time I told them about CND or student politics, and how we were campaigning for an optimistic and peaceful future, they would smile sadly, hoping I might be right, and that a better world, a second Eden, could be created if only people had the will to make sacrifices for it. And yet the look in their eyes as they smiled at me showed that they never quite believed it to be possible. They had seen too much of human nature, too much suffering, disappointment and violence.

But I still kept on at them, convinced they had given up too soon, and still they smiled indulgently, furrowing their brows in the way mothers and fathers do when they look at their children, with love and sadness, hoping we might be able to correct the errors that they made when they were young themselves; so that they could live on through their offspring rather than the memory of their own past.

I told them how my generation believed we could change the world, rebuilding its virtues and its decency after so much bloodshed; and if we could not do so then, at the very least, we would make a difference.

Martin and I would not be like them. We would leave an imprint of goodness.

Martin

Whereas Linda's clothes were always tight to her body Claire's seemed to float and unfurl around her. She had shoulder-length auburn hair and when it had been newly washed it was allowed to fall freely back over scarves, cardigans, blouses and jewellery. She told me that it had once fallen as far as her thighs and her mother had never forgiven her for cutting it. Everything about her was in movement, not only her hair but also her clothes, in layers of deep russet, burnt orange and dark ochre, stretching down to the knee-high boots she always wore for cycling through Cambridge.

Claire wouldn't eat meat, she gave money away, and she appeared to know instinctively what was right and what was not. That was why I fell in love with her, I suppose: her energy and her confident optimism, her determined attack on life, her refusal ever to accept the word no.

She shared a house with three other girls in Portugal Place and her room was a mass of books, music and manuscript paper. There were shawls and tie-dyed drapes over the chairs; there was a sewing machine and material from the market to make new clothes; and her jewellery was arranged like a series of still lifes. Necklaces dangled from picture hooks; one of miniature mussels and pearls, another threaded squares of orange and brown plastic in differing sizes, a third consisting of scallops of burgundy glass.

A wide-brimmed black felt hat hung on the music stand. On the walls were photographs of her family on a corkboard, and posters that had come from Italy: a Botticelli, a Raphael and a Masaccio. Studded around them were CND badges, postcards from friends, the timetable of her lectures and tutorials.

Each morning she made a careful selection of jewellery to match the colour and fall of her clothes: ethnic wooden bangles, beads and a bracelet made out of dried flowers and melon pips.

At the weekends we went for long walks over Coe Fen past the old Sheep's Green bathing sheds and out towards Grantchester. Claire told me of family holidays in France by the sea and the remembered sounds of late summer; the returning tide, a child practising the piano, the shouts of her brother and sisters as they pulled canoes ashore with their father.

We liked to get out of Cambridge and find ourselves out in the flat lands under immense skies, by river and fen, amidst the frosts and snows of winter. We walked past isolated windmills into the emptiness of old tracks and forgotten streams: Fleam Dyke and Fen Ditton, Upware and Wicken Lode. I told her about the land of my childhood and the way the landscape had been formed: reclaimed, unstable, and yet prepared, at any moment, for the waters to return. Claire said that she had been in Florence just after the floods of sixty-six and it had been the first time she had realised that water could be as dangerous as fire.

I persuaded Claire to play the violin: airs, jigs and English folk songs, pieces of Bach and Haydn. She told me that she didn't like me listening; she preferred to play on her own. It was a kind of prayer, she said. The music had a completeness that made her feel restored, as if there was one part of her life, however small, that could always be healed.

We were careful with each other and we didn't force things because we didn't want to endanger what we already had. Claire never came to Canvey and I never went to her home in Oxford-shire. I think we were frightened of what our friends might think. I certainly couldn't see her going down the pub with Ade or Dave, sitting in the Labworth Café or spending a Saturday night down at the Monico.

But as graduation approached we knew that if we were going to continue we should at least look for jobs in the same part of the country. We should also meet each other's families, however alarming that might sound. I told Claire that as long as she was with me I wouldn't be frightened at all.

'In that case,' she replied, 'we'll start with my parents . . .'

'When I said I wasn't frightened . . .'

'My father's a vicar, for God's sake. He's not going to bite.'

'But what if he disapproves?'

'He can't. I won't let him. Besides, it's my mother you want to worry about . . .'

The family home was an extended Georgian rectory by a tributary of the Thames near Farringdon. An English sheepdog was asleep by the back door but sprung to life as soon as we arrived. Across the drive Claire's father was tinkering with his motorbike.

'Ah, here you both are. "Do the elm clumps greatly stand, still guardians of that holy land?"'

'Daddy.'

'Rupert Brooke. Lovely to see you with your golden hair down, my darling.' He turned to me. 'Don't you think she looks like a Burne-Jones? Or possibly a Rossetti? You must be . . .'

'I'm Martin.'

'Ah yes, Martin. Am I allowed to use the word "boyfriend"? Good to meet you. I would shake hands but, as you can see . . .' He waved an oily hand at his motorbike. 'Bonnie's been overheating. My wife's in the kitchen. Perhaps you'd like to go for a spin when it's fixed?'

'I'd be honoured.'

'Honoured, eh? You have been brought up well.'

The house smelt of baking and old dog, of sherry, furniture polish and fading freesias. There were photographs in silver frames, oil paintings with their own overhead lights, and copies of *Country Life* mingling with the *Church Times*. Claire's mother was baking scones for tea. The heat of the day made her appear flushed and it was clear that we had arrived sooner than she had anticipated.

'I thought I said supper?'

'Do you want us to go away again, Mummy?'

'No, of course not. I just haven't got enough hands.'

She told us that the twins were playing tennis with friends down the road and that 'Jonno' was at a cricket match. I was shown to my room, which was located as far from Claire's as possible, and told I might want to 'wash and brush up'.

'Well, he looks all right,' I heard Mrs Southey pronounce. 'Quite presentable. Although his voice is a bit quiet . . .'

'He's nervous . . .'

'He's not fussy, is he? He's not going to want roast beef and Yorkshire pudding?'

'No, Mummy, Martin's lovely. You'll see.'

'I think I'll be the judge of that.'

My room was painted Wedgwood blue, with prints of Cambridge on the walls and a standard lamp that had been made from an old rowing oar. I opened the window and looked out over the garden with its smooth lawn, its separate areas for roses, vegetables, herbs and even a netted section for fruit in the fullness of summer.

When I came downstairs I was offered elderflower cordial and we sat in the garden where Claire's parents asked me polite questions about my prospects. They weren't particularly interested in any of my answers until her father discovered that I was reading engineering. He asked me if I knew anything about mechanics because his motorbike was still playing up and he thought it needed a new rocker arm.

'It's a twin-cylinder sixty-horsepower screamer, Martin. Goes like the wind. Terrifies the parishioners.'

Claire's mother lit a cigarette. 'Sometimes my husband thinks he's Lawrence of Arabia. I only hope he doesn't come to the same end.'

We were interrupted by the girls coming back from their tennis. They were laughing about their partners, and as soon as they started on the news of the day it became clear that the family felt most at home when speaking to each other in some kind of code. At times it consisted entirely of acronyms and Claire had to provide a whispered running commentary. Amanda said that Victoria's partner was NSIT ('not safe in taxis') but at least he was RGL ('reasonably good-looking') whereas her current admirer was simply NPA ('not physically attractive') and it would have to be a PBJ ('paper-bag job') if there was going to be any progress.

We went for a walk to the village and drank a couple of pints in the pub garden before returning home to change for dinner.

Claire kissed me on the landing and only stopped when she realised that her twelve-year-old brother was spying on us. 'Go AWAY, Jonno.' She apologised and said she would see me later but I couldn't think how it would be possible to make nocturnal visits over creaking floorboards.

When we came down to help with the final preparations for dinner Claire's mother beckoned me into the kitchen in order to open the wine.

'Come on, Martin, make yourself useful.'

This was a family that never appeared to have had any problems. No one had ever died as far as I could see, at least not recently, and they had all booked their place in heaven long ago. They were continually at ease, laughing and interrupting and looking forward to summer garden parties, musical evenings, fêtes and cricket matches. It didn't occur to them that there was any kind of life outside their own.

On the Sunday morning Claire's father preached on the subject of contemporary morality. He began by quoting St John's account of Jesus's farewell to his disciples – 'No one shall rob you of your joy' – and spoke of the ultimate bliss awaiting those who put their trust not in the world but in the divine.

It was difficult stuff, taking on the sorrow and the mystery as well as the joy of love, but as soon as the service ended the mood lightened. At the parish breakfast no one appeared to pay the slightest attention to anything Claire's father had said. It seemed that the service had been something everyone had to get through simply to reach the coffee. The lady parishioners choreographed their cups, saucers and buns and were called by old-fashioned names like Veronica, Margaret and Patricia. Most of them were in love with the vicar.

The Sunday lunch that followed was not the traditional roast but grilled asparagus and mushroom risotto with an apple and celery salad. Afterwards there were to be the first strawberries from the garden. It was a world away from Vi's boiled ox tongue.

'You should never eat anything you're not prepared to kill yourself,' Claire's father was saying, 'isn't that right, Celia?'

His wife explained. 'In this family, Martin, we think there's enough killing in the world as it is.'

'Martin likes fish,' said Claire. 'His father is a fisherman.'

Matthew Southey smiled. 'And Jesus, walking by the Sea of Galilee, saw two brethren, Simon called Peter, and Andrew his brother, casting a net into the sea; *for they were fishers*. What is the quotation, Amanda?'

' "And he saith unto them, follow me, and I will make you fishers of men." '

'Well done, my little cream puff.'

They began to talk about cricket and the game Jonno was due to play that afternoon. His father offered his advice: 'Every day you should look at the weather and think: "Is this a bowling day, heaviness in the air, a bit of moisture in the pitch; or is it a batting day, a clear sky and a pitch that's true?" What do you think, Martin? Today, would you choose to bat or decide to bowl?'

'Bat, I suppose . . .'

'No suppose about it, I would have thought. And what do you plan to do when you leave university?'

'Don't start interviewing him, Daddy,' said Claire.

'I don't see why I can't. So many people these days are living a DNB kind of a life.'

'DNB?' I asked.

'Did not bat.'

'Well,' I said.

No one shall rob you of your joy.

'I thought I'd make a start by marrying your daughter.'

Claire's father wondered whether he had heard me correctly. 'Aren't you supposed to talk to me about it first?'

'Well, I thought I'd ask her. I don't mean to be rude. I thought it might be more appropriate.'

'And have you?' He examined a piece of risotto on his fork.

'Not yet.'

'Bit sudden, isn't it?'

Claire's sister Victoria laughed. 'You're discussing this, in front of all of us, and you haven't even checked it with her?'

'No, I haven't. I'm sorry. Claire, will you marry me?'

Her mother interrupted. 'You don't have to answer, darling . . .'

'Yes,' Claire said. 'Of course I will.'

'Well,' said her mother. 'This is a bit of a surprise on a Sunday morning.'

'It certainly is,' said the vicar. 'Are you sure about this, Claire?'

'I've never been more sure of anything in my life.'

'Well, I don't know what to say.'

Claire smiled. 'That must be a bit of a first then, Daddy.'

'I suppose we had better congratulate you,' said her mother. 'Matthew, you know where the champagne is? Didn't the doctor give you some after his wife's funeral? We might as well use it up now. Seems as good a time as any.'

Matthew Southey rose from his chair. 'It won't be cold, of course.'

'Oh, I think Mummy's already provided the ice,' said Claire.

Violet

You wouldn't call Claire thin, which was a bit of a surprise after Linda, especially since she was a vegetarian. You don't see many plump vegetarians, do you? I thought Martin liked the skinny type, but now he'd gone for someone much more, well, voluptuous, I suppose, although she hid it well enough. We'd noticed the engagement ring: an emerald. It went with her eyes and matched her hair: very Irish. On a good day you might even have mistaken her for Maureen O'Hara until she opened her mouth and that posh English came out.

'This has all happened very quickly,' I said when Claire was safely in the bathroom. The taps were running so I knew she couldn't hear us.

'But when you know,' Martin replied, 'you know. Wasn't it like that with Uncle George?'

I wasn't having him change the subject as quickly as that. 'Your father's worried it won't last,' I said firmly. 'He's concerned.'

'I don't need his concern.'

'You're both so young, Martin. You should listen to him. He knows a thing or two.'

'And what does he think is wrong?'

'We only want what's best for you,' I said. 'We're just trying to help.'

Len came into the room with a bottle of beer. 'Class. That's what we're worried about.'

'You're wrong,' Martin said, stubborn as ever. 'You don't understand.'

118

Well, thank you very much, I thought.

'Have you met her parents?' I asked.

'Of course I have.'

Martin was so abrupt that Len had to cut in. 'And what does her father do?'

'He's a vicar.'

'A VICAR?' Len said. 'Every time I see a vicar I think I'm about to die.'

'Is he going to do the wedding?' I asked.

'He's going to give her away.'

'How touching,' I said, fetching the Babycham from the cocktail cabinet. I wondered if Claire was pregnant. Perhaps that would explain it.

'I like a bit of a party,' I said, 'and it's about time you settled down; especially after Linda and everything . . .'

'That was a long time ago.'

Long time! It was only a couple of years. 'Have you told her?'

'Why should I do that?'

'Might be polite.'

Len tried to help but it didn't come out right. 'Sometimes I think you'd have been better off with Linda.'

I could see that things were getting a bit difficult so I went to check on the fish pie. Martin hadn't told me about the vegetarianism until it was too late so I felt a bit embarrassed but Claire did have manners, I will say that for her. She said she'd be perfectly happy with the vegetables and some bread and cheese.

While in the kitchen I kept an ear out for the two men talking. Martin was getting quite shirty.

'Why are you telling me this now?' he was saying. 'I don't love Linda.'

'You did.' Len was always fond of that girl.

'I know I did. But now I don't,' Martin replied. 'You didn't even like Linda. You said you could never tell what she thought.'

'No, I didn't.'

'You did, Dad, don't deny it.'

'I don't know what I did or didn't do. It's nothing to do with me anyway. All I'm asking is why you want to be with this other woman?'

119

'Claire, Dad, she's called Claire. What is your problem?'

'I don't have a problem, son. You can marry whoever you like. Don't mind me.'

'Good,' said Martin. 'So you approve?'

I could hear Claire draining the bathwater. I didn't want her overhearing and so I came back and tried to calm things down. 'Maybe it makes your father feel old: you getting married,' I said.

'Too right it does,' Len said. 'Makes us both feel old.'

'Have you set a date?' I asked.

'We have to check with Claire's mother.'

'Will it be a posh do?' Len asked.

'I hope so. And we expect you to be there.' Then Martin looked at me. 'And George, of course. You're all invited. No excuses.'

Len could see I was worried. 'George is a bit of a liability. You know that, Martin.'

'He's family. He should come.'

I was trying to work out some of the costs. I'd have to get a new frock, Len would need a new suit, and I'd have to persuade George into his uniform. That was about the only chance I'd have of keeping him still. I began to dread the whole thing, but I had to go through with it for my sister's sake. God knows what Martin thought he was playing at. A vicar's daughter! That really took the biscuit.

Martin

Dad was right. It was a posh wedding. April 26th 1969. Cup final day. Just as well it was Leicester v Man City. If it had been Tottenham we would have had to change the date because he would have kicked up a fuss.

I think it was the first time I felt embarrassed about my upbringing. Dad looked smaller than he normally did, Vi was blousy and overdressed in a yellow outfit that showed too much of her cleavage, and my old school friends seemed to think they were only there to look at the women and get drunk. At one point I was worried if I even belonged myself, if this was really me, here on my wedding day dressed in a morning suit. I kept expecting a tap on the shoulder and a man saying, 'Come on, Martin, admit it, you don't really fit in here. This is far too good for you . . .'

Ade, my best man, had brought a packet of condoms and put one in his right hand so that after he had greeted me I was left with sticky handshakes from then on. He even put one in the cucumber sandwiches. George pulled one out and started to blow it up. Claire's mother thought he'd done it on purpose.

'*Who is that revolting man?*'

And then there were the speeches. Claire's father had written a poem to his daughter that said her smile was like the sun coming out and even when she cried as a child there was always a rainbow after the storm. Then he began to cry himself, holding it back as much as he could, but ending by saying that the best present everyone could give would be their love and understanding throughout our marriage. Loyalty mattered more than anything in the world.

'Be ye steadfast,' he said, 'unmovable, always abounding in the work of the Lord.'

I thanked him and said what an honour it was to be part of their family. I tried to be generous without upsetting Dad or Vi, and I could tell they felt out of place, sitting apart with all the Canvey people, toying with their sparkling wine and chickpea vol-au-vents.

Ade made a drunken speech beginning with the old joke: 'The trouble with being the best man at a wedding is that you never get to prove it'; but that didn't get a laugh so he upped the ante. 'Martin, old son,' he said, 'I'm telling you that your wedding night is going to be like a Christmas dinner: a bit of leg, a bit of breast and a lot of STUFFING . . .'

Claire's father tried to pretend he wasn't there and her mother did her 'boys will be boys' look.

'She's a vegetarian,' Amanda shouted.

Ade then moved on to perform his trademark impersonations of a dog being sick and the boys got behind him and started jeering along ('Bone up, Mart! Go for it, Mart! Hey hey hey!'). Then he said that although marriage could and should last a long time, it came in six-inch instalments.

Half of the room was silent.

'Sorry, perhaps I shouldn't have said that. Anyway. I'm stopping. Yes, I'm stopping. Claire, Martin, may the blue bird of happiness crap all over your wedding cake. The bridesmaids!'

Linda

I wasn't invited, of course. Instead I went down to the Lobster Smack by the jetty for a few drinks. It was Saturday lunchtime and there were the regulars and a few couples out for a bit of a blow but it was too cold to stay out long. I found a table in the corner and tried to look like I was waiting for someone, smoking and drinking lager tops. I got the odd stare and by the time I ordered the third drink anyone could see that no one was joining me. I did a bit of doodling in my sketchbook and a few people gave me dirty looks because they thought I was drawing them. Eventually this man came over and asked me if I wanted another lager. He had a red shirt and a cowboy hat. He was tall and much older than me, and he had the kind of moustache I never liked, just curving round the upper lip and down the side of the mouth, but I didn't care.

Stan, he was called. He worked at the Bata factory in East Tilbury making shoes and told me he knew what it was like to be lonesome. *Please*, I thought, *I don't need your pity*, but it was getting near drinking-up time and I didn't want to leave. Two-thirty: the time of the wedding.

Stan told me he had some Cointreau back at his house and it was just nearby. It would be a privilege, he said, a privilege, if I joined him.

We walked back and the light was shining through dark clouds like something out of *Whistle Down the Wind*. Stan's house was just off Canvey Road in the Dutch Village, an ordinary semi with cracked crazy paving and roses that already had black spot on the leaves. It smelt of gas and fried food like it needed a good airing. We went into the kitchen for the drinks and I could see there were family photographs, the children grown up, and three different cowboy hats on the walls.

'Deirdre bought them for me.'

'Deirdre?'

'My wife.'

'Nice.'

'She died.'

'I'm sorry.'

'I didn't want you to think I was divorced.'

'I didn't.'

'I don't want you to think there's anything wrong with me.'

'I don't.'

I could see the remains of breakfast in the kitchen sink. The plate and the cutlery, a frying pan with dried-up fat and half a sausage on the gas ring.

'Would you like to come through? I've got a drinks cabinet. Perhaps I could light the fire in case it gets a bit chilly? We could sit on the sheepskin.'

'That'd be nice,' I said, expecting him to move the coffee table out of the way. That was how he wanted it, I could see, on the rug by the fire. He put a match to the gas.

'Would you like to see my collection?'

'Of what?' I wondered if it might be pornography. Ideas he wanted to try out.

'Boots, of course.'

'What do you mean?'

'Samples. Everything I've made. A whole career. They're in the basement.'

'Take your hat off,' I said.

'No, I'm shy,' he said. 'I'd like to show you the boots first. I don't have all my hair. I like to keep my hat on.'

'OK,' I said. 'Show me the boots.'

'It's a bit dark on the stairs but there's no need to be frightened. I won't harm you.'

'That's a pity,' I said, trying to be jokey and then regretting it. What if he had his mother down there like in *Psycho*?

'You should look at the wellingtons first. That's how I started. It was my idea to make them in pink and blue rather than green and black. Then I did white for the young ladies. Then protective and safety. I'm good with steel caps too. But I expect you don't want me going on about that. Rubber's best.'

'No,' I said. 'Tell me about the steel caps.'

He wasn't going to talk to me about floods or mothers or changing the world. He was going to talk to me about shoes. That was as long as he didn't murder me. Then we'd go back up, drink Cointreau and fool around for a bit. Not much harm in that, I suppose.

'Shall we go upstairs and put on some music?' he asked.

'Yes,' I said, 'I'd like that.'

'We've got lots of country. Lynn Anderson's good. Do you know "Ride, Ride, Ride"?'

'Have you got any Neil Diamond?' I said. He looked like the type of man who would.

'I've been to his concerts. With Deirdre, of course.'

Stop talking about your wife, I thought.

'Let's have something else,' I said. 'Johnny Cash. "A Boy Named Sue", something like that.'

'You're not a country person, are you?'

I took off my jacket and lit a cigarette. 'Then I suppose you'll have to teach me.'

'You don't need that . . .' he said, looking at the cigarette.

'Just dance with me, Stan.'

He was a good mover. I only hoped he wasn't thinking of his wife.

Eventually when I'd finished the cigarette we started necking and we sank to the floor, right by the rug and the fire like he had wanted. After a while he broke off and asked if I wouldn't prefer to be more comfy in the bedroom.

Comfy.

That wasn't how I would have described it, since the sheets were yellow nylon and the room wasn't heated, but we made the best of it and I managed not to think of Martin or the wedding or where my life was heading. I looked up at the ceiling and listened to the rain until Stan came. Then he turned away and I think he began to cry, although he didn't want to let me see that. Perhaps his wife wasn't dead after all.

By then it was six or seven o'clock and I felt a bit sick. I went to the bathroom and had a shower to let the smell of sex and Cointreau run away from me. There was some Imperial Leather, which was a relief because the only other scent on offer was the great smell of Brut and I didn't want that.

I came back to the bedroom, sat on the edge of the bed, and put my clothes on.

'You going?' Stan asked.

'Best get back.'

'Where do you live?'

'Maynell Avenue.'

'Can I see you again?'

'If you want,' I said. 'There's not much to see and you've seen most of it.'

'Was it all right?'

'Yes,' I lied.

'We should do this again some time,' he said, leaning back in the bed. I noticed he had put his hat back on. It was the only thing he was wearing. 'So long, partner.'

The next day Mum wanted to stay in and watch *The Sea Shall Not Have Them* with Michael Redgrave and Dirk Bogarde but I went to Dave's house so he could tell me about the wedding. We smoked some dope and listened to Deep Purple singing 'Wring That Neck'.

I wondered if I'd ever have feelings again. I thought about Martin and all that middle-class crap he wanted, clawing his way up into respectability. He still hadn't got his head round the idea that this was 1969. He didn't understand that once you'd sorted out your attitude to money and how much you needed then everything else followed. Did any of us want to have friends round for fondue suppers at a Habitat dining table? Did I really want to sit in a Vauxhall next to a husband in a Burton's suit who was always the wag at the Christmas party? I'd rather be poor. I'd rather be desperate.

FIVE

Claire

We began our married life in a terraced house in Brighton. We couldn't afford a home directly on the seafront so we found a dilapidated building three streets back with a balcony and a bit of a view. In the evenings we would ignore all the work that needed doing, open the windows and sit out drinking white wine, watching people walking on the esplanade and the gulls circling overhead. I had always liked seagulls as a child but once they start nesting in your roof you develop a more hostile attitude and I started to hate the bastards.

I was specialising in music and teaching a Primary 4 class in a Church of England JMI. Although Martin and I were lucky to find work I think we were surprised by the responsibility and the lack of freedom that went with it. For the past few years we had been the carefree generation with a conscience but once we were employed it was as if we had opened a door and walked straight into middle age. 'This isn't us,' I wanted to say, 'we're not ready for this, it's all a mistake,' but we had to accept that we weren't students any more.

Our house had once been divided into bed-sits and so we spent much of our early marriage knocking down flimsy dividing walls, sanding, polishing and choosing soft furnishings. Consequently most of our car journeys were either to Habitat, the local DIY store or the municipal dump.

I think we became almost careless of time; our marriage a procession of work, cooking and gardening, of *Morecambe and Wise* on the telly, and friends coming round for buffet suppers, music and the odd joint. Brighton was lively in the seventies, 'a good place to bring up kids', everyone said so, and we were invited almost every weekend to parties where we were offered nut loaf and potato salad, and where the decade's greatest invention, the clip-on plastic wine-glass holder, had become the quintessential lifestyle accessory.

After a few years, and as soon as they thought it polite, people began to ask when Martin and I were going to start a family but there were enough children for me to be going on with at the school. I told everyone there was plenty of time and, besides, we wanted to enjoy being the two of us for as long as we could. I wasn't ready to turn into my mother, a housewife in Oxfordshire, preparing endless batches of soup for the freezer, making marmalade in spring and chutney in autumn, and praying each day 'because it does make a difference, darling, it really does'.

I think my parents were disappointed that I had to earn money. Although they could hardly disapprove of my being a teacher they clung to the notion that it was in some way shameful for a wife to work. They always looked at Martin with a faint air of regret because they didn't think he earned enough to support me. Whenever they asked him a question it always came over as slightly patronising.

'Still straightening out rivers, Martin? Still shoring up cliffs?'

They never understood that I actually wanted to teach. I loved the joy on the children's faces as they sang together, happiness for which I was, in part, responsible. It wasn't like maths or spelling where they were continually assessed; they came to music lessons as equals. No one had kicked the confidence out of them by telling them they were no good, and even the ones who all the other teachers said were trouble could always bang away on a glockenspiel. We warmed up with rounds, 'Frère Jacques' and 'Non Nobis Domine', and then got out the recorders for 'Au Clair de la Lune' and some old folk songs. I had a little music trolley and gave triangles, Indian bells, tambourines and a bass xylophone to those who couldn't play the recorder and we rehearsed songs for school assembly extolling the joys of youth and creation, from 'Farmer, Farmer, Sow Your Seed' to 'Glad That I Live Am I'.

Living in Brighton we didn't have to travel far for our holidays and Martin worked all through the hot summer of 1976, examining the cracked and dried-out coastline, assessing the increased risk of landslip as the cliffs crumbled away. The reservoirs were depleted and the rivers low. Martin warned of a future of hot summers and flash floods. There was a hosepipe ban, you couldn't wash your car, and the water board threatened to shut off the supply to household taps from two in the afternoon until seven the next morning. Even the fountains in Trafalgar Square were turned off.

In the garden I tried to mulch the roses with old dishwater and wet newspaper, but the thirstier plants all began to wither away in the arid soil. Only the lavender survived. I had always wanted to make a garden as my mother had done but there wasn't the space or the money in Brighton. Of course I didn't have the ability or the patience either, but at least I had the excuse that now we didn't even have the water.

Then sometimes, when I was in the garden or out in the town, I would stop and wonder what the hell I was doing with my life. I couldn't understand how I had ended up dead-heading roses or carrying a shopping basket and why everyone kept asking me about my 'hubby' and what I was going to cook for him. At our wedding I'd been given a hostess trolley and a fondue set and I think everyone assumed that Martin would have the primary career and I'd be a dutiful wife who would simply dwindle into domesticity. But I just couldn't do that.

I joined a women's group where we shared experiences and talked about how the personal was as political as anything else in life. We sat round each other's kitchen tables swapping Germaine Greer and Kate Millett, discussing patriarchal attitudes and whether or not sex with men was inherently oppressive. Was marriage a form of domination disguised by love? Had male power and female submission been eroticised? Should there be wages for housework?

Soon I could bandy about phrases like 'the price of beauty' and Martin became increasingly anxious, especially when I started talking about a woman's right to refuse sex and control her own fertility. I think he thought it was a phase I was going through and he could tease me out of it by saying that he didn't mind what I did provided I didn't start wearing dungarees. I told him that I planned to start dressing for health and comfort rather than looks and if he didn't watch out I would make him read all the articles in *Spare Rib* about the politics of appearance and the nature of women's pleasure.

'I thought I was quite good at women's pleasure, my darling.'

'All men think that, Martin. They never think there's any room for improvement.'

'Then you'll just have to show me.'

'And you'll have to earn the right to be shown.'

Everything in my life seemed to involve presentation, some means of putting on a feminine mask to face the world, whether as teacher, wife, daughter or friend. I loathed being called 'Mrs Turner' at school and I hated being subject to what my friends called 'the male gaze'.

'Sometimes I'm not sure I know who you are any more . . .' said Martin.

'But wouldn't it be boring if we stayed the same all the time?'

'Yes, but I don't want you turning into a completely different person. I could have married anyone if that was going to happen.'

'Aren't you supposed to be helping me fulfil my potential, Martin? Isn't that the point of marriage?'

I'd given him a tea towel on Valentine's Day, the one saying how you start marriage by sinking into his arms and end up with your arms in his sink.

'I know. But it's hard. I wasn't brought up to think like this.'

'I hope you weren't expecting a *wife*.'

'Well, I did think that was the general idea.'

'Then I'm sorry to disappoint you.'

Martin liked me being feisty just as long as it wasn't with him.

'It's all right, Linda, I . . .'

'What?'

'Sorry.'

'Did you just call me Linda?'

'I didn't mean to. It just came out. Perhaps it was the word "wife".'

'I can't believe you did that. And now you're smirking. It's not funny, you know.'

'I'm sorry.'

'Well, don't smile about it.'

'I'm nervous. You make me nervous.'

'Perhaps you should have married her after all,' I said. 'She wouldn't have given you so much trouble.'

'It has occurred to me.'

'Oh, it has, has it?'

'But then, of course, my life wouldn't be so delightfully combative, would it?'

'Don't push it, Martin . . .'

One day I found him looking through an old sketchbook Linda had given him. He thought I hadn't noticed and he put it away quickly enough, but I knew what he was up to. It's so irritating the way men romanticise former girlfriends. You can see the phrase 'If only . . .' hovering over their heads even if the whole thing was a disaster. In fact, very often the more dreadful it was at the time, the more they miss them.

Then there was the small matter of children. We didn't speak about it much at first because we enjoyed our freedom and I think we were both scared by how much a baby might change us. I felt that I wasn't ready and Martin was frightened by the idea. It was part of his general anxiety, the old fear of tragedy returning. How could I guarantee that our child would be healthy, that I wouldn't die, or that nothing would go wrong?

We spent Christmas 1978 with my parents. Jonno was there with his little boy and Amanda was six months pregnant so much of the focus was on them. My mother kept giving me patient, loving looks but I could tell that hers was the smile of disappointment.

'We don't like to pry, dear, but is everything all right?'

'It's fine, Mummy, fine.'

'If you need any advice, dear, you just have to ask. Or if you'd like your father to talk to Martin . . .'

'No,' I said, 'please don't do that.'

My father pretended he was unconcerned about the emptiness of my womb. Instead he asked me to play a piece of Bach on the violin. It was the only present he wanted, he said, just to listen to my music.

We went to church on Christmas Day, Martin and I all too aware of our unexercised faith but grateful for the ritual of lessons, carols and the half-forgotten certainties that had defined my childhood. Dad read from the Gospel of St John and stood in the pulpit dressed in a simple white surplice, telling of the Christ child as a light in the darkness, a fragile hope against all the unpredictability of the world.

It was a love, he said, that was as strong as death.

He talked of the power and the freshness of new birth, the child as source of peace and joy, and of comfort from fear, and I thought, suddenly, and for the first time, that he was preaching only to me.

Martin

Every time I went back to Canvey Dad and Vi were as embarrassed
to ask as Claire's parents. I could sense them starting to steer the
subject round and then giving up and talking about football or the
weather so it was a relief when we could finally tell them that Claire
was pregnant.

'Well, we *were* wondering,' said Vi.

'Thought there might be something wrong with you.'

'Thanks, Dad . . .'

I watched the children coming out of my old school in Long
Road and recognised some of my former friends waiting outside
the gates, already parents. They looked tired and bored and were
older than I had ever imagined they could be. Ade's wife Kate was
talking to Patsy Warner. I remembered how she used to let boys
look at her knickers for a shilling a show. Linda told me that she
was the first of her friends to lose her virginity. Then there was
Henry Williams who used to invite the girls to watch him streak
every night, and Alison Watkins, and Rosie Atkinson who everyone
said had the best breasts in the school even though none of us had
ever seen them.

Some of the old teachers were in a Portakabin: Mr Lister, Miss
Dovedale, Mr Wheatley, Mr Keating, their names a roll-call of
memory. I remembered Mr Dodd going through French irregular
verbs until his mouth started to dribble, and Mr Longstaff who had
left one afternoon and never come back. Why was that? we
wondered. A nervous breakdown? Infidelity? Indiscretion?

When I was a child they had been tall and authoritative but now they seemed either eccentric or desperate. If we ever returned to Canvey they would teach our child and Claire would be one of their colleagues.

I wanted to be seventeen again, with Linda and the future all before us. I didn't want to be middle-aged.

I tried to remember what it had been like in the past, when I had loved without imagining a future. Any consummated desire, any happiness, had always contained the possibility of its absence. This was how I had lived my life, holding back and protecting myself, still conscious of the loss of my mother, knowing how swiftly love could be taken away.

But now, with a child, love would have to be unconditional. I would have to provide the certainty and trust: a life without doubt.

Claire

It was 1979, the winter of discontent: freezing fogs and the roads not gritted; oilfields blockaded by fishermen and a national rail strike inevitable. There were drifts of snow fifteen feet deep, the snowman outside the school had an 'Official Picket' sign stuck round his neck, and the temperature was twenty-nine degrees below zero. Martin's dad telephoned and told us that four men from Benfleet had gone missing at sea. Freak tides had breached the defences at Jaywick and a thousand people had been evacuated. A man had been found dead and covered in snow in a car park at Stanford-le-Hope.

There was rubbish everywhere. Water workers, ambulance drivers and dustmen were on industrial action, and Martin had stayed on to help keep a pumping station open. We didn't tell too many friends about that but he couldn't afford to strike. He was management not production line and there wasn't much of a choice with a baby on the way.

The first sign had been the surprise of my waters breaking before I felt any contractions. I awoke just before dawn to a feeling of wetness and the faint smell of protein, and I guessed what my doctor called 'the unstoppable adventure' had begun. The spontaneous rupture of membranes was like a wave unfurling over my baby's head.

I woke Martin and told him to make a cup of tea and phone the hospital. I wanted him to be calm, and we had tried to anticipate every eventuality, but in the end we panicked like everyone else. When the contractions eventually came they were only four minutes apart and we had to make a mad dash.

We reached the hospital at nine in the morning and Lucy arrived at three minutes past five. Martin joked that it was the only nine-to-five job I'd ever done but I was too exhausted to find it funny. Instead I think we both cried.

There weren't the words. I had started going into labour in a dream and woke to find my world utterly altered: Lucy's crumpled face smoothing from old age to a baby, the grey-blue blood-streaked flesh slowly gathering colour like dawn. It was the reverse of dying; the eyes slowly opening, the head lifting to the air rather than sinking in the last gasp of death.

I could not believe the beauty of her presence; the nuzzling smell of her, the softness of her skin, the fragility of delicate fingernails and miniature curled toes. I could not understand how I could feel so much love and so much fear at the same time. If I lost this child I would have to live with an exploded heart.

But I found motherhood harder than I had ever imagined. It hurt as the baby took the colostrum, and when the milk eventually came in my breasts felt engorged, the areolae were swollen and hard. Lucy found it difficult to latch on, so much so that I couldn't accept the fact that the bluish watery foremilk could ever be any good for her.

Martin and I were attentive, over-anxious parents, determined to be better than our own, but neither quite trusting the other, our panic due to a surfeit of love we could neither define nor resolve. We argued about feeding and how quickly Lucy should be weaned. I accused him of rocking her too slowly, of carrying our daughter like a parcel even after he'd made the effort to support the head, and of leaving her to sleep with too much light. In turn he told me I was wrapping the baby too tightly so that she was hot and tempera-mental; that I let her sleep too long in the afternoons so that our nights were disturbed; and that she spent so much time in our bed we no longer had any marital privacy.

What marital privacy? I thought. *Surely he doesn't want that already?*

There was no time for anything except Lucy. She didn't settle into any pattern and although people told me to let the baby take the breast every four hours and cry in between I couldn't allow her to go without. I was determined to feed on demand even though my breasts were sore and the nipples were cracked. Milk got everywhere, through the pads and the T-shirts, because Lucy didn't take that much. Little and often, that's what she wanted, but I couldn't get the hang of it. The shock of her dependency was overwhelming. I began to wonder who I was and to hate myself: my breasts, my body shape, even the sound of my own voice.

I tried to talk to Martin but he didn't understand the tiredness and the tears and the hatred of my own body; my fear that it would never regain any of the tautness that it once had. I lost weight, watching what I ate because everything found its way into the milk, and the maternity wear fell off me. But even when I regained what was left of my figure all my old clothes felt wrong. I was reduced to wearing fishermen's smocks, drawstring tracksuit bottoms and slippers. Bits of food and sick and house dust kept sticking to me and I had no time to clean anything because I was so preoccupied with each change for the baby. The midwife came and told me to rest when Lucy slept but there was always so much preparation and tidying up to do, I couldn't keep up.

The kinder Martin was to me, the more irritating I found him. When he told me I looked beautiful I thought he was lying. When he said he was proud of me I didn't believe him. When he read that cabbage leaves could calm the pain in the breasts I shouted back that he had never understood anything about my breasts and never would. I wanted him out of the way; and then, as soon as he was gone, I wanted him back to help me.

I felt sadness and then guilt about being depressed. How could I be sad when I'd had a much wanted baby? None of the books I'd bought went into sufficient detail. They simply said I might get tired or feel like a treat: steak and champagne if we could afford it, liver and beer if we couldn't. Liver! The thought made me gag.

Some of my friends suggested some new clothes and a bit of shopping but I hated my body so much I couldn't imagine looking good in anything. I was tense and fearful, and Martin's voice took on a pained tone of sympathy that was never convincing because I knew he was wondering how long this was all going to last.

He walked slowly round the house, carefully trying to institute a feeling of serenity, which only made me more angry. I couldn't believe how anyone could take so much time over anything. Eventually I lost my patience and shouted, 'For God's sake, what are you doing? Get a move on. There's so much to do.'

'Calm down, Claire.'

'DON'T TELL ME TO BE CALM.'

'It doesn't help when you're like this,' he said. 'I have pressures too.'

'Of course, silly me, it's you who have been putting yourself out. Forgive me for being so selfish and thinking it was about me, my baby and my stitches.'

'I know it's difficult . . .'

'Oh, do you now?'

'Of course I don't know exactly . . .'

'No. Not exactly.'

'But it would be nice,' he said quickly, 'if I knew when you were going to get over this so we could start being a family, instead of having to put up with all this . . .'

'All this what?'

'I don't know. Attention seeking.'

'Is that what you think this is?'

'I'm sorry. I didn't mean it like that.'

'You bloody did.'

'Look. I'm doing my best. I can't help it if you're so bloody difficult to live with.'

'Well, fuck off then,' I said. 'Fuck off and grow up, Martin Turner.'

I could see that he was shocked that I'd called him by his full name but instead of leaving me or putting his arm around me, he gave me one of those infuriating smiles of his, like he'd thought of a joke, and said: 'What shall I do first then, fuck off or grow up?'

I threw myself at him, beating his chest with my fists, hating the man I loved, not knowing how I could ever experience such fierce fury, or why I was so out of control, or when these feelings would ever leave me.

Violet

Martin and Claire couldn't sit still for a moment; they were so worried about Lucy, the world and each other. It was as if they thought life was going to catch them out if they didn't move quick enough. When she was in the kitchen Claire spent all her time watching the baby and checking where the food had come from: if any of the vegetables on the market had been sprayed with insecticide, if eggs from battery hens contained salmonella, if ratatouille, or whatever it was called, was safe to freeze.

Her voice was strained and high and she couldn't trust anyone with even the simplest of tasks. She was always fussing over her child and telling me I should change the way I ate and the washing powder I used, talking about additives and chemicals and how it was a sin to bleach. But her clothes had that grey look about them because she had started to use some new-fangled non-biological rubbish. I do think ecology has its limits.

Her conversation was filled with a running commentary on Lucy's every look, need and gesture, as if her daughter was the most interesting thing in the world and everyone else was irrelevant. When I suggested that she and Martin could do with a bit of a rest and were in danger of spoiling the baby, they just pointed to their motherhood manual and said: 'No child suffers from too much love.'

Honestly. They never made it easy for themselves. I even caught Martin changing a nappy but when I said I was surprised to see him doing such a thing he told me that I had a lot to learn about the gendered nature of domestic responsibility. I didn't know what he was talking about.

I tried to remember what he had been like at the same age, but I could only think how pink he had been and how his ears might need to be pinned.

'I remember when you were a little boy, Martin,' I said. 'Do you remember cutting the fringes of the rug in the living room?'

'No, Auntie Vi, I don't.'

'You thought it was growing; said it needed a haircut.'

'I can't remember.'

'Then you found the scissors and started cutting away at it. Snip, snip, snip. Your father was so angry. I had to stop him giving you the slipper.'

Len interrupted. 'Don't bring that up now, Vi.'

Claire came over all prim. 'We don't believe in hitting children.'

'Well, I'm sorry I spoke.'

I was only trying to make a bit of conversation but next time I wouldn't bother. Neither of them could see past the baby.

When Len got to sixty-five I thought we should celebrate by going out for a meal but Martin and Claire even made a fuss about that because they were worried about leaving Lucy with a baby-sitter. At one stage it looked like they were going to try and bring her with them but I wasn't having any of that.

'The restaurant does not welcome children in the evenings,' I said. 'They have to think of the other guests.'

'In Italy parents take their children everywhere,' Claire said.

'But this isn't Italy,' I answered, 'and that's where all their problems come from, if you ask me. No backbone and too much aftershave. All the men are in love with their mothers . . .'

'Have you ever been there, Auntie Vi?'

'I don't need to go there to form my opinion, thank you very much.'

They were so chippy but eventually we got it sorted out and settled down to a good no-nonsense menu: melon balls or prawn and avocado cocktail, plaice or fillet steak, Black Forest gateau or fruit salad. You could choose between Hirondelle and Blue Nun if you wanted value and there were old bottles with little foun-tains of dried candle wax from previous dinners. Of course I wouldn't have the gateau or the Blue Nun because I didn't like to eat anything German. That was something of a rule in our family. My mother wouldn't even dance the waltz because she said it was German.

A couple at the next table were describing Mrs Thatcher as 'the best man for the job', and I nearly joined in. *Quite right,* I thought, but I knew if I said anything too political there would be trouble. Claire said she'd like a cheese omelette even though it wasn't on the menu, and Martin went AWOL and ordered the plaice. Len had a bit of a laugh about that and tried to jolly things along because he could see that Claire was cross. It was far too warm a day for plaice, he said.

'I just want the fish, Dad.'

'Order what you like,' said Claire. 'Don't mind me.' I was surprised she let him have it.

Then Linda appeared all dolled up at the bar with a gentleman friend. She had some kind of glitter in her hair and was making a good job of showing the little bit of cleavage she had – just the right side of common, it was – and I could see Martin fall for it straight away.

'Hello, everyone,' Linda said, and then, 'Hello, Martin.'

Martin should have introduced Claire but he was too distracted for manners. He and Linda had all the embarrassment of former sweethearts, not kissing each other, standing awkwardly, neither quite knowing what to say.

'Linda . . .' Martin looked at her so fiercely she had to turn her eyes away. As soon as she did so he said, 'I'm sorry I haven't . . .'

'That's all right . . .'

It was like watching something you shouldn't have. Len was about to ask Linda to have a drink with us but I put my hand on his knee to stop him and thank goodness he knew what I meant.

'It's lovely to see you, Linda,' I said. 'Keeping well?'

'Not bad . . . you all right, Martin?'

'This is my wife,' he said, gesturing to Claire.

'I guessed as much.'

Claire kept looking at Linda. 'I couldn't really be anybody else.'

'It's nice to meet you,' said Linda.

'I'd always wondered what you were like,' said Claire.

'Well, I hope I'm not a disappointment.'

Martin could see that it was getting a bit tense but he couldn't think of the right thing to say. 'We're old friends,' he explained to his wife.

Claire smiled. 'I do know who Linda is, Martin.'

'Long time ago now,' said Linda. Her boyfriend was signalling he'd got the drinks. 'I'd best get back.'

'You don't want to lose him . . .' I said.

She gave a little smile. 'Bye then, Martin,' she said. 'You all have a good evening.'

As soon as she had turned to go, and still within her hearing, Claire picked up her wine glass and announced: 'So that's the famous Linda.'

'Nice girl,' said Len. 'Though not as nice as you, of course, Claire . . .'

I could tell he was thinking that he'd been right all along and that Martin would have been better off with his first girlfriend. She was far less opinionated and had always been more like one of us. The restaurant had to make such a fuss about Claire being a vegetarian and you never got that with Linda.

'Couldn't you just have our vegetables?' I said, but Len was trying to get on her better side and made sure they cooked her the omelette.

Then Martin piped up, quite unexpectedly, 'Pity George couldn't come.'

'Don't you worry about George,' I said. 'He's much happier where he is. You know he can't tell what's going on these days.'

Honestly. I don't know why he had to start talking about George. Neither of them had any idea what it was like and I could tell they were judging us even though no one would call their marriage perfect. Then Len changed the subject and said it was time for a dance. Of course Martin and Claire didn't join us; didn't know how, I suppose, even for the rumba, which any old fool can do.

I tried not to let them get to me. Even when Claire had recovered from her depression (of course we weren't allowed to call it that out loud) she still spoke as if she didn't expect anyone to be clever enough to understand her. I think she thought she felt things more deeply than anyone else but she wasn't exactly the first person in the world to have a child.

I only hoped their marriage would survive. At least mine had, despite its troubles. No one could say I hadn't been good to George, looking after him for all those years.

George

Sometimes the old woman came to see me. She was losing her looks but I pretended not to notice. You have to be careful with ladies. They can be touchy. She kept talking to me as if I was married to her. But if that was the case then why weren't we in the same house? And where was my tea? I said, 'I can't be married to you, my wife's much younger than you, and she's attractive, so what are you talking about?'

Days went by and I remembered seeing the child that everyone said was Martin's and I was confused and I couldn't stop thinking about how no one came to visit me any more. I preferred sleeping but I couldn't always be sure it would be all right. If I had dreams or woke up I couldn't get back to sleep and the waking was always a disappointment. It was like when I was in the hospital and they made me sleep for weeks and weeks, before they put the electric probe in the throat to make me speak. 'Narcoanalysis,' the trick cyclist called it. Woken for an hour a day for a bit of soup and a wash, then the medicine and back to sleep where no one could harm me.

> She's my lady love.
> She is my dove, my baby love.
> She's no girl for sitting down to dream.
> She's the only girl Laguna knows.

The jungle juice was so strong I didn't even dream. It was so peaceful then. It was a bit like being dead, I imagine. You got sad to wake up.

Now I either liked to be asleep or fully awake. I hated the bits in between but that was the time in which I lived. The voices in my head kept coming back again like it was a dream but not like the old days when there were orders and everyone knew what was what. Now it was different.

I knew that they were doing some decorating next door and there was scaffolding. The men had a radio but I couldn't make much sense of it. Someone was singing about going underground, and then another man with a lively voice said it was jam but I couldn't understand. How can jam go underground? It must have been like picking the flies off the sandwiches in the trenches. My dad had told me about that.

Then there was a woman singing about Bette Davis eyes and someone else saying it was all a joke and that suicide was painless and all these voices started to come together, the songs from next door and up in the sky and in my head: *The ratings are drowning . . . I'm watching the rivets . . . come on, Georgie, look lively . . . what are you doing, mate?*

I thought I should get better. Really I should. But then why get better when I might have to go back?

Watch them drown all over again.

I don't mind death; it's the dying, I think: the fear of being afraid; always waiting for the surprise, things coming at me.

But I keep surviving. Nothing kills me. Ever. It's like I'm being punished for the ratings. They keep drowning and I keep surviving.

Sometimes I hear their voices calling me from underwater. And I see their faces. I want the voices to stop but they keep coming. Even in my sleep I hear them.

You still alive, Georgie? Fancy that. Lucky old George.

Then I hear them calling me.

Come on, George.

The slightest noise affects my heart.

I know she likes me.
I know she likes me
Because she said so.

147

I think I'll go for a walk, blow the cobwebs away, only this time I'll walk as far as I can. Keep right on to the end of the road.
   Straight On for the Sea.

> *She's my lady love.*
> *She is my dove, my baby love.*
> *She's no girl for sitting down to dream.*
> *She's the only girl Laguna knows.*

We'll have this big reunion under the sea. I'm sure the men are waiting.

> *I know she likes me.*
> *I know she likes me*
> *Because she said so.*

All I have to do is keep walking towards the sun. Best foot forward.

> *She is my Lily of Laguna.*
> *She is my lily and my rose.*

Violet

They used to train them, the postmen, because they always knew. I hoped for a young one coming up to the door because they only told you good news. It was the older ones you had to watch, the ones with kind faces. You could tell before they said anything, holding the envelope and wishing they weren't. 'Priority,' it said.

I was with Mother in our old house in Thames Road when the news of George came the first time. 'Is it good or bad news?' she asked and the postman looked embarrassed.

I couldn't understand how you could go missing from a boat except to die in the sea. And people would know about that. I heard bits of news; that there was a hospital there, not just a military one but a big civilian one, and I thought he might have gone off with one of the nurses and started a new life. Russian children running through the woods, and him drinking vodka and pretending he never knew me.

When he came back he had horrible dreams. He cried out that he was on fire with superheated steam or that some of the ratings were drowning.

He had given the order to flood the watertight compartments, and he'd had to do it to get the ship on an even keel again. Four of the men had been trapped below the waterline until their air gave out. He thought it was his fault.

'Come back,' I wanted to say, 'come back to me,' but he couldn't. I don't think he ever knew who I was, not really, not the laughs we had or the fun or the dancing. Instead all I got were those terrible eyes, the kind you see in the heads of people when

149

they're about to die, glittering. When I asked what was wrong he said: 'I'm watching the rivets.' He thought he was in the water again, seeing if the ship was sinking, trying not to get sucked under. And then there was that shaking he did, and the moments of temper when he'd mutter and then stamp about angrily or bang on the table and shout, 'Stop.'

Every Guy Fawkes I had to close the windows and doors and bandage his head so he couldn't hear the noise. But the bandages reminded him of the wounded he'd seen and the friends he'd lost and he started to pick away at them. And then when they came off he thought the lights were too bright and he heard the sounds from outside, fireworks, children and laughter. He thought he was being laughed at and that they were coming to get him to put him in the middle of the bonfire. He curled up under the bed and I had to lie beside him, holding him with his teeth chattering, his body shaking, waiting for it to go away and not knowing when it would.

Sometimes he came back to me a bit. He had these moments of sense when I remembered that in his day he was cleverer than anyone I had ever met. He was brilliant, it's the only word I can think of to describe it; brilliant in his eyes and in his mind, shining like he knew something nobody else did. And you got a glimpse of it before bang, out it went, quickly, like a light – not when you turn it off but when it snaps or explodes, gone, and his whole body slumped and it took ages to get him right again.

At the inquest the two witnesses said he looked at them but he didn't notice they were there at all. They shouted at him, told him the jetty was closed for the day, but either George couldn't hear them or he didn't want to. I don't know whether he'd waited until all the day-trippers had left or whether it was just a coincidence that there was hardly anyone there but he walked straight past the Old Bay Country Club, across the beach and on to the jetty without breaking his stride. He knew the currents were strong and he'd weighed himself down just in case but I wonder if he knew which step would be his last, if he'd paced it out or if it came as a surprise when he was falling, the way people who've survived say they wish halfway down that they hadn't done it.

He had a roving eye and I knew he fancied Lily rather than me, but she was too young for him at the time, only fifteen, and so I decided to take my chance. Of course I didn't realise that he was going to keep fancying Lily even after we were married. God knows where they went or how they did it without anybody noticing. It was hard to find any place for yourself in those days. Perhaps a friend of his had a room or something.

Afterwards I got so depressed that I began to think that he had only married me in order to be closer to her. People always thought Lily was a soft little creature but she was all steel. That weakness, that 'look after me, I'm so frightened', was an act.

George was always going on about her. Some people thought it was sweet but it was humiliating to me. There was nothing I could do to shut him up. Then one Christmas he blurted it out. 'My son Martin.' Luckily Len was out of the room and I slapped him across the face and told him he had to stop that right then and there, but Lily went quiet like she couldn't keep it a secret any more and said, 'It's true, Vi, it's true.'

I looked at George and I was filled with such hatred I couldn't describe it. I think I wanted to murder him on the spot: kill the both of them.

I decided not to tell Len. I never have. I've never told anyone. Not even Martin. Knowledge was only going to make things worse and I'd lived with it for so long. Sometimes a family needs its secrets.

Sixty-six, George was. Not old, is it? I dream about it. Sometimes I'm there, telling him to stop, shouting and shouting, but the wind is too strong and he can't hear me and he doesn't even want to hear me and he keeps on walking until he falls.

People say I could have done a bit more, but George needed such a lot of looking after. I wish they realised that. And he'd let me down so badly. I wish I could have told them what it was like. But you have to keep things to yourself sometimes. You have to have grace.

Len

Everyone thought we'd get married. I still found Vi attractive, I always had, and we joked about it, but it wasn't right that a man had to die in order for us to be together. It came home to me at the funeral. It was one of those grey days when you're sure it's never going to get light; the sky had all the hope drained out of it.

Burial at sea. I've always dreaded those words. The priest said we might as well take out the fishing boat but it was a bit of a squash with all of us on it and I was worried about the wind. I didn't want George's ashes blowing back in our faces.

'How far out do you want to go?' I asked.

'Chapman's Light,' said Vi.

'You know it's just a buoy these days.'

'I want to go where there's no river any more. I don't want to see any land.'

'Hard to see anything in this,' I said.

Martin and Claire looked like they'd had another of their arguments and were still fussing over Lucy's life jacket. I don't think Claire trusted it. She kept asking about the dinghy and if the radio worked and how soon help could arrive once it had been summoned. They'd even brought special food for Lucy and some children's binoculars like it was an outing we'd organised especially for her.

'Look,' I wanted to say, 'this isn't about you, it's about George,' but I knew it wouldn't have done any good. As Vi said, it was like no one in the world had ever had a child before.

I let the boat idle and the priest began: *O most powerful and glorious Lord God, at whose commands the winds blow, and lift up the waves of the sea, and who stillest the rage thereof: we thy creatures, but miserable sinners, do in this our great distress cry unto thee for help: save, Lord, or else we perish.*

I'd had a few drinks before we set off. I never normally do anything of the kind, but then it's not every day you take your best friend's ashes out. I don't know whether it was the alcohol, or nerves, or the fact that I felt for the first time that I was a bit too old for the fishing, but whatever it was I wasn't so steady on my feet. I had to cling on to the edge of the boat. I had never before felt frail, and on the boat too, where I always knew what I was doing.

We therefore commit his body to the deep, to be turned into corruption, looking for the resurrection of the body (when the sea shall give up her dead) and the life of the world to come . . .

The priest helped Vi unscrew the urn and I watched her cradle it with both hands and hold it over the edge of the boat and everyone line up downwind of her.

'Ready?' she called, checking everyone was looking.

The ashes caught on the wind and swirled away from us, dust on the dark waters.

Violet

You forget how official death is and how long it takes afterwards. It's such a kerfuffle of grief and administration and you can't understand what you're supposed to be doing next. It's hard to believe any of it matters: the paperwork, the letters, the certificates and the meetings with the bank. I had to keep proving my husband was dead. Len helped but there were some things I had to do on my own, like meeting the man from the Navy who came to talk about my pension and the conditions he had to impose if I was to stay on in my house on the reduced rent.

'We're happy to let you continue here, Mrs Lancaster, but there are a few things we need to go through. You have no dependants?'

'I have a nephew, Martin.'

'Visit you regularly, does he?'

'He used to. Before he had a daughter.'

'Ah yes . . .'

'What do you mean?'

'Sometimes, with the elderly, visits tend to diminish.'

'He lives in Brighton,' I said, 'and I'm not elderly.' I knew what the man was getting at: disappearing relatives who come back all too quick as soon as there is any sign of money.

'And you have friends?' he asked.

'Oh, I've plenty of friends,' I said.

'But no one special?'

'No,' I said. 'No one special.'

The man made a note like he wasn't sure if he believed me. Then I realised where I'd seen him before. It was at the Christmas

154

dance in the War Memorial Hall. He was with a dowdy woman and they'd made a pig's ear out of a reverse turn in the waltz. He must have heard some of the gossip about Len.

'So you have no plans to marry again?' he asked.

'Would be a bit quick, wouldn't it?'

'I only point it out because of the conditions. I am obliged to do so.'

Oh are you? I thought. *Obliged.* 'You mean the will?'

'Not so much your husband's will but our provision for you here. There are conditions.'

'I am aware of them.'

'Then you understand my need to remind you. This is a delicate matter. If you marry again we would expect your new husband to provide for you.'

'That would only be proper.'

'Which means you would lose some of your benefits.'

'This home?'

'And the pension.'

'You would expect a new husband to keep me?'

'You would have to decide, Mrs Lancaster, if you preferred a new husband or an old pension. You wouldn't be able to have both.'

He smiled like he had made a joke, but I could tell it was one of those false smiles because only his mouth was animated. The rest of his face stayed still, and the smile disappeared, like he could turn it on and off.

'Do you think this is the time to tell me?' I said.

'I'm sorry,' he was saying. 'This is always difficult.'

These people were quicker in cutting my pension than they were in arranging the funeral.

I knew they didn't approve of suicide but if they hadn't made him mad in the first place then he'd never have done it. 'You'll have to go,' I said. 'I don't feel well.'

'I'm sorry.'

'I'm a bit upset.'

'Can I get you anything?' the man asked. 'Some tea? Or some brandy? I carry a hip flask.'

I bet you do, I thought. I wondered how they trained men like him.

'I'll be all right,' I said. 'I'd like some time on my own. Gather my thoughts.'

'I understand,' the man said. I remembered that he had told me his Christian name was Gavin. He had said I could call him that if I liked or I could be formal if I preferred. Well, I did prefer. I didn't want to be on the sort of terms where he could presume to call me Violet.

He got up from the settee and then stopped by the door. He seemed to be wondering where he had left his umbrella.

'As I said, these are difficult times.'

'Will you see yourself out?' I asked but I could tell he couldn't leave fast enough. He was probably trying to work out whether it was worth sacrificing his umbrella in exchange for a quick exit. I imagined him sighing as he walked to his car. *Well, I may have lost my umbrella but at least that's another widow done for the day.* A bit of rain would serve him right.

As soon as he was gone I felt depressed all over again. I stared at the wall, the dark green below the dado, except there was no real dado to speak of. People had pity but I couldn't help feeling that in their heart of hearts they thought I deserved this; that I was even responsible. They were embarrassed by what had happened. Perhaps they thought suicide was a disease they could catch simply by speaking to me.

I thought about what the man had said. Gavin. I could give it all up: the house and the pension. I could persuade Len to let me live with him, even marry, I was sure, but I wasn't going to beg.

Perhaps Len wasn't being selfish in not asking me to marry him; maybe he knew or had guessed about the pension and was being practical and understanding. We would just have to carry on in our separate homes with the same standard of living. No difference. It wasn't romantic but I suppose it made a kind of sense.

But I felt a bit giddy. Len could at least have asked me to marry him and I could have politely declined. Or we could have discussed it. Now I would have to be above it all because of the money and the need to stay respectable. It was so hard to do right, to keep my dignity and think the best of people.

I wished I'd had some of the man's brandy but it was too late now.

Five o'clock. Two hours until *East Enders*.

I sat in the chair and tried to picture George as a young man. I wanted Len to come round and I wanted him to understand.

Cheer up, old girl.

I was lonely in that room and I was frightened of growing old. Of losing my teeth. Or my mind.

I remembered my old mother. We had to put signs up all over her house. 'This is a kettle. Put water in it first. This is a tap. Fill the kettle with water and put the lid on. This is the electricity socket. Turn it on when you have filled the kettle with water and put it back. This is a teapot . . .'

Then she forgot how to read and everything was hopeless. I thought of her saying the last time I visited her: *Please remind me how I know you.*

My own mother.

I didn't ever want to be like her. I didn't want to die on my own.

SIX

Claire

By 1983 Martin was travelling all over the country, working out suitable strategies for different sections of coastline, bringing back samples of rock, chalk and limestone so that the upstairs rooms of our house began to look like the lair of a Victorian fossil hunter. He kept talking about the fragility of cliffs and high-ridged sandstone, rippled and crumbling to the touch like spice, insisting that land was only loaned from the sea. He said that one crevice he was working on looked like a giant vagina. I told him that he should either keep quiet or develop a better knowledge of the female anatomy.

I was busy with Lucy, loving her with the same desperate and protective passion I had always had, but I still couldn't shift my feelings of worthlessness. There had to be more to my life than washing, baking and looking after a child. I wanted to make a difference, to do some kind of good in the world, and here I was, turning into my own mother. I wasn't bored exactly, but sometimes, out in the Lanes of Brighton, I would drift off and think about shoplifting or going missing or having vigorous sex with a complete stranger in the Royal Albion Hotel. I just didn't know who I was any more. Whatever happened to ethical ambition? Where was that Aldermaston spirit now?

Then, towards the end of the summer term, the women's group started to talk about the peace camp at Greenham Common. The installation of cruise missiles was set for November and the women there were appealing for others to join them. I heard one of them on the radio telling people not to be afraid: 'You might think that you are alone, sitting at home. You may think that your contribution won't make much difference, that you only have a tiny voice in the middle of this dark time in our history, but together we can shout, "Enough. Stop this insanity." '

I was angry that common English land should be appropriated and endangered by weapons controlled from another country. What was the point in having children if the government was so reckless with their future? I had marched at university and sent money to CND but here was something I could do that was practical and immediate. I even got to the stage of thinking that if I didn't go and the cruise missiles came then any nuclear incident would be my fault because I hadn't been there to stop them.

I knew Martin would worry as soon as he discovered my plan and so I decided to organise it in secret and then break the news to him over supper in the garden. I didn't want there to be any doubt or for him to put on his dependent face that always made me feel guilty.

'Can't you go for a weekend?' he asked.

'That doesn't count, does it?' I said. 'The missiles aren't there for the weekend. War doesn't break out for a weekend.'

'But you have a family . . .'

'Yes, but there won't be much of a family left if I don't do something about it.'

'And what about Lucy?'

'I'll take her with me.'

'For God's sake, Claire. She's far too young.'

'I can look after her there. There are lots of children.'

'So you've already made up your mind. Before talking to me?'

'I'm not doing this for me; I'm doing it for the future. Please,' I said, 'don't make it hard for me.'

Martin picked up the plates and went back into the house. 'I'll have to think about it, Claire.'

Don't you dare, I thought. *Don't you dare try and stop me.*

Further down the street I could hear a barbecue in full swing and everyone singing along to Spandau Ballet's 'True'. I couldn't understand how people could be so unconcerned.

When I came to bed Martin turned out the light and we lay for a while in the darkness without touching each other.

Then I heard his voice. 'I don't want you to go . . .'

'I know.'

'But it's not much of a marriage if I try and make you stay.'

I took his hand. 'I do love you,' I said. 'You do know that, don't you?'

I felt for the side of his face and began to stroke it. People talk about love going stale and of marriages becoming sexually lazy, but just because we knew how to please each other didn't mean our love-making was any the less exciting. It was tender and familiar, and I think we were gentler than when we had begun our life together. We were aware this separation would not be so much a test as a sign of confidence that we could love each other despite absence.

As I turned away from Martin to sleep, my body on its side but my hand stretching back to touch his, I thought how strange it was that in the past men had left home for war: now women were leaving for peace.

Violet

Claire had a bit of a goodbye party and we came down to see her off. That was a bit of a shock. The house was a tip with all the washing and the toys and there was nowhere to get your Hoover round. It had that warm smell of old milk that you get in those family homes where you can't be sure anything is ever really clean.

I had managed to ignore the Mods and Rockers in the sixties, and to smile as kindly as I could at the long hair and glitter of the seventies, but some of those women were eye-popping. They had either shaved the sides of their head or dyed their hair purple and they wore those boiler suits that made them all look as if they were plumbers. Some of them had bright stripy knitwear – alpaca, I think it was, with bits of twig in it, quite rough to the touch. Not much chance of finding a single man between the lot of them, I'd have thought. And hardly any of them were wearing make-up, not even lipstick. I always have to have my lipstick. It helps me concentrate.

At the kitchen table, eating aubergine lasagne or some other Italian muck, Claire was entertaining her new friends: Gail, Pasha and Franny. I think they were the ones who told her that make-up was a sign of masculine domination. Honestly. They were about as exciting as a box of billiard balls.

It was the little girl I felt sorry for, always watching her parents, not sure what any of those women were doing in her home. With a hippy you knew where you were, but with this lot you felt anything could happen. God forbid that any of them would ever want to live near me.

Claire told me I should think about joining them. 'You are joking,' I said, but I could see that she was either testing me or making fun. She had that ambiguous tone clever people always adopt, half-joking, half-serious, and you're supposed to guess which one they mean. If you think they're joking they say they were being serious. If you take them seriously they say that they were joking. You can't win.

'Well, Violet,' Claire said, using my full name to make me listen, 'it's quite simple. Are you on the side of death or are you on the side of life? Because that's the only decision you have to make.'

'Well, Claire,' I replied, 'I don't think you can achieve world peace by going camping.'

'And so are you going to do anything about it, Violet? Anything at all?'

'I've been in enough wars,' I said. Her tone of voice was starting to give me the pip. If you ask me, the world was messed up enough as it was without that lot trying to sort it out.

Claire

Before Greenham we went on our family holiday to Dorset and it rained all the time. We dressed in bright-blue cagoules and tried to pretend we preferred wet weather. We'd given Lucy a camera and she took photographs of everything: not only the views and the boats but Coke cans, bits of rope in the road, Martin shaving, the food on her plate in a restaurant, even her own knee. Strangers were commandeered to take snapshots of the three of us together. We took a trip to Lyme Regis and walked on the Cobb, not talking about Greenham at all, and watched various girls with hooded coats trying to look like the French Lieutenant's Woman each time a wave came over.

You could see we were going our separate ways on the return journey by looking in the boot of our clapped-out Volvo: a suitcase for Martin returning to Brighton, a rucksack and camping gear for the intrepid mother and daughter. I packed clothes that didn't need any maintenance, candles, tins of food, matches, a camping kettle and a couple of sleeping bags. I took lavatory paper and, in a moment of vanity, I threw in some moisturiser and a bit of lipstick. Vi would have been proud of me.

'You're quiet,' said Martin, as we left Newbury.

'I don't know what to think,' I said. 'But I feel my life's about to change.'

'As long as I can still recognise you when you both come back.'

'We're not going for that long,' I said.

'Be home by Christmas then?' said Martin.

'Don't . . .'

It was Hiroshima Day, 6th August 1983, and there were Stop the Arms Race marches from all over the country. As we neared the base we could see processions of women with banners making their way towards the main gate.

We parked on a verge and Martin asked if I wanted him to stay and put up the tent but I didn't want to look dependent in front of the other women. I could hear one of them with a loudhailer: 'This gate is a women-only area. Please respect this and follow it.'

Martin smiled. 'I suppose I can take a hint.'

I put on the rucksack and made sure Lucy had hers. Then we stood together by the side of the car. Martin hesitated, and for a moment I wanted to say, 'No, it's all right, I'll come home.'

'I am proud of you,' he said. 'And I'll try to be as brave as you. As both of you.'

'Thank you,' I said. 'Lucy. Give your father a hug.'

She clasped him to her and he picked her up and swung her round. 'Look after your mother, darling.'

'Don't make her dizzy.'

Then Martin kissed me on the lips, but briefly. We watched him drive off, his hand out of the window, waving back but concentrating on the road ahead.

'How long are you staying?' a woman asked. She had cropped grey hair and wore dungarees over a yellow T-shirt.

'I don't know,' I said. 'As long as it takes.'

'Not just the weekend then?'

'Oh more, far more than that.'

'We get a lot of tourists. Some of them even ask where the Ladies' is.'

'No, no, no,' I said. 'We're staying.'

Then she turned to my daughter. 'And what is your name?' she asked.

'LUCY.'

'Well, Lucy, my name is Joyce. I'll get you a peace bracelet. Would you like that? Then we can make some paper doves. I bet you're good at making things.'

The light was falling but the common was still warm from the heat of the day. There were fireflies in the haze and I could hear women singing in the distance.

Don't want to cause no sorrow
Don't want to cause no pain
I'm only gonna cause what I have to cause
Until this land is free of shame
Till this land is free of shame.

I couldn't wait until morning.

Martin

Back at home I shopped for single servings of ready-made food and
I didn't care even if they were meat or fish. I filled my trolley with
ocean pie, beef casserole, steaks and fish fingers. It wasn't cooking
so much as heating, but each time the aroma of warm food made
me think of family life and reminded me of its absence. Sometimes
in the evenings I found myself staring at Lucy's pink plastic
hairbrush in the bathroom, at her first winter shoes, or at Claire's
jewellery by the side of the bed. She had left her engagement ring
behind, saying that it gave her eczema and, besides, she didn't want
to lose it at Greenham. It was hard to remember what it looked like
on her finger.

I wondered what kind of world my wife was trying to defend and
what kind of England we were both attempting to save. I remembered my geography teacher at school in Canvey holding up a
piece of chalk and telling us that it was a symbol of everything we
needed to know about our country. 'If you study the history of this
substance,' he had said, 'this simple piece of chalk, you will know
how this land became separated from the continent, allowing the
Channel to fill; you will appreciate the white cliffs of Dover, and the
glory of Beachy Head; you will know why beautiful horses are
carved on the downs and you will discover how pure England can
be when it wants to be.'

I had forgotten the racism, but the image had made me think
about the ground beneath my feet and the nature of chalk; how
the backbone of England was porous and crumbling, that I lived in
an osteoporotic country, bent over itself and its history. In the car I

listened to a clergyman on the radio saying that if nuclear war brought the world to an end then it would bring us closer to Judgment Day and that time when we shall all, at last, see the face of God. I couldn't imagine Claire's father being so reckless with his faith.

I was working on a project to preserve the Norfolk coast from further erosion. Each week I drove up through the familiar geology of England towards the downs, following the variations of outline and contour, the confusion of sea, sky and horizon.

Men in fluorescent jackets over white T-shirts and shorts were walking up and down the hard shoulder spiking rubbish from the roadside trees, picking up shards of polythene bags, nappies and polystyrene cups. I could see sofas and mattresses left in the straggle of woodland. This was the England of abandonment, of tipping in country lanes and cars dumped in rivers. I remembered my first experience of contempt for the landscape: a rusted sky-blue Cortina, its front lights missing and its hubcaps gone, rammed into the stagnant summer waters of the Colne.

As I neared Canvey I could smell methane and burning rubbish from the council tip. A summer shower fell on the windscreen. I turned on the wipers but they only blurred my visibility with the smear of half-dead insects. Their rhythm reminded me of being rocked, of my mother's voice:

> *It's raining, it's raining,*
> *There's pepper in the box,*
> *And all the little ladies*
> *Are picking up their frocks.*

Once into Norfolk I took first to the back roads and then the coastal route. I could almost feel the tarmac pressing down on soil and scrub, tracing the memory of hollow ways and ley lines, following the rural England I was trying to preserve: grass meadows flowering with comfrey and hemp-agrimony, sedge and milk-parsley fringing the river banks.

I stayed in a pub and worked in an office in Cromer where I

continued to study wave and tidal processes. I gathered samples from the cliff face, recorded the geological differences from Sheringham all the way down to Great Yarmouth, and measured the absorbency of the coastline: how much water it could retain, and how much it could repel.

There were heavy rains and high tides throughout September and there had already been small slips and random cliff falls. Soon there would be a much greater collapse but none of us could predict where that might be or how much it might take with it.

It was a Saturday, on Halcyon Beach, and a hint of blue sky had tempted families on to the sand to enjoy the last of summer. The sun broke through high clouds, illuminating the virulent green of the rising sea. By the afternoon the clouds began to move swiftly across the horizon, darkening against the last of the light, rising into a grey bank of shadow.

The gulls and waders disappeared, leaving the sky to itself. It was as if a stage was being cleared for some long-planned realignment between earth and sea. Only after the first high rolls of thunder did people begin to pick up their possessions and hurry back to the car park, dropping their newspapers, holding beach mats and towels against their faces. By then the sands on which they ran had taken on a metallic sheen, the seaweed dulled by cloud.

At the beach café the white plastic chairs that hadn't blown over were stacked in haste. All over the bay people were racing against the oncoming storm and the speed of the tide. Children were crying 'Daddy, carry me' and 'Mum, Mum, wait for me' as their parents tried to be authoritative without appearing afraid.

I saw a family to the south, sheltering at the back of the bay, anticipating the storm but failing to understand the pace of the tide or the danger of landslip. I came down from the car park, shouting at them to get out, away from the cliff, but my cries were against the wind.

I ran towards them, gesturing that they should come out from the cove but they waved back jauntily, as if I was a friend on his way to share a picnic.

As I ran the sand became heavier underfoot. The rain kept switching direction in the wind and the spray was all around me. Now I could make out the family: a couple with two children, a boy of seven or eight, and a girl of three or four. Their windbreak had already blown over and they were trying to keep the rest of their possessions together in a narrow hollow.

If I reached them in time they could still wade to safety. But when they began to hear my shouts they made cancelling gestures with their arms, telling me everything was fine and I should go back. They even pointed up to the cliff above them, suggesting they could climb up there if things got difficult, but I knew that any foothold would crumble and that their children would never manage the ascent.

'Get out,' I yelled. 'Come on. Start running.'

The father could not understand the danger they were in. 'It's all right, mate,' he called back. 'We're OK here.'

'You're not. The cliff could go . . .'

'We can climb up it . . .'

'Didn't you hear me? You've got to get away from it.'

'What do you mean?'

I knelt down and turned to their little girl, imagining she was Lucy. 'Come on, get on to my shoulders. I'll carry you.'

'What are you doing?' the mother screamed. 'Leave her alone. You're mad, you are.'

The dad shouted at me, 'Don't you touch our little girl.'

'I'm trying to save your lives.' I stood back up. 'Can't you see the danger? The storm's coming.'

'But it's miles away,' the man said. 'And we've got shelter here. The tide never comes this far up.'

'Today it will,' I said. 'And it's not just the tide, it's the cliff.'

I could see the veil of rain approaching, the sky whitening now from dove-grey to an almost arctic-white blur.

'Come on,' I shouted. 'I'm a water engineer. I know what I'm talking about.' I crouched and said to the little girl, 'Get on my back.'

'What will I do, Mummy?'

'You're a what?' the man interrupted.

'A water engineer.' I looked at the girl. 'Come on, darling.'

172

She climbed on to my back even though her parents had not decided whether to obey me or not.

'All of you.' I grabbed the boy's hand. 'We have to get out of here.'

'What are you doing?' said the woman. 'You can't just take our children off like this.'

'Look,' I said. 'Can't you see that I know what I'm talking about? Why else would I be here? Stop buggering about and come with me.'

'There's no need to swear.'

I stopped and looked at the man. 'You have to trust me. Come on. Move.'

'All right, all right,' he said.

His wife grumbled as she grabbed at their beach stuff. 'We're coming as quick as we can.'

'I told you we should have gone home before this,' said her husband.

'Leave it, Malcolm.'

'Come on,' I called, setting off with their children. 'We have to beat the tide.'

Behind us both sea and sky had become a whiteness brightened only by lightning.

'I can't see,' said the little boy.

'It's all right,' I said. 'Hold on to me.'

The waves had reached the edge of the cliff and were striking the boulders at the base, rebounding in white sprays of foam. The rocks began to shake from below.

'Run,' I shouted.

We made our way through leftover picnics, broken deckchairs and abandoned sandcastles. I could just make out the coast-guards near the top of the cliff chasing people back, cars turning in the middle of the road, people bent forward and heading for shelter.

I looked back, checking if we were still together. The little girl cried that she wanted to get down. She was frightened of falling.

'It's all right, darling, it's all right.'

Her brother kept holding on to me. 'Come on,' I shouted, 'we're nearly there.'

At last the sands began to harden beneath our feet as we neared the shore. The storm was relenting, moving beyond us.

'Are you all right, love?' the man called to his wife.

She looked back at the sea and at the bay where they had been sheltering. 'Are we safe yet?'

'I think so,' the man said, waiting for her to catch up. 'It's all right, love, it's all right.'

He held out his arms and his wife tried to smile. 'I know, Malc. I'm sorry I was cross with you.'

'I love you, Kath.'

At last we reached the safety of the dunes, throwing ourselves down on to the grass. The two children cuddled into their mother. The man was about to say something to me but gestured that he was waiting to get his breath back.

And then we began to hear a deep rumbling, not from above, but from under the ground, a low dark sound amidst the weight and the drama of the storm, building in volume until it dominated all the noise around it.

The cliff under which the family had sheltered now began to wrench itself away from the land. The earth was so sodden that the fall wasn't so much stone rent apart, cracking and tumbling, as a great implosion of overhanging mud, grass, road and housing. The cliff disintegrated from all angles and slid heavily down, sloughing itself off from the mainland and splitting against the sea.

I had organised boulders and stone, scaffold and cement to restrain just such a storm and just such a tide but the water had found each weak spot, surging through the defences, the sea greedy for the land, hungry for the fabric of the cliff.

The bay became a mass of mud, water and storm. I watched a house teeter uneasily and then slowly tip over and inch away down the remains of the exposed cliff face. It broke apart as it fell, the windows of its conservatory bulging out and cracking, the brick walls fracturing and the furniture tumbling: sofas, chairs, televisions, beds, wardrobes and tables, all falling in a dull roar of earth, stone, rubble and chalk.

I saw a red dress caught in the wind, floating down like a parachute above the debris, and an exposed bedroom wall with a mirror still hanging. A brass bed slid across the last of the flooring and down into the sea, before the rest of the home followed: its garage and garden shed, its front porch and bird bath, its swing and its sandpit. Everything was given over to the sea.

I looked at the people around me and I heard my mother's voice:

> There was an old woman called Nothing-at-all
> Who lived in a dwelling exceedingly small
> A man stretched his mouth to its utmost extent
> And down at one gulp house and old woman went.

'Bloody hell,' said the man. 'You saved our lives.'

Afterwards he bought me a drink and we sat with our pints at the window of the pub. Still the rain fell, streaking the glass, each drop skittering down, leaving tadpole trails.

'We're a close family,' the man said. 'I don't know how we'd cope if something bad happened to any of us. The kids, Kath, I don't know.'

His wife was drying the children in their camper van. Then they were going to join us. He'd decided to have a few drinks and then order a family fish and chip supper as a treat. Malcolm said he knew that's what Kath would like.

'The thing about our family,' he went on, 'is that we always know what everyone else wants without them saying. It's incredible. I can even tell what my children are thinking.'

Well, I can't, I thought. *I rarely know what Lucy thinks at all. And as for Claire . . .*

How was I supposed to know anything when they'd taken themselves away from me?

I wondered what they were doing. I wanted them to come home and to love me and to understand what I had been through. I wanted Claire to sympathise with what I could not do and to be proud of what I'd actually done, at least in saving the lives of these people. I could have died and she wouldn't have known anything about it. She didn't even know where I was.

I wanted her to return and tell me that she loved me. Because, for all the good she was doing at Greenham, I couldn't help but think she was causing damage elsewhere: to Lucy, to our marriage and to our future.

I didn't know how much longer I could hold on without her. I decided that in the morning I would drive over and bring them both back. It was crazy that we weren't together.

Claire

When the women found out I was a teacher I soon had my own little children's class: informal school in the week and crèche at weekends. I slanted the lessons to suit the situation. We used maths to count policemen and missiles, art to make banners, and English to write letters to members of parliament. We even made trips round the perimeter fence and I talked about the geography of England and why it had to be preserved. I realised that sometimes when I talked I was using Martin's words, adapting his thoughts, and I began to miss him all over again. I wanted him to be with us and felt guilty when so many of the other women spoke of how glad they were to be free of men. They made jokes about the smell of them, their endless exhaustion, their selfishness and laziness in bed. Some of them impersonated their former partner's pomposity, ridiculing their sense that life was so much more difficult for them if only we women knew. We remarked how men's clothes were such depressing colours – taupe, beige, grey, slate, mud and fawn – how they kept hoisting their belts in an attempt to show that they were losing weight; and how they leant back and swayed from side to side as they spoke, sometimes closing their eyes so that they could not be interrupted.

I laughed with them even though I knew in my heart that Martin wasn't like that at all.

But Lucy and I soon made friends. There was Joyce who wanted to be one of the first women priests; Martha who had been training to be a doctor; and Kate who was also a musician. We started by staying at the Green Gate, the one nearest the silos, but then moved to the Orange Gate, because it had become the official musicians' area and from there we organised much of the singing. Together we played ballads and folk songs of unity and protest: 'Last Night I Had the Strangest Dream', 'Where Have All the Flowers Gone?' and the Phil Ochs song 'Do What I Have to Do'.

The women told us what they had done so far: wedging potatoes deep into the exhausts of the trucks, bolting security gates together to hamper movement in and out, and keening repeatedly whenever large vehicles came near.

The previous Hiroshima Day they had gathered a hundred thousand stones and placed them round the Newbury war memorial, one for each life lost to the atomic bomb. A veteran shouting, 'Where would we be if we hadn't fought the Japs?' had slapped Joyce in the face. Another woman had yelled, 'My husband died for the likes of you.' There were even anti-peace protests in Newbury town centre, with 'Women for Defence' in floral skirts, carrying handbags that matched their shoes, brandishing banners saying 'Squatters Out' and 'Greenham Women, you disgust us'. They looked like the local Conservative Association on a day out.

I suggested we bought a great swathe of red material and held up a sign with it saying: 'The blood of one family; imagine the blood of one nation.'

My first action was a die-in at Orange Gate. I had the idea of painting outlines round our bodies, like a mass-murder scene, so that even after we had been dragged away people would think what it meant. Lucy was given one of the paint pots but she found it difficult to keep up.

'It's so hard, Mummy.' She was painting round Julie, a woman who had already been arrested five times for causing criminal damage to the perimeter fence.

'Just do one pot. Then you can lie down and I'll paint you.' I wanted the outline to look like a dead mother and child. I thought it would be more shocking that way.

Lucy lay down and I told her to cup her hand to her cheek to protect it from the hard surface of the road. Then I began to paint around her. A local photographer came up to us and started taking pictures. Lucy smiled, almost posing for the camera.

'Keep still,' I hissed. 'You're supposed to be dead.'

'But I want to look pretty even if I am dead.'

'That's our girl,' said Julie.

'Thanks,' said the photographer. 'You can get up now.'

'We don't want to get up,' Julie said firmly.

'No, it's OK,' he said. 'I've finished.'

'We're not doing this for you.'

'Then what are you doing it for?'

'We're doing it for the future,' I said. 'For all of us.'

'Shame you have to drag your child into it.'

'She wanted to come. Perhaps if yours came too we could get rid of the missiles and be done with it.'

'I don't have children,' he replied. 'But when I do I'm going to look after them properly. I'm not going to make them lie down in the middle of traffic with a bunch of bloody lesbians.'

We decided we had to 'increase the peace'.

We planned to embrace the base once more, thirty-five thousand women in a human chain round the nine miles of the perimeter fence.

We started singing and dancing in groups, forming small circles and gathering hands with all who came near. When the circles broke up or we needed a break for a cup of tea, we started to fill the fence. We wedged photographs of our children, cardboard doves and poetry inside the gaps, turning a wall of destruction into a frieze of colour. When we saw the helicopters overhead we held up shards of glass, cathedrals of light, to deflect the negative energy. We wanted to lock in the violence and surround it with healing.

The helicopters flew low over the base. I think they were trying to blow us away from the fence, but we kept holding on to each other. Inside was the dead grey cement of aggression and destruction. Outside lay the green of summer. When the police accused us of being lesbians in need of a good man we sang back: 'We're here because we're queer because we're here because we're queer.'

I tied Lucy's pale-brown hair in purple, green and white ribbons, the colours of the suffragettes, and gave her a packet of seeds wrapped in mud to throw into the base so that life might re-grow there. There were white poppies, sweet violets and lily of the valley. Lucy sat on my shoulders and lobbed the ball over the fence. We watched its soft arc against the sky and its flight downward on to the ground, the smallest gesture, a simple act of hope. Then one of the policemen smiled and I heard him say, 'I wish my daughter could do that,' and I knew that we were winning.

It was so obvious that what we were doing was right. I couldn't understand how anyone could be against us. All we wanted was a gentler world.

Martin

When I arrived the women were lighting candles and holding up signs: 'Grannies for Peace', 'No Cruise', 'Give Peace a Chance'. There were banners that at first I thought contained bizarre spelling mistakes – 'Womyn for Peace', 'Womyn for the Future' – until I realised there were no 'men' in these 'women'.

I was surprised how close to the roadside they were camping. There was a communal area of tipis and Elsan toilet tents jostling ramshackle structures made of polythene, tarpaulin and branches. Inside the doorway of the main tent was a cauldron surrounded by orange box seats and camping chairs. Beyond stood a caravan with message boards, posters and sheets for making banners.

Lucy was juggling with three red balls. She smiled, let them fall and ran towards me.

'Have you come to take me home?'

'I hope so.'

Claire gave me a wave. Her hair was muddy with ties and ribbons and she was wearing a baggy hand-knit jumper I hadn't seen before.

'You look very settled,' I said.

'I am. We're in it for the long haul.'

'A bit like marriage then . . .'

'Don't, Martin . . .'

There was a kitchen area which they called 'open-plan', with bread, butter and spreads for quick sandwich breaks; plastic bins with beans, muesli, tinned food and vegetables; and then a pallet with plastic water containers, a plate rack and washing bowls. Claire had organised a water rota to make sure they never ran out. If I hadn't wanted her to come home so much I would have been proud.

In the distance I could see a draped plastic tunnel. Inside some of the women were resting.

'Do you sleep there?' I asked.

'Depends.'

'On what?'

'Whether I have to be up for an action.'

'Does Lucy join in?'

'When she wants to. Most of the time she likes making things round our little tent. Ask her to show you. She's good at art.'

'I know that.'

'You should see what she's done, doves, mosaics, all kinds of things. She's learning such a lot.'

'It would be nice if we were a family again.'

'We *are* a family, Martin. Don't make it difficult.'

'Come home,' I said. 'I need you. My work's horrible and I'm lonely.'

'My work's horrible too.'

'Come home then.'

'When the missiles have gone.'

'They're not going to go, Claire.'

'They are. This is common land. It doesn't belong to the Ministry of Defence or the government. Wait for me, Martin, and then we can walk across it together. I'll come if you insist. But please don't make me resent you.'

'What about Lucy?'

'She's happy. We're coping. Trust us, Martin. We love you. It's all right. We're going to win.'

The police were lining up outside the gates expecting a delivery or further action. I couldn't help feeling they'd rather be in an office solving an impossible murder case than stuck out on a cold night in front of a group of women who were never going to give up.

'Why am I so kind to you?' I said.

'Because we love each other. You can come and see us whenever you like. It's not a prison. And we do miss you. But you know we have to do this. And you letting me be here only makes me love you more. You must know that?'

'I'll try to keep remembering then.'

'Don't try. Just remember. Please . . .'

When I got home her father phoned. 'Claire not back?'

'I'm afraid not.'

'You couldn't persuade her?'

'No.'

'I'm used to Claire being a wildcard. I was one myself, although you may find that hard to believe. But I'm worried about my granddaughter. Lucy's far too young for all this. Celia thinks so too. We can't let Claire bully us with her idealism. Lucy's just a child, for goodness' sake.'

'That's why I went to fetch them.'

'Then why didn't you bring them home?'

'I don't know, Matthew. Perhaps I can't. Perhaps I can't control my wife like people did in the old days.'

The only thing was to go out and get drunk, somewhere close to home so I wouldn't have far to stagger back. I found a pub away from the seafront that was sufficiently down at heel for tourists to ignore. It was dark and filled with ship memorabilia, bits of driftwood and faded newspaper cuttings. The only concession to modernity was a blackboard in the Gents' for the graffiti.

I sat on a stool by the bar and asked for a pint of IPA and a double whisky chaser.

The barman looked a bit surprised. 'You all right, mate?'

'A bad day, that's all.'

'Then you've come to the right place. We make this pub so crap you can't help feeling better. Give it five minutes and you'll think the sun shines out of your arse.'

'I've never thought that.'

'But you've never been here, have you?'

I ordered some food, the largest rib-eye steak they had, with mustard and chips. At the next table a girl with a Frankie Goes to Hollywood T-shirt and blonde hair piled high on her head was getting rid of her boyfriend. 'I'm sorry it hasn't worked out . . .' she was saying. 'I know this has meant a lot to you, and it has to me too.'

Her companion had almost finished his pint and it didn't look like there was going to be another. 'I understand.'

'I haven't been good at disguising things . . . how I haven't been happy . . . and I think you haven't been happy either.'

'I understand, I understand,' the man replied.

'So it has to be for the best . . .'

'It's all right.'

'Really, it is. It has to be. We can't go on like this.'

I tried to imagine what it would be like to be these people, away from the comfort of marriage, where friendships were tested for sexual tension and where love could begin or end at any minute.

'You don't need to say this,' said the man, trying to get out of his seat even though it was pinned between the table and the wall.

'I know but I want to. You've been so good to me.'

'I haven't done anything.'

'You have but we both have to accept that it's over.'

'Well, if that's what you feel . . .' He sat down again.

'It is and I'm sorry. I wish things could have been different.'

'So do I.'

The girl rose from her chair and swung her bag over her shoulder. 'I'm really sorry. I'm sorry. I'm sorry.'

'I understand,' the man repeated, looking back down at his drink. 'It's all right.'

But it isn't, I could see him thinking. *No one will love me again. I'm washed up. It's all over. Fuck you. Fuck everything that has ever happened to me. Fuck this town and this bar and this career and this day and this life.*

I wondered what I would think if I ever broke up with Claire. Would it be like that, the two of us in a pub, talking about how we had tried but there wasn't enough love left to support us and that it would be better, yes, better for us both if we parted?

We would not be able to look at each other, perhaps, and Claire would be pale and hollow-eyed and I would not know what to say.

Or perhaps she would be happy. She would be relieved and confident and try not to show it. Perhaps she would have found someone else: a woman at the camp or a man with money and stability and calm; someone not so filled with some foolish ambition to save a crumbling cliff face from disaster in memory of a mother he could hardly picture any more.

I thought of Linda and how we had broken up all those years ago. I remembered her on the beach at Aldeburgh, dressed in black, sitting on an upturned boat while I tried to measure the tide.

I had taken so much for granted and now I couldn't imagine anyone else loving me as she did then. And what had I done with that love?

Perhaps I could go back and make amends, say sorry, do something right with my life. I didn't know. I didn't feel certain of anything.

I heard Linda's voice. *Come on then, I'm cold. Need you to warm me up. Let's go back to the hotel. A bit of whisky and each other.*

I remembered how we used to lie in bed, our faces close together, cupping each other's heads with both our hands to form a sphere so that we blocked out most of the light. We had looked at each other as intently as we could, our focus on each other's eyes, and pretended that the whole earth was contained in the circle created by our hands.

Linda had told me that our eyes were the seas of the world, our noses the mountains, and our mouths the dark caverns underground. If we closed our eyes and kissed then the world would disappear. We would cup our hands and build a new world, with new seas and new mountains, and it would be ours and no one would know about it. It would be like a distant, uninhabited planet, millions of years from here, contained in our heads and our hands, and lit by the moon.

It was 1964 then, and we were seventeen.

Linda

Ade came round and said that Martin had phoned him to get my address and was it all right if he gave it to him?

'What do you think?' I said. 'Bit of a surprise, isn't it? Why does he want to come now, after all these years?'

'It's a free country,' Ade replied.

'Do you think he's got bored of his wife?'

'I don't know. But be careful. You can do what you like, Linda, but don't go getting yourself hurt all over again. Married men are nothing but trouble. I should know.'

'You're no trouble, Adey,' I said.

'Wanna try?'

'Don't be silly.'

'Are you going to see him then?'

'There's not much point, is there? He's still married as far as I know.'

We'd probably meet in a pub: neutral territory. I began to imagine what it would be like and the kind of things we'd say to each other. Then I worried that he'd be able to tell I wasn't happy. Sometimes I think men can smell the desperation.

I still hadn't met anyone who was right; they were gay, or they were married, or they were screwed up. There wasn't such a thing as a normal man of my own age who was single and wanted someone to love.

Martin was probably another of those men whose relationships have dwindled into friendship and they want to prove that they had once had a life. He was hardly the first to have come calling. People think that because you're single and you live on your own you're available. It makes it easier for them than having an affair with a married woman. Then they have to go to the expense of hotels and the affair can only last until the money runs out or they're discovered. Whereas with me they all imagine it's going to be discreet and easy and the only problem they'll have is the guilt of sleeping with their wife afterwards.

I wasn't going to do anything stupid and I was determined not to be hurt. But we had loved each other. And love always feels stronger when you remember the past. Him getting in touch after all that time was a relief in a way. It meant I wasn't the only one wondering what might have been.

SEVEN

Martin

Canvey was two different places at the same time. There was the town of seaside fun and the town of aggression with its prohibitive signs warning incomers that the people who lived here were not going to put themselves out for anyone. 'No Vacancies. No Loitering. No Entry.' I walked past a pub. 'No dogs. No working clothes.' White faces. Chips. Early drug use. *Don't look at me. Don't touch me. What do you want?*

I stayed with my father, pretending I'd come to see him rather than Linda, and we lived a bachelor existence. In the kitchen there were stale cornflakes, tea bags, powdered milk and peanut butter; Ritz crackers, vacuum-packed Cheddar and a six-pack of Tennent's. I thought of the care boxes ordered by ex-pats in Spain and realised that I could probably fill one simply by emptying my dad's store cupboard.

My old bedroom had been made feminine by a lace cloth on the bedside table. The view to the back yard was obscured by nets and faded velvet curtains, salmon pink and falling like an old belly. I could almost hear my father knocking on the door, telling me to get ready for school, and Vi leaving a cup of milk on the floor outside. I could still picture my duffel coat on the hook with my satchel and the money pouch which my father sometimes binned for drinks. It was a house in which I could never sit still for long: *Shouldn't you be getting on? Haven't you got homework to do? Be a good boy and run to the shops, will you?*

I think Dad guessed why I was there and he certainly knew that I was having problems with Claire being away. He kept banging on about how life was like climbing a mountain.

'You think the ascent is the difficult part, growing up, getting a career, having a family, and then you get to forty-five and you realise you have to start coming back down and it's far harder than you ever imagined.'

'I'll bear that in mind, Dad,' I said. 'But I don't think I've reached the plateau yet.'

'Just got to make sure you've made the right foot-holes, son . . .'

'Yes, *all right*, Dad.'

'And you don't slip up.'

'I *know*.'

Ade told me that Linda lived above a newsagent's on Long Road. It was at the end of a row of shops that had changed owners but remained the same: the off-licence, the charity shop (it had been blind, now it was cancer), the minicab office, the bookie's, the hairdresser with specials for senior citizens, and the newsagent selling anything you couldn't get elsewhere.

It was two days before I met her. I saw her walk into the off-licence and come out with a bottle of vodka. I was about to get out of the car but she was already heading towards me.

'Are you following me?'

'Of course not.'

I thought she would smile. I had imagined we might even kiss each other, but Linda wasn't having any of that.

'I saw you yesterday and I nearly came out but I couldn't believe it was you. What do you want?'

'I thought we could go for a drink.'

'Well, I've got a drink, thank you very much.'

'I'm sorry,' I said. 'I just wanted to see you.'

'Oh.'

'Didn't Ade tell you?'

'Yes, but what was I supposed to do? I didn't know when you were coming. You might have changed your mind. It's been a long time, Martin.'

'Too long.'

'I don't know about that.'

'Well, what do you say, Linda? One drink. For old times' sake.'

'I don't think "one drink" was ever enough for either of us. But I'll be in the Smack at six. You can buy me a vodka and tonic, easy on the tonic. Don't be late.'

She didn't wait for an answer, but opened the door to her flat with one hand and barged it open with her shoulder. She didn't look back.

I had so few ways of remembering her: a photograph taken by Vi so that her smile to the camera was guarded and false; some letters that she had sent to Cambridge; and singles she had given me for Christmas and birthdays: the Turtles singing 'Happy Together', 'All I Really Want to Do' by the Byrds. By driving along the back lanes, visiting the pubs and sitting on the same concrete bench in the sea wall, I hoped to remember more: the smell of soap on the back of her neck and paint on her hands, the bump on her left index finger where she held her pencil, the way in which she would ask 'Now what?' whenever she was bored.

It had begun to rain when I headed back for the pub. A middle-aged couple dressed in cagoules had been braving the weather and were eating their scampi outdoors. They could have been Claire and me having a drink before going to see Dad. Inside a group of boys were playing snooker while some women were preparing for a hen night, putting L-plates on to the bride's jeans.

'You got them then?' I heard Linda's voice. I was so lost in my memory of the past that it reminded me of that first time when she had asked about condoms.

'The drinks . . .'

'Oh. Yes.'

'You look surprised. We did arrange to meet here. Is there something wrong? Were you expecting me to be seventeen?'

'No. Of course not.'

'Bet you were.'

Behind her was a photograph of Canvey from the 1950s: the parish pump and the Red Cow before the flood. I remembered that this was how we often defined the time in which we lived; not 'before the war', or 'after the war', like everyone else in England, but 'before the flood', 'after the flood'. It made the island biblical.

'Well, cheers then,' I said.

I looked at the hen-night women, and the boys playing pool, and

I wondered how many of the couples in the pub having a quiet drink were either getting together or breaking up.

'It's funny seeing you again,' said Linda.

'We had some good times.'

'I'm glad you think so.'

'We did,' I said. 'Don't you remember?'

'I'm not so sure about that.'

'Riding all over the island. Dancing to Dave's band. Whatever happened to him?'

'He's all right. Still trying to make it. But he drinks a bit too much. You know Dave.'

'Not really . . .'

'You made me a necklace. I remember that. I've still got it somewhere.'

'I didn't behave very well. I'm sorry.'

'Yes. I remember you saying sorry at the time.'

'That was the end, I suppose. At Aldeburgh.'

'Well, we haven't seen each other since so I guess you must be right; unless you count the time in the restaurant when you were so embarrassed you could hardly speak.'

'It threw me, seeing you and Claire in the same place.'

'I couldn't work out whether you were embarrassed about me or embarrassed about her. Perhaps it was the both of us. And your awful Auntie Vi.'

'She's got a bit better.'

'She could hardly have got worse. Do you want to get me another?'

I made my way through the hen night to the bar ('*You need company, mate? Fancy a bit of an evening?*' – '*No, I'm all right, thank you*' – '*We know you're all right, that's why we're asking*').

'Made some friends?' Linda asked when I got back to the table. 'Don't mind me.'

'I came to see you, not them.'

'Well, that was kind.'

'I keep thinking of something we did, just us. Do you remember that cupping-hands thing? Pretending we had created new worlds?'

'Show me.'

'I put my hands in front of my face, cupping them forwards, see?

Then you put your hands in front of your face and we made a kind of ball.'

'Looks daft.'

'Don't you remember?'

'Are you sure it wasn't someone else?'

'No. Of course it wasn't.'

Linda downed her vodka. 'I remember Aldeburgh all right. Couldn't forget that. Bloody cold it was. And you being hung up about the tide.'

'I can't remember how it went wrong.'

'I'm not sure if it was ever right.'

'It was,' I said.

A girl from the hen party put Gloria Gaynor on the jukebox and they all started to sing along. Linda shuddered. 'I can't stand that crap. What a load of desperate middle-aged bollocks. No, I will *not* survive. Let's go.'

We climbed the bank up on to the sea wall, avoiding the steps as we had always done in the past. I held out my hand to Linda but she didn't take it. When I looked down I could see her breasts showing through her T-shirt. We walked down to the jetty and watched a man flying his son's kite for him.

'I know what it was,' Linda said at last. 'In the end I gave you the confidence to leave me.'

'I suppose I never realised . . .'

'Did you ever get round to changing the world?' she asked.

'I tried . . .'

'Job a bit too big for you?'

'The other week a whole cliff collapsed in the area I'm responsible for.'

'It can't have been your fault.'

'I don't know. Perhaps it was. I don't feel I've done much with my life, Linda.'

'Well, you're not alone there.'

The sun broke through a bank of cloud and caught her eyes. She shielded them briefly from the light.

'Why?' I asked. 'What's happened?'

'Nothing.'

'Is that the problem?'

'I don't know if it's a problem. I just haven't found anyone to love.'

'A girl like you. There must be hundreds of men.'

'Believe me, Martin. There aren't.'

'Come off it . . .'

'You get to the stage when you realise the time when you can choose has passed you by. And then there's no choice left.'

'Perhaps your standards are too high.'

'I went out with you, didn't I? They can't be that high.'

We walked on across the stones and broken seine nets, keeping to the harder parts of the shore, past the car tyres and the abandoned bottles, the bits of driftwood and strands of seaweed. I didn't want Linda to think that I was staring at her, but she looked even thinner than I had remembered. I wondered if she was eating enough, or if she had enough money. Then she stopped to light a cigarette, cupping her hands away from the breeze. Her nails had been bitten right down. In the pub she'd managed to hide the worst of them but now she needed both hands for the cigarette. I think she saw me notice them because she gave me a quick glance that told me to say nothing.

'I sometimes wonder what would have happened if we'd stayed together.'

Linda laughed. 'Disaster, probably.'

'Why do you think that?'

'Don't you?'

'No,' I said. 'I don't. Sometimes I think it would have been the best thing I ever did. Losing you was such a careless thing to do.'

'Don't say that.'

'I mean it.'

Linda bit at a nail. 'Let's not talk about it.'

'Why not?'

'Because I don't have anything to say to you. In fact I don't know why you're here.'

'I wanted to see you,' I said.

'But why? We weren't even friends in the end. You hurt me. You hurt me so much.'

'I didn't mean to.'

'No. No one means to.'

The light was bright off the water. I didn't want Linda denying our past or changing it. But I didn't know what to say.

She picked up a pebble and put it into the pocket of her jeans. 'I should go.'

'I'll walk you home.'

She stopped. 'All right. But you're not coming in. I don't want you getting any ideas. I remember what you're like.'

'Did I ask?'

For the first time she smiled. 'You're OK, I suppose.'

We bought some chips and walked back up Haven Road, past the gas installation. A man jogged past us, plugged in to his Walkman. A couple ahead were strolling with the girl's hand in the back pocket of her boyfriend's jeans. 'Are you seeing anyone?' I asked.

'Nosy.'

'Just taking an interest.'

'And what if I am?'

'I'm only asking.'

'You still married?' she said.

'Can I see you again?'

'You haven't answered the question.'

'Sorry.'

'I'll take that as a yes then.'

'I did love you,' I said. 'I can promise you that. I absolutely loved you.'

'Not enough.'

'No, perhaps not enough, but more than I realised. More than I had ever known.'

'How long are you here for?' she asked.

For the first time she looked interested. *Perhaps it could begin again*, I thought. Perhaps it had already started.

Linda

When I thought about it I was angry. How could Martin come round after all those years and turn up like he'd just popped out to the shops?

It made me remember the emptiness I had felt when it was over: the staring into absolute nothingness, the going back to bed at eleven in the morning, the vodka and the crap afternoon telly, the rubbish food and the dressing gown with bits of crisp and chocolate stuck to it, the unmade bed and the unwashed hair, the pointlessness of every single activity other than lying down.

Two days later we drove over to Southend. The car smelt of his wife's perfume but I didn't say anything. We went for a walk on the pier, watching children screaming on the rides high above Adventure Island and their parents queuing for the ten-pin bowling. A handful of birdwatchers were chattering about black terns and a couple of punks with green hair were waiting to be photographed for a pound a time.

'Why are you here?' I asked Martin. 'Remind me.' Although it was good to be with him again I wasn't going to make it easy. 'I can't believe you still fancy me.'

I had seen the confusion on his face when he had looked at me the last time. He had tried to pretend that he hadn't been eyeing up my breasts. It's amazing how men think women don't notice.

'And we can't be seventeen again, Martin. Life doesn't work like that . . .'

A Punch and Judy show was in full swing and Judy was handing Punch the baby, leaving him in charge. *That's the way to do it.*

'There's a pub at the pier head,' he said. 'If we can get through the crowds we can have a drink there.'

We walked by the abandoned railway line and up to the lifeboat station. A group of Southend fans were singing:

Super, super, super Shrimpers
Super, super, super Shrimpers
Super, super, super Shrimpers
And our pier is fucking long, long, long.

I said to Martin, 'You took my dreams away. Have you come to bring them back?'

'I don't know the answer to that.'

'What do you know then?'

'All I can say is that it's good to see you again. You've still got that spark.'

'It's an act,' I said. 'Show the world a bit of attitude. It's a game.'

'I've missed you,' Martin said.

'Steady.'

'It's true. I've missed talking to you. When I'm away, I think sometimes you're still with me.'

'Don't be daft.'

'Walking here with you, it feels right. Everything is, I don't know, possible again.'

'Have you gone soft?' I said.

'No. It's true,' he said. 'I mean every word.'

'No, no, no, Martin. You don't get me that easily. It was a long time ago. We had some good times, I know that, but you can't dredge it back.'

'But I can remember it all.'

Three blonde women were singing old Supremes numbers. They had finished 'Baby Love' and were launching into 'Where Did Our Love Go?' Martin smiled. 'Appropriate or what?'

'Don't push it,' I said. We had reached the pub at the head of the pier.

'I'm telling you. Sometimes the memory of you fills my head and there's nothing else. It's you and only you and I feel this pain behind my eyes like I'm about to cry but there are no tears left.'

He held the door of the pub open for me. 'Don't speak like that,' I said. 'You can't feel that.'

'I do. I can't help it.'

'You can't mean it.'

'I can. And I do,' he said. 'I've told you. I mean every word.'

'I should go,' I said. 'We can't talk like this.'

'I thought you wanted a drink?' he asked.

'I'll have one to be polite,' I said. 'But don't think this is going to work.'

I knew it wasn't right. Why was he doing this if he was still married, and where was his wife anyway? I hadn't asked about his daughter. That might have stopped him, I suppose, if I'd asked about her.

Then I realised I didn't want to know about either of them. I'd rather he kept it secret so that I could pretend that we were young again, and that we hadn't messed up our lives, and that the whole idea of a future together was possible once more.

Perhaps if I gave in to him I could find some of that hope again, some of that love.

Len

Today people want to tell each other too much. I've never thought that's right. I don't want everyone knowing what I get up to and what makes me afraid. I'm a great believer in secrets but Vi kept saying I had to have a word with Martin.

'If you can't be straight with your own son then what's the point?'

We were having a bit of sausage and mash. Martin reminded me he was a vegetarian but I liked to corrupt him now and then. That was the easy part. It was the conversation that proved tricky.

'You all right, son?'

'I'm fine, Dad. Just a bit preoccupied, that's all.'

I remembered what Vi had said and I didn't want to let her down. 'I don't mean to be nosy or anything . . .'

'Well, don't . . .'

'But if you ask me it looks like you're letting someone get to you.'

'What do you mean?'

'You want me to spell it out? I mean Linda.'

'Look, Dad, I just wanted to see her again. I haven't done anything wrong.'

'Not yet, you haven't.'

'Anyway, how did you know?'

'Never you mind about that.' Vi had seen them getting fish and chips. 'You be careful, son. Claire's a good wife to you.'

'You don't need to say anything, Dad.'

'I'm not saying anything. You know what I think.'

'I'm not sure I do.'

201

'I don't want your brain going south.'

'It's not like that.'

'It's the truth. You've just got to hang on to what you've got. There isn't such a thing as a one-hundred-per-cent marriage. The best you're going to get is seventy: the very best. Sometimes you might meet someone and you think she can get you up to a hundred but it only lasts an instant and as soon as it's over you're down to ten. Stick to seventy per cent. That's the best you're going to get and I'm telling you, son, it isn't bad.'

'But what if I aim for seventy and get stuck with forty?'

'You've got seventy, son . . .'

'It doesn't feel like it.'

'That's because it isn't a hundred.'

'You don't need to worry, Dad. It's under control.'

That's what people say when it isn't, I thought.

I didn't like my son lying to me. I could tell from his reaction that it had already started up again with Linda. I'd rather not have known.

Claire

We almost got used to the night attacks by vigilantes: the rocks that were thrown, the buckets of maggots, the ox blood and the pig shit. Our tents were daubed with paint, trampled and slashed with knives. People started fires to try and smoke us out, hurled fire-crackers and shouted that we were either slags, lesbians or fat cows who'd never had a shag. They couldn't make up their minds which. One night I heard an American voice saying, 'If it was up to me I'd pour gasoline over them and torch the lot.'

Newbury District Council revoked bylaws which made Greenham common land and announced that they were now private landlords. Our squatting was illegal. Eighty police and fifty bailiffs came at dawn with warrants and bulldozers to destroy the camp, arrest us for trespass and take our possessions away. A fat man in a black leather jacket that was far too small for him got out a knife and ripped into our tent. Then he started pulling it up from the pegs. Other men began to kick away whatever was in front of them. They weren't so much clearing the site as taking revenge. Some of the women were in tears, others shouted back, but whatever they did to us, and however aggress-ive they were, we knew that we could not be violent. I saw my friend Cathy pick up a rock but four other women immediately stopped her.

'We're not doing it that way,' one of them said. 'If we start to behave like them then they have won. We have to remain non-violent. Then we can stay here for ever.'

'You're not staying anywhere,' said one of the bailiffs.

We circled the men and Joyce got us singing to show that we weren't afraid.

> Which side are you on?
> Which side are you on?
> Are you on the other side from us?
> Which side are you on?

The first dustcart drove off with our tents and belongings to ironic cheers. Black plastic sacks had been filled with personal things the bailiffs couldn't possibly sell on: diaries, quilts and children's toys.

> Are you on the side of suicide?
> Are you on the side of homicide?
> Are you on the side of genocide?
> I ask you: 'Which side are you on?'

It rained throughout the day and we still had a few umbrellas to protect the children but the police wouldn't allow us to fix them into the ground because they said it turned them into a structure. Even the Portaloos had been removed. When we asked why, we were told it was to stop people camping in them.

Lucy had had enough. She had been brave not to cry amidst all the destruction but once everyone had gone she let go. 'I want to go home, Mummy.'

'Soon, darling, I promise.' If a car had passed and I could have hitched a lift, I would probably have done it there and then.

'Can we only go home when the men behind the fence go?'

'Yes, darling.'

'I miss Daddy.'

Joyce had managed to get to Newbury and returned with matches, firelighters and a few blankets from the local charity shop. We still had our sleeping bags but the ground was a soggy mass of grass, mud and heather. We were going to have to live off the donations of well-wishers and build shelters amidst the trees. I wondered if I could sell the idea of a tree house to Lucy to make her stay.

Then the council came back with tons of rocks and rubble and dumped it all by the Yellow Gate so we could not resettle. They said the area was due for 'landscaping'.

As soon as they had gone, we began to rearrange and paint the rocks, making them the perimeter of a new camp. Then we gathered reeds from the side of the River Kennet and formed them into frames for makeshift tents. Friends arrived with cars full of polythene sheets, blankets and booze and we started to build our benders: wigwam-like structures with polythene walls and ground cover, straw and blankets. We decorated the interiors with wildflowers. I told Lucy that we were playing at being Red Indians and she began to holler in the same way that the women keened whenever a vehicle came near the base. Someone gave her a pack of felt-tip pens and a pad of paper so she could do a series of drawings of all our friends, Joyce, Cathy and Julie, and we pinned them up inside the bender along with beads, necklaces and mementoes of home. There was even a photograph of Martin with Lucy in a blue-striped buggy eating her first ice cream, vanilla all round her mouth, father and daughter smiling like they had both done something secretly naughty. It made me remember the first time we had offered Lucy chocolate and she had given us a bemused look of surprise and indignation, as if she was saying to us: 'Why have you denied me this pleasure for so long?'

'It's cosy here, isn't it?' I said.

'No, Mummy, it isn't. But I like it for now. Just for now. Then we can go to our proper home.'

In the evenings, we sat and sang and lit candles and fires. We had to be careful with all the straw around us, we didn't want to do the bailiffs' job for them by setting light to the camp, but in a way we were even more comfortable than we had been before they tried to evict us. The men kept coming back, but by then we had learnt not to give our real names and they couldn't work out who lived in which bender. As a result, they had to pin their eviction notices in big brown envelopes on nearby trees and the camp began to look like something out of the Wild West.

Joyce taught Lucy to weave a spider's web out of black wool. She said it was a web to bind us so that when we next did our die-ins or any direct protest it would be harder to move us because we would all be tied together. To move one of us would mean moving us all.

A few weeks later, a group of workers came to lay the fuel and sewage pipes for the base. Stopping them was our next action and we became a continuous wave of women lying down in front of the JCBs. We webbed ourselves up with Joyce's black wool and it took them a whole day to cut us apart and lift us away. But even then, we returned individually, continually obstructing their progress. As soon as one woman was pulled up, another lay down in her place. We were a revolution of women, turning over and over in front of the trucks.

> We are women, we are women,
> We are strong, we are strong,
> We say no, we say no,
> To the bomb, to the bomb.

The police kept yanking us away, and we kept singing:

> We say no-o, we say no-o.

Still we were determined that whatever happened there would be no violence towards the people moving us. I think I went into a kind of trance in order to avoid the pain of continually lying down in the road and being pulled out and away by the arm sockets. I tried to remain so calm that the protest was almost like an out-of-body experience. Every time I thought, *Why am I doing this?* I heard the reply in my head like a mantra: *Because I have to. Because there is no choice.*

A police officer was shouting, 'These missiles are to protect you. They will be for your own good. Can't you see that?'

'We would rather die than see that day,' I said.

'I'd rather have missiles than live under the Russians.'

'This is our land,' I said. 'We don't need to live under anybody. We want to be free of all this evil.' I lay down again in the road.

'Haven't you done enough?' said the policeman. 'Aren't you tired of all this?'

'You can't do anything to me. You can't stop me.'

'Try me.' The policeman leant down to pull me away once more.

I turned on to my stomach to make it more difficult for him. 'I'd rather die doing the right thing than survive and do nothing.'

'Well, you're a daft bitch. Coming back for more all the time.'

This time he grabbed me by the legs and started to drag me so that my head bounced on the road.

'Careful,' I shouted.

'What's there to be careful of? Why should I care about you?'

'Oh God, forget it,' I replied. And then, just as I was nearly clear of the crowd, I gave him a playful little kick and added: 'No wonder your wife's unfaithful.'

'Right, that's it, you can say goodbye to your career, smartarse.'

Suddenly there were five of them, one for each limb and a fifth for the hair. I tried to collapse my weight, make myself as heavy as possible.

'What are you doing?' I asked.

'You know what we're doing. We've just told you.'

'Let me go,' I shouted. 'My little girl's here. I must get back. She needs me with her.'

'Well, some mother you are, assaulting a police officer.'

It had just been a little kick and a joke but now I saw the sky wobble and policeman faces all around me: sweat, spit and moustache, steamed-up glasses and toppling helmets. I could hear the women still singing and the sound of bulldozers revving their engines but none of it seemed to have anything to do with me. There was the noise of doors being opened, then of handcuffs, and I felt my wrists go tight before I was swung into the back of a van, the metal floor coming up to meet me, slamming into my side and my shoulder. The door was banged shut and then locked. I couldn't move. My hands were strapped together, the floor was throbbing against my face (or was it the other way round?) and I could smell petrol. The engine was running and women were beating on the sides of the van, whooping and keening, and in the momentary darkness I wondered where I was, and if any of this was part of my life. I couldn't tell whether everything was happening far too quickly for me to understand or if it was all as slow as a dream.

But then my eyes began to adjust to the dim light inside and I could make out the other people in the van: Sasha, Bridget and Min. They were smiling at me but I could tell that they were tired smiles that couldn't stay up for very long. Kate started a chorus of 'Show Me the Prison', trying to make the whole thing sound like an adventure.

The woman next to me was wearing a badge. It said: 'Pregnant. Handle with care.'

'I'm frightened,' she said.

Martin

I kissed Linda on the cheek and I saw her eyes and it was the look
that I remembered. I knew that I should not be there, in her flat,
and that nothing about it was right. But I couldn't stop, I didn't
want to stop.

She was wearing a dark-red T-shirt, jeans and some beaten-up high
heels that matched her top. 'I haven't done much. It's only pasta.'

'That's fine,' I said. 'I'm not that hungry.'

The living room was painted a dark brown, with raffia blinds out
to the street. There was a television with an internal aerial, a three-
piece suite that had seen better days, and on the coffee table there
was a full ashtray and a bottle of vodka. I looked at the bookshelf:
*The Rubáiyát of Omar Khayyám, Zen and the Art of Motorcycle Main-
tenance, The Prophet.* There were cassette tapes round an Amstrad
music system and some old jazz LPs.

'I didn't know you liked this kind of stuff,' I said.

'Charlie Parker or Duran Duran? John Coltrane or Spandau
Ballet?'

'Bessie Smith or Sade?'

'You get the idea.'

There were two other rooms, one of which had been turned into
her studio. It was the brightest space in the flat, and I could see a
series of canvases facing the wall by the open door.

'Drink?' she called. 'I've got the vodka.'

'I brought some wine.'

'The vodka's open.' She came towards me and put a glass into
my hands.

'Cheers.' She drank, still looking at me, smiled and then kissed me full on the lips. 'There. That's better, isn't it?'

I was about to hold her to me when she turned and went straight back into the kitchen. To the left I could see a dark-red bedroom. On a high shelf were bottles of miniatures from all over the world.

'How do you do this?' I asked.

'Oh, same old stuff. The dole. I help Masood out downstairs in the newsagent's when they're short. Sometimes I tell a fortune or sell a painting. And then there's always the dealing.'

'What?'

'Only joking,' but I couldn't tell. 'Do you want this pasta or not?' she called.

'All right.'

'Well, put some music on then.'

I found some Sarah Vaughan and we sat on the floor, side by side, our backs leaning against the sofa, and ate our tagliatelle. I opened the wine and Linda smiled.

'Can you remember?' she asked.

'What?'

'You know, the two of us, together.'

'Of course.'

'And what do you remember about it?'

'I don't know,' I said. 'It felt right.'

'Even the first time?'

'No. I wasn't so good the first time.'

'You made up for it later.'

'I did my best.'

'You were good, you were. I remember.'

'Well. We loved each other.'

'Do you think so?'

'I know so.'

We sat in silence, drinking and listening to 'The Nearness of You'.

Then Linda stood up and took off her T-shirt. 'I think we've got the message by now.'

She slipped off her shoes, unbuttoned her jeans and pulled them down. 'Come on.'

Her skin was darker and fuller than I had ever remembered.

210

'It's what you want, isn't it?' She threw her jeans on to a chair and walked off into the bedroom in her bra and knickers.

I followed.

When it was over we lay side by side and I felt Linda curl up against me as she had done in the past.

'Happy?' she said, stroking my chest.

I had promised my father I would be home. 'Of course. But I should go soon.'

'Why? We're not seventeen any more.'

'I know that.'

'Then what's the problem?'

'My dad. He disapproves.'

'He knows?'

'No, of course not. How could he? We've only just started.'

'I can never tell with your family. They get to hear things pretty quick . . .'

'He knows I've seen you.'

'You told him?'

'I think Vi saw us.'

'God, some things never change.'

'I don't want him suspecting. I promised I'd sort a few things out for him. I'll come back tomorrow if you want,' I said.

'Of course I want. I want you now.'

'Again?'

'Yes, again, Mr Married Man. Don't be lazy. You're in for it now.'

We made love slowly and more tenderly. I did not know if it was regret that we had taken so long to find each other or whether there was already an awareness that it could not last. Then I started to get dressed.

'I can't stay,' I said.

'Of course you can.'

I pulled on my shirt. 'I know I can, but please . . .'

'Why?'

'I can't stay here for ever . . .'

'Why not?'

'You know why . . .'

'Then promise you'll come back.'

'I promise.'

She turned on her side and watched me try to find my shoes. 'Don't leave me this time.'

I leant down and kissed her on the lips. 'I won't,' I said, and headed out into the night, the streetlights stretching away before me, the last drinkers silhouetted against car headlamps.

Claire

We were charged with trespass, resisting arrest and breaching the peace. We gave false names, the levellers and suffragettes who had gone before us, women hidden from history: Elizabeth Lilburne, Mary Overton, Katherine Chidley and Milly Fawcett. I was Emily Davidson.

When the police took statements and asked for our professions we didn't say we were schoolteachers or nurses or homemakers but that we were restorers of free speech, recoverers of liberty, servants of the people. We asked to be considered political prisoners but were refused.

'You have broken the law.'

'These are not laws we recognise.'

We spent the night crammed into the cells. We had a lawyer who gave her work for free, and she phoned home and tried to reach Martin. I didn't want him to read it in the papers. Joyce had got a message to me to say that Lucy was fine and she was looking after her.

Then the lawyer came back and told me that there was no one at our house. Perhaps Martin was working away from home?

I gave her the office number but they said he had taken some leave and they didn't know where he was, and so, out of desperation, I told her that she should ring Martin's father. He was always good about phoning his dad.

I began to worry that something was wrong. I thought of all the terrible things that could have happened: illness, accident or a freak event. I realised how much Martin had done for me and how badly I was missing him.

Martin

'Here,' she said. 'I want to give you this.' It was a pebble, with the sea at night on one side and dawn on the other. Underneath Linda had written the date when we had made love again in tiny white numerals. 'You're supposed to guess what it means.'

'Dawn and dusk?'

'Night and day . . .'

She told me she had once taken a job on local radio to earn a bit of money. One of her first 'how to be a DJ' lessons had been what to do in the event of a nuclear attack, and behind the turntable was a fading copy of *Frank Sinatra's Greatest Hits*. As soon as she heard the three-minute warning, she was supposed to slap it on and head under the nearest table.

'From then on, any time I heard Frankie on the radio I began to panic: have we only got three minutes left or are they having a laugh? His music always makes me think of the end of the world.'

We drove up the coast and stayed in a country-house hotel with a spa and twenty-four-hour room service. The receptionist looked disapprovingly at Linda's ripped jeans and scuffed shoes, but said nothing. She didn't even remark when we asked for a bottle of champagne for the room, but I could see the smirk at the corner of her mouth that said: 'I bet you're not married.'

We went upstairs. 'Happy?' I asked.

'Of course I am. You?'

'I can't believe we're doing this.'

'Well, we are,' she said. 'You see how happy you can be if you just let go.'

'I didn't think it was possible to feel like this again.'

'Let's stay here for ever,' she said, 'or at least until the money runs out. Have you got enough?'

'Of course,' I lied.

'Then you're richer than I thought.'

We ordered late breakfasts, had a swim before lunch, and made love in the afternoons. 'Our honeymoon,' said Linda.

I tried not to think of Claire but on the second night it rained hard and it reminded me of university where the girl in the next room had a tape of 'natural sounds' and rewound to the thunderstorm whenever she was about to have sex. Claire and I always remembered it as our little joke whenever there was thunder.

Linda was in a dreamy mood, drinking champagne, reciting bits of poetry and falling asleep:

> *A book of verses underneath the Bough*
> *A jug of wine, a Loaf of Bread – and Thou*
> *Beside me singing in the Wilderness –*
> *Oh, Wilderness were Paradise enow!*

'I had forgotten you could recite poetry,' I said.

'Well, I like to impress you from time to time; keep a bit of mystery going.'

'What was it?'

'Edward Fitzgerald. *The Rubáiyát of Omar Khayyám*. He's buried down the road. There's a rose from Persia on his grave. Do you want to go?'

'When?'

'Whenever you like. We can do anything we want, remember? Once you take away the fear of responsibility you can do anything.'

Her hand closed slowly into a fist in front of my face. 'Look, here's your old life, scrunched up in my hand, and lo,' she blew and unfurled her fingers, 'abracadabra, I make it disappear . . .'

We drove to the village of Boulge and found a squat church with a sixteenth-century tower and a Victorian nave. We parked by the side of the main road and approached through early autumn fields. It must have been the darkest interior in Suffolk, the only light coming through small windows of thick coloured glass: Faith and St Nicholas, the Annunciation, the Baptism of Christ.

As we walked up the aisle Linda said, 'Just think: we could have got married here. I could have been Mrs Martin Turner after all.' She took my arm. 'Here comes the bride . . .'

'Don't.'

'It might have happened.'

'Stop it, Linda.'

'And it still could, of course. It just takes a bit of courage. In two years' time we could be here again like it was supposed to be. I could even wear scarlet. That would get people talking . . .'

'Don't . . .'

'We could have our child baptised in the font. Look, black marble. Why not?'

'Linda, we should go. I don't want anyone seeing us here.'

'Who's going to see us? It's the middle of nowhere.'

'Someone might come . . .'

'I'm going to sign the visitors' book.'

'Don't,' I said. 'Please don't.'

'Why not? Martin and Linda Turner. What's wrong with that?'

'You know what's wrong with it. Why are you being like this?'

'Like what?'

'Not yourself. A bit hysterical.'

'Well, why do you think? Nothing about any of this is normal.'

'What do you want then?'

'I want you to accept me and for us to be together in public like normal couples.'

'But we're not a normal couple, are we?'

'I hope you're not ashamed of me all over again.'

'No,' I said. 'Of course I'm not.'

'I don't want you starting to have doubts.'

'Let's go outside. I'm sorry. Look, it will be all right. I find it a bit difficult.'

'And you think I find it easy?'

We looked at Fitzgerald's grave, and it began to rain. The rose from Persia looked withered. Linda grabbed my arm and stood up on the railing round the stone. She lifted up her face and shouted to the sky:

> *Some for the Glories of This world; and some*
> *Sigh for the Prophet's Paradise to come;*
> *Ah, take the Cash, and let the Credit go,*
> *Nor heed the rumble of a distant Drum!*

'Sometimes I think you're a bit mad,' I said.

'Of course I am,' she replied. 'That's why you love me.'

When we got back to Canvey Linda told me that she wanted me to stay at her flat rather than my father's. We didn't even need to tell him we were there. I could pretend I was going home but then stay on secretly. It would be the start of my double life.

I took another week off work, knowing that if I didn't start explaining myself soon I could run the risk of losing my job. I was aware that I could not go on much longer and my head began to fill with fear: of discovery, of Claire, and the choices I had made.

Two days later, we were woken at six-thirty in the morning. It was Masood from the newsagent's below.

'Miss Walker, there's a phone call for the man staying with you.'

'Who is it?'

'His father. It's urgent.'

I pulled on yesterday's clothes, unable to think what could be wrong. Perhaps Dad had been burgled or something had happened to Vi. In the shop, Masood was writing the addresses on newspapers and his son was sorting them ready for delivery. The boy looked about ten. I turned my back but could feel him staring at me as I picked up the phone.

'Dad . . . How did you know I was here?'

'I'm cleverer than you think, son.'

'Are you all right?'

'Never mind me. Claire's been arrested.'

'*What?*'

'Some of the women are looking after Lucy, but you've got to get over there and pay the fine. Claire's refusing to do it and said she'd rather go to prison but we can't have her in the nick.'

'I'll get my things.'

'And don't tell anyone.'

'It'll be in the papers, Dad.'

'I don't mean about Claire, you idiot. I mean about Linda. Don't tell anyone. Especially don't tell your wife. Don't go home and dump it all on her.'

'I'm not that stupid.'

'I'm serious, son, even if she asks; don't make it worse by telling her. Keep it to yourself.'

'I don't need your advice, Dad.'

'You're getting it anyway. You've got to shut up about it unless you're planning on doing something daft like leaving her altogether. She's a good woman, is Claire. Don't keep messing it up.'

'I'm not messing it up.'

'Then what are you doing?'

I put the phone down. Masood and his son pretended they hadn't been listening. I couldn't work out how much they might have guessed from my end of the conversation.

When I went back upstairs, Linda was still half-asleep. 'Come back to bed,' she said, 'I want you.'

Claire

In the past, I'd always been frightened of police officers. They made me feel guilty, as if I'd forgotten that I'd murdered someone and they were coming round to remind me. And I'd never been in a courtroom in my life.

But the magistrate looked nervous. Perhaps his only experience of women was a compliant wife and placid old ladies up for driving without due care and attention. He could tell he was in for a rough ride when Sasha refused to swear on the Bible.

'You must give the oath, madam.'

'I will not swear by Almighty God. That is a male construct.'

'Then what will you swear by?'

'I'll swear by the goddess, but not by the god.'

We had packed the court with supporters who, when asked not to speak, began to hum 'We Shall Overcome', swaying from side to side: Abby who had given up work as a therapist, Sue who wanted to start a Greenham newspaper, women from all over the country: Catherine, Mandy and Emma; Ali, Amy and Morwenna.

When it came to my turn, and I was accused of invasion, assault and giving false evidence, the women stuck their fingers in their ears and started ululating so the charges could not be heard.

'This is the law of the land,' the magistrate announced.

I told him that no person should have to live under laws to which she has not personally given her express consent.

The women cheered.

'I ask you to be silent or you will go down for contempt.'

'We believe in the sovereignty of the people,' I said.

The judge replied, 'I have one sovereign and I am grateful to say that it is not you. You are faced with three charges. How do you plead?'

'I do not need to plead.'

'I think you will find that you do. I repeat that I would rather not have to add the charge of contempt.'

'I'm not going to beg. I have done nothing wrong.'

'That is for the court to decide.'

'I know in my heart that anything I have done I have done out of love for my fellow woman, and even, dare I say it, for my fellow man. Such is my love for humanity I have even done it for you.'

The police gave evidence, told the magistrate that I had trespassed on to MOD land, obstructed vehicles, kicked a police officer and given a false name: Emily Wilding Davidson.

'Wasn't that the woman who threw herself under the king's horse?'

I was almost impressed that the judge knew. 'I understand that you have been a teacher,' he said, 'and I imagine that one day you might like to return to your profession. I will therefore be lenient. We ask you to enter into recognisance and to keep the Queen's peace for the next twelve months for the sum of twenty-five pounds. Are you willing to accept?'

'What do you mean, "keep the peace"? That is what I have been doing.'

'The law must be upheld,' said the magistrate.

'Surely, I am the one keeping the peace: not you.'

My friends began to sing 'Give Peace a Chance'.

'I understand that to be a refusal.'

'I'll keep the peace but I will use my own definition.'

I was on a roll, performing more to my friends than answering the questions put to me, and I believed I was invincible. But then I heard a voice interrupting me.

'I will pay her fine, your honour.'

'And who are you?'

'Her husband.'

'Then I pity you,' said the magistrate.

The women began booing.

'He will not pay the fine,' I said. 'I will not let him. I'd rather be in prison.' I turned to Martin. 'If you pay then the money goes to the Ministry of Defence.'

'I have already written the cheque.'

'Shame,' sang the women. 'Shame on you, shame on you.'

'I've collected Lucy and we're taking you home,' said Martin.

'Shame,' continued the women. 'Shame on you, shame on you.'

'I assume you still believe in a democracy. Even if you want to stay it's two votes to one.'

'Don't do this to me, Martin. I thought you understood.'

'I have to do this.'

'We say no,' shouted the women, 'we say no.'

But Martin was adamant. 'We're leaving. Our family. Together.'

I was so tired.

'Lucy's already in the car.'

I started to follow my husband.

'Come back, Claire,' Abby called out. 'We love you. We need you.'

Driving out of the car park, I could hear Kate singing:

> *Show me the country where bombs had to fall,*
> *Show me the ruins of buildings once so tall,*
> *And I'll show you a young land with so many reasons why*
> *There but for fortune, go you or go I . . .*

Linda

As soon as Martin had gone, I couldn't do anything. I smoked and drank and stared at the walls. Then I wrote down everything we had done in my notebook: where we had walked, what we had eaten, and how we had made love. I wondered if I could keep repeating those days in my head until Martin came back so that I would not have to live in the real world at all. I kept going over what he had said. When I stood up it was only to move across the room and sit down again. I had the record player on continual repeat so there was endless Billie Holiday.

When I did manage to go out I found that all the music in the pubs and supermarkets on the island was aimed directly at me. It was always the Communards singing 'Don't Leave Me This Way' or 'Never Can Say Goodbye'. I kept thinking of the questions that needed answering. How could Martin have made love to me that morning already knowing that he had to leave? Perhaps that was why it was so tender. But in that case why did he need to go? Why couldn't he stay? His wife had left him and got herself into this mess.

If I could at least have talked to him everything would have been easier to bear but I didn't even know his address. I tried Directory Enquiries but his wife was a teacher and so they'd obviously gone ex-directory. Bitch.

I couldn't wander round Brighton hoping to bump into him. But that's what he had done to me. All right, he had asked Ade, but he had staked me out like a private detective. If he needed me so much and he was happy when we were together, I didn't see why he had to go at all. He could just have sent his wife some money.

I tried to pretend that he hadn't really gone, and he would be back at any minute. He would sort things out at home and return. How could he leave me twice? He couldn't be that heartless.

Claire

When we got home, Martin bundled us out of the car and said that he would unpack everything. 'You both need good long baths.'

I could see that it was going to be difficult to be the three of us again. I could hear Martin being especially nice to Lucy, running her bath, leaving presents in her bedroom, and making sure it was warm. His blatant bribery made me even angrier.

'Let me know,' he called, 'when you'd like to ask me about how I am, whether I still have a job, and how I've been coping without you. My life is as nothing compared to your great project, but it does, in its small insignificant way, have a bearing on how we decide to bring up our child.'

'Oh fuck off, you pompous prig,' I said. 'Just fuck off.'

'Don't you tell me to fuck off. I saved you from prison. I've looked after you. And now I'm going to look after our daughter. Which is a damn sight more than you've been doing.'

I had never seen him so irritable or aggressive. 'She's happy. She's fulfilled. She's alive. She has seen what matters in the world.'

'She should be at school. I should have thought a teacher like you would have appreciated that.'

'Of course I know that.'

'Daddy!' Lucy called. 'I'm ready to get out now.'

'Coming!'

'I'll do the supper then,' I said.

'I've left some things out. It's ready.'

'Good. Then I'll have a bath myself.'

Hot water. Space. My own towels. I was amazed by the affluence of our home: the size of the bath, the waste of water, taps left running. There was so much food and so much stuff in the cupboards. I could see that Lucy was happy to be back in her bedroom, talking with her My Little Ponies, brushing their hair and arranging their dream castle. I remembered her saying when she was feeling tired and upset that she just wanted normal parents. *Well*, I thought, *here is our chance to be normal again.*

Later that night, when we were in bed, I said I was sorry for the things I'd said, and how I'd let Martin down, and how I would try to be better at everything and that I did love him.

'Even if I am a fucking pompous prig?'

'Yes, even if you are a pompous prig.'

I couldn't get used to the idea of being in my own bed. 'I'm sorry,' I said. 'I'm sorry if my going away has made it hard for you.'

'It's all right,' he said but I couldn't tell what he was thinking.

'Is something wrong?'

'No,' he said. 'Nothing's wrong.'

'Tell me.'

'No. It's nothing.'

'Then look at me,' I said.

'It's too dark.'

'Tell me.'

'I missed you, that's all. It's so long since we've been together.'

'It doesn't feel right?'

'I'm not used to it.'

'We need time, Martin.'

'I'd forgotten how, I don't know, ordinary it felt, to lie here beside you.'

'Ordinary? That doesn't sound very exciting.'

'Perhaps we've had enough excitement.'

'We've been through so much, Martin. Let's not try to force it. Think of all that's happened and how much we mean to each other. I couldn't have done any of this without you.'

'You could.'

'No. I'm not sure if I could,' I said. 'I'm not sure if I could do anything without you.'

Linda

Of course I couldn't phone him when I wanted. In fact, I couldn't phone him at all, and so I was always waiting. Even when we did get to talk, it was impossible to speak about what really mattered. I couldn't see his face, I couldn't tell what he was thinking and I didn't ever know if I was saying too much or too little.

I lived a suspended life: reading without remembering what I had read, looking without seeing, hearing without listening. Ade came round because he hadn't seen me for a while. He said I wasn't looking so good (thanks, Ade) and that I should put a stop to it all before I got hurt. I told him it was too late for that.

Then he announced that the first affair in a marriage is the one that doesn't last: people sometimes have two or three affairs before the eventual break-up, didn't I know that?

'You want to be the last-affair girl, not the first.'

'How do you know I'm the first?'

'I don't. But Martin isn't the type to play away.'

'Then what's he doing with me?'

'You're the exception. But you want to watch it, Linda. I can't see him leaving his wife. Can you?'

'He's got to.'

'That doesn't mean he's going to, though, does it? He's not going to come back and live here.'

'Why not?'

'In Canvey? The place he ran away from?'

'He didn't run away. Anyway, we'll find somewhere else.'

'We were never good enough for him, Linda. We couldn't give him what he wanted . . .'

Everything Ade said came out harder than he meant it. 'I think you should take a deep breath, dump him and start getting over it. It's not doing you any good, all this.'

'I can't.'

'That means you don't want to.'

'You're right,' I said. 'I think I'd rather have this and be unhappy than nothing at all. I don't ever want to feel nothing again.'

'You're mad, you are.'

'I know. But I don't want to be normal. I can't stand being normal. If I could just talk to him. If I could just see him then he'd know. I could talk to him and persuade him. I know I could.'

'This isn't good.'

'I know it isn't good. You don't have to tell me it isn't good.'

'I don't like seeing you like this.'

'Well, I don't like being like this.'

'Come on,' said Ade, 'let's go to the pub.'

Of course that was the one time Martin phoned. Masood left me a note.

Your boyfriend called. No message.

It was Friday night; at least forty-eight hours before I could speak to him again unless he escaped the family and got to the phone box down the road.

I started to write to him, I could always send the letter to his work, but I couldn't find the words. I didn't know whether to be grateful to him for coming back in the first place or to be angry that he'd gone again. I kept drinking and smoking and scrunching up bits of paper through the night.

'Dear Martin . . .' (Was that enough? Perhaps it should be 'Darling Martin' or just 'Darling' or 'My Love'? But was that being too keen too soon?)

'Dear Martin, Thank you for coming back to me . . .' (Too dependent.)

'Dear Martin, I love you . . .' (Too raw.)

'Dear Martin, I don't think you know how much it means to me . . .' (Too accusatory.)

'Dear Martin, I miss you already . . .' (Too desperate.)

'Dear Martin, I don't understand why you had to go . . .' (Too demanding.)

'Dear Martin, I understand why you had to go . . .' (Too placatory.)

'Dear Martin, Stay with me . . .' (Too honest.)

I gave up, found an old postcard and wrote: '*However quick the stream may be, it does not carry away the reflection of the moon.*'

I wrote the phrase 'Linda Turner' in my sketchbook. I wrote it a second and a third time. Then I found I couldn't stop writing it.

Violet

It was Martin's birthday and Claire insisted that we came down to celebrate it with her family. She said he'd been under a lot of stress and everyone getting together would cheer them all up. Stress. Well, that's one way of putting it. I don't know how much her parents knew but Len and I had decided that as far as we were concerned we were happy to pretend that Martin hadn't had an affair, Claire hadn't been arrested, their daughter was perfectly well adjusted and everything was hunky-dory. We only hoped that the Reverend Matthew and Lady Celia took the same line.

As soon as we arrived, Lucy started to play up; well, you could expect as much after the attention she must have received at the camp. We had to obey each whim: looking at the souvenirs she'd brought back, the paintings she'd done, and watching the show she wanted to put on. It was sweet at first, even if it did involve a lot of her falling about and pretending to be dead, but after a while it appeared that she wanted some kind of audience participation. I whispered to Len that I wasn't going to start lying down and pretending I was dead in front of a cruise missile. Not before dinner, anyway.

The meal was all right, I suppose, because at least we were getting used to Martin and Claire's ways. Personally, I don't understand how anyone in the world can enjoy comfrey-leaf fritters but there's no accounting for taste. I think they prepared it just to see the looks on our faces.

I noticed Claire had lost some weight and I thought it might be polite if I told her so. She replied it was the Greenham diet and I should try it.

After that most of the meal was conducted in silence, apart from Lucy singing songs and pretending the adults were policemen. She made us listen to her like she was still at that awful place.

'And so, Claire,' said her father, 'tell us your news, your stories from the front. The battles you have fought and won, your tales of derring-do.'

'Don't, Daddy.'

'No, I'm interested. We've seen it on the news, of course, the mud and the singing and the dungarees. Some of my parishioners even went on a coach trip. Funny kind of holiday.'

'It wasn't a holiday.'

'You know what I mean.'

'You should have come, Mummy.'

Celia looked startled. 'Oh, I think I'm a bit old for that kind of thing.'

'If every woman in Britain came then no one could stop us. Imagine . . .'

'But that's hardly likely, is it . . .'

'What's happened to you both?' Claire asked. 'When I was growing up you were full of such ideals. We travelled to Africa, we went all over the place installing water pumps and converting the heathen, and now you spend all your time stuck drinking sherry by the Thames.'

'I wouldn't say we were stuck, my darling.'

'Where's your courage? Where's your vitality?'

She was beginning to rant and Martin asked her to calm down.

'I've told you before. Don't tell me to calm down. It's so patronising.'

'You're all right, Claire,' said Len.

'Do you know what it's like to see your friends kicked in the stomach and being pulled away by their hair? Do you know what it means to be frightened every day that something terrible is going to happen? It's not a joke, lots of women getting beaten up. It's not just a nice story to tell at a coffee morning. You can't imagine it.'

'I can imagine it,' said Matthew.

'I don't see how. You only became a clergyman so you wouldn't have to fight.'

Her father coloured up. 'That's below the belt, young lady.'

'I wonder, Celia, if you would like some of this delicious salad?' I interrupted.

I could see she was starting to get in a state. 'Your father always wanted to be a cleric. Don't you dare put it any other way.'

'We KNOW,' Claire was almost shouting. 'It's hardly a secret. You should be proud of it. Conscientious objection. It has a noble history, even if people did get shot for it.'

'Don't bring that up now. That's family.'

'We ARE family,' said Claire. 'This is my family. Martin and Lucy. And Len and Vi. We're one family. Don't you think they should know rather than we all keep pretending?'

'Your father has nothing to be ashamed of.'

'Except in front of people who actually fought.'

Matthew was dignified. 'You don't know what it was like. You can't even imagine the horror, sitting there with your friends on a campsite. It's easy enough to protest in a time of peace. It's a lot harder in war.'

There was silence.

'I'm sorry, Daddy, I didn't mean to hurt you.'

Her father looked at Len and me and said, 'I got as far as the bayonet training. We were told it was important to hate your enemy. We had to run at sandbags in this field outside Aldershot. I couldn't do it. I couldn't imagine hating anyone.'

'It's the one word Matthew won't allow,' said Celia. 'The children have always been able to swear if they want to but we won't have the word "hate" in our house.'

'And yet so many of my friends were killed. And my brother, of course. You would think I would be able to hate but I just couldn't do it.'

It all came back to me. Not that it had ever gone away. Claire's father saying 'of course', like the death of a brother in war was the most natural thing in the world.

He turned to his daughter and spoke quietly. 'It was a lot harder to say no then. You were stigmatised. Some people never recovered.'

Len put down his knife and fork. His fingers were resting on the edge of the table like they always did when he was waiting to speak. 'I think you should put a stop to this conversation,' he said. 'You're all right, Matthew. Let's not go into this. Long time ago. Things are different today.'

'I'm sorry this has come out,' said Celia. 'I do think it's best if we change the subject.'

'And anyway,' Len went on, 'plenty of padres were killed. They were there with the troops. That was brave enough. They saw enough death. Lots of burials to get through.'

'That's what Matthew did,' said Celia. 'He was always by people's side when it mattered. He has high moral principles.'

'Not high enough for some, alas.'

'But I'm sure that's where your daughter gets her ideals from,' said Len.

'I'm sorry, Daddy. I didn't mean it. I'm very tired.'

She stood up and kissed her father on the top of his head. Then she put her arms round his shoulders and he took her hand.

'That's all right,' he said. 'I forgive you.'

'I'll get the pudding. It's lemon meringue pie.'

Her father rubbed his hands together. 'My favourite.'

When his daughter was in the kitchen Matthew said, 'Claire always did have such high expectations of people. Perhaps that's what happens to the children of clergymen. They want so much goodness and then they find that there just isn't enough of it in the world to go round. They get so disappointed.'

I could hear Claire singing as she took the pie out of the oven.

> *You can forbid nearly everything*
> *But you can't forbid me to think*
> *And you can't forbid my tears to flow*
> *And you can't shut my mouth when I sing.*

Linda

I made Martin promise to ring me twice a day: as soon as he had
left the house in the morning and then again at six o'clock when
he was on his way home. He didn't like to call from work, and he
wasn't at his best on the phone, but I was determined not to lose
him. We would have a life together no matter how much pain we
had to go through.

The phone calls weren't ideal. Sometimes Martin was distracted
in the mornings by all that he had to do in the day and then, in the
evening, he was tired and he wanted a drink and a bit of a relax,
preferably with me. A phone call was never going to be enough, he
said.

'Well, you know what to do about that. Just get in the car.'

He told me it was a bit more complicated than that and he was
going to come and see me and talk about it all. He hadn't told his
wife about us yet because it was difficult. I suppose he thought I'd
understand.

'What's so difficult about it?' I said.

'It just is.'

I knew that the longer I left it the more likely he was to stay with
her. He would get used to everything being normal again and she
would make it impossible for him to leave.

'You don't still love her, do you?'

'There's a lot between us. It's hard to throw it all away.'

'There's a lot between us too. I was first; remember? You haven't
got over me; neither of us has got over each other. That's what this
is about.'

'I know, but it's hard, Linda. I do love you but . . .'

'Don't start giving me any buts,' I said. 'Don't even think about speaking to me if you're going to use the word "but".'

Martin

Sometimes when you wake you know that there is something wrong or something you have forgotten. But then it comes, back again, the trouble you hoped sleep would take from you, reasserting itself in the daylight. Claire was sitting on the edge of the bed. As I began to focus I saw that her towelling gown was belted rather than left loose.

'What?' I asked. 'What are you doing?'

'Waiting for you to wake up.'

'Do you want me to make the coffee?'

'Not yet.'

'What is it then?'

'I'm looking at this pebble. I haven't seen it before.'

'Where did you find it?'

'In your jacket pocket. I was sorting out the dry cleaning. And I found this. Quite special, I imagine.'

'I've had it for ages.'

'But there's a date on it. Didn't you notice?'

'You'd need a magnifying glass to see anything on that.'

'Well, it's just as well I've got one.'

I turned away from her. 'It's a pebble. There's nothing to see.'

'I think there is. And I think there's something to tell.'

'There's nothing. It doesn't matter.'

'Well, I didn't give it to you.'

'No.'

'So that makes me wonder who did.'

'It's nothing. It's not important.'

'Turn round and look me in the eye. What kind of marriage do you want to have, Martin?'

'I thought we knew.'

'What if I think you've changed your mind?'

Had my father, or even Vi, said something? Claire couldn't know anything for sure.

'Stop being aggressive,' I said. 'You were the one who went away.'

'Oh, so it's my fault now, is it?'

'I'm not saying that.'

'I was trying to do some good in the world. One little bit. I was trying to make a difference.'

'What?'

'Are you sure you haven't got something to tell me?'

'Don't be ridiculous. There's nothing to tell. I missed you.'

'I know, Martin.'

She couldn't.

'And do you know how? I could tell from the way Vi looked at me. She's a nice enough woman but she can't keep a secret. I could see it in her eyes. She knew something. And your father. They were different with me.'

'No, they weren't.'

'Yes, Martin, they were. They were kind to me. They've never been that kind to me in the past but on your birthday they were kind to the point of *pity*. Anyone could have seen that. Even my father noticed, for God's sake. Everyone knew except me. You've embarrassed me. Embarrassed and humiliated me in front of my own family.'

'Don't get upset. It's all right. I haven't done anything wrong.'

'Don't get upset? What am I supposed to do?'

'Nothing happened.'

'Really?'

'Really. If you're going to go on like this then I wish it had.'

'So there *was* something.'

'No,' I said. 'There wasn't.'

'You've never got over her, have you?'

'Who are you talking about?'

'Oh, for God's sake. Who do you think? I'm not stupid but I'm not going to acknowledge it by saying her name. I'm not going to pollute my own mouth.'

'It was ages ago.'

'But you've seen her again, haven't you?'

'I went home and she was there.'

'I thought this was your home.'

'You know what I mean.'

'No, Martin, I don't know if I do. I see you didn't feel the need to tell me about anything.'

'There's nothing to tell. And anyway you weren't here, in case you hadn't noticed. It's not me that's in the wrong. You're the one that went away and got arrested. I came home. I'm here. I would have looked after our daughter and supported you both if you hadn't taken her away. What do you want from me?'

'Honesty.'

No, I thought, *no, you may think you want it but you don't want that at all.* I heard my father's voice in my head. *Don't make it worse by telling her.*

'I didn't do anything,' I said.

'No? Then what is this pebble then?'

'It's nothing.'

Still she sat on the edge of the bed. 'No. That's not good enough, Martin. You remember when we agreed we would always tell each other the truth?'

'Yes, but . . .'

'I want to know the truth. There's no point pretending everything's all right when it isn't. I want a marriage with truth in it.'

'I've told you,' I said.

'You haven't.'

'I have.'

'Oh. Don't tell me. She threw herself at you. There was nothing you could do. You didn't intend it to happen. You're sorry. Look at me when I'm speaking to you.'

I had to keep lying. 'There's nothing to say,' I said.

'I see. So she gave you this stone as a thank-you present.'

'We went on a walk.'

'A walk? Is that what you call it?'

'Is there something wrong with that?'

'Think about it. And then I'll tell you what you've done.'

She stood up, took off her wedding ring and put it on the bedside table. Her eyes had become blood-red at the corners.

'Well?' she asked.

'It's difficult, Claire.'

'What's difficult?'

'This conversation.'

'Did you sleep with her?'

Claire was staring at me and I tried to look away but I knew that she wouldn't let me. I had to keep going but I couldn't see how it was ever going to stop.

'I asked you a question. Did you sleep with her?'

'Yes,' I said.

'Linda?'

'Yes.'

In the silence I tried to imagine everything she might do – sink to the floor, hit me, walk out and never be seen again.

'Why?' she asked.

'I don't know.'

'You don't know?'

'Because I missed you. Because you weren't here.'

'Is that all it takes?'

'What do you mean?'

'A few weeks apart? After fourteen years?'

'I wanted somebody to love me,' I said. 'I wanted some kindness.'

'Is that what you call it?' she said.

Claire

I tried to remember what my father had taught me about forgiveness; how he had stood up to preach about gentleness really being strength and how love was always stronger after it had been tested but it was so hard to put anything like that into practice.

All my life I'd been told that if you were good and decent and trusted others, if you were honest and did your best, then people would recognise what you were doing and be kind to you. I'm not saying I was trying to lead a good life so that people would love me in return, a kind of selfish altruism; I just thought we had a marriage in which truth telling was paramount, and provided we had that then nothing could hurt us.

But what now? Perhaps I demanded too much honesty. I had forced it out of Martin. What had happened could have been buried, an undetonated explosion, always there but far too deeply mined to trouble the surface. All our marriage we had kept some of our feelings from each other in order not to cause hurt. But now I had excavated the whole damned thing. I remembered all those essays I'd done at school – 'When is a white lie not a lie?' – and I thought of my mother telling me the importance of discretion. *You should always tell the truth but the truth need not always be spoken.*

Martin hadn't wanted to confess because he didn't want to hurt me and, besides, it was all over. At least that's what he said. And so I began to think that it was my fault: for leaving him, for not being enough for him, for forcing out the truth.

But then I stopped myself. We could have talked about it. He did not need to seek her out. And he had betrayed me.

Had he loved her all through our marriage or was it a fantasy? If he had always loved her then why hadn't he said anything? And if it was only a fantasy then why did he need it?

For weeks we lived without referring to anything that had happened, sending Lucy to school, avoiding difficult subjects, steering clear of anything that might cause upset. But in the middle of the night I couldn't stop feeling. The rage was so intense and I found myself writing her name repeatedly on bits of paper and picturing how she might die. I went through old photographs, cutting Martin out of them or scratching out his face: the three of us on the beach at Bridport taken by a stranger with Lucy's first camera; the two of us at Cambridge, long-haired radicals, when I had a fringe and looked happy; Martin helping at the summer barbecue, pointing out the courgettes in case anyone had forgotten we were vegetarian. I rummaged in desks and cut and gouged and threw things around, anything to rid myself of the feeling.

When Martin found me I told him to leave me alone. I didn't want him to see me like this. I didn't know where my anger might go.

'What are you doing?' he asked.

'It's nothing.'

'Do you want to give me the scissors?'

I didn't realise I was holding them. Neither they nor my hands seemed real. I kept the scissors open and stared down as he took them from me. Nothing made sense any more. Then he put them down on the table and opened his arms and held me and said he was sorry. I could feel his fingers against my back. He was pressing me to him and I wanted to go back to how it was when we were first married but it didn't feel right. I didn't want him to think he could just be nice to me and everything would be fine.

I heard him say that he wished he hadn't hurt me. He said that he wished he hadn't told me the truth. He'd always promised himself that he would do nothing to upset me but now he had. He kept talking and talking and I didn't say anything but I realised he was crying. He said he wouldn't let go until he had said everything and he told me again and again how much he loved me and how he couldn't bear it if we ever stopped loving each

240

other and that his life meant nothing, absolutely nothing, without me.

I stood there in my velour nightdress that was old and black and torn, feeling cold with my hair sticking up and needing a bit of colour, and my eyes that must have been red, and I couldn't believe that I was letting him say all this, and that he still loved me and that I, despite it all, loved him.

I thought it must have been so much easier for him to be with her, with their past and the sea and the advantage of never having lived together.

Oh God, I didn't know anything any more.

But I understood I had not to think about her and what she had done and why they had ever been together. I only wanted to think about us, Martin and Claire, how we had met and found each other even though it was so long ago, our first love and our marriage, and our child, and all the depression I'd felt, and the love we'd shared. We had so much that was past and even though it was distant it was mad to throw it away, mad, it had to be preserved, it was too precious, we were nothing without it, and so surely we had to stay and fight and learn and love now, in the middle of the night, with both of us looking terrible, we had to fight, we couldn't let anything about us, anything we had ever shared, go.

I realised that Martin had stopped speaking but we were still holding each other, neither of us letting go because we both knew that if we did then the moment would be over and we would fall and there were things we still had to say and there was so much of the love that still needed repairing.

Repairing. That wasn't the word. Nothing was the right word. Perhaps if we just stayed together, holding each other, that would be enough.

Then he said, 'I love you. I love you and I love you best. Better than anyone.'

'You wouldn't rather be with her?'

'No.'

'Tell me to believe you.'

'I'm sorry for everything I've done. I'm sorry about being distracted and thinking only about the present and forgetting so much about us . . .'

'You loved her once. Like you loved me.'

'I still love you.'

'And you still love her?'

'Don't make me say these things.'

'When you were with her . . .' I said.

'Don't . . .'

'No. I want to.'

'I don't want you getting upset . . .'

Getting, I thought. *What do you mean* getting?

'When you were with her, did you think of me?'

'Of course.'

'All the time?'

'A lot of the time.'

'And what did you think?'

'I thought, *Why am I doing this?*'

'Did you love her?'

'I love you. If you want to force it all out of me of course I'll tell you but I don't want to hurt you any more.'

'But I don't want you thinking of her . . .'

'I can't control what I think. All I know is that I had to give her up. For us. That's why I'm here.'

'I was asking if you loved her.'

'Not as much as you. Never as much as you.'

'You're not just saying that?'

'It's why I'm here. Not there. I never ever didn't love you.'

'Then that's what I have to remember.'

I must have been looking at the same patch of floor for half an hour.

Martin pulled back. 'I wish I hadn't told you. I wish I hadn't upset you. I think I'd rather live a lie than have this truth.'

'No. I wouldn't,' I said. 'I'd rather have truth. I'd rather we knew exactly what we thought even if we hurt each other.'

I didn't know where we were or what I thought but the words came out and I said: 'You have to never see her again. You can't write, you can't phone, you have to be totally silent and you have to promise me that you'll do this, because if you can't and if you don't we'll never get better, and we'll never be able to love each other again.'

242

'I know.'

When people in the past had told me that they had no secrets from each other I had never believed them. I always thought they were the most deceived; like those who professed they had open marriages. You knew it could only last until one of them fell properly in love. But now I believed absolutely in the idea of telling one another as much as we could even if it was hurtful. I wanted there to be no surprises, no moments of discovery.

'And you must tell me everything,' I said to Martin. 'Tell me everything, even if it hurts me.'

'And do you want to tell me everything?' he asked.

'I want you to want to know,' I said. 'I want to be first in all that you think and do. I want you to tell me things before you tell anyone else. I don't want other people to know things I don't. When you walk into a room I want you to come to me first, whatever else I am doing or whoever else is there. I do not ever want to be embarrassed or hurt or humiliated by not knowing what is going on in your life. I do not want other people to know secrets that I do not. Wherever you are and whatever you are doing, I should be able to walk in and feel loved. Unembarrassed. For you to look up and know that you need nothing other than this, the two of us, as we are.'

'Nothing?'

'And at any time. And I will make the same promise to you. This is how we have to live. And that, in itself, is a secret. That, in itself, is what should be at the heart of our marriage.'

I wondered what we were going to do with the rest of our lives: how fragile, fast and short the past had been, how much of it we had wasted, and what little time there was left to redeem what lay before us.

Linda

Martin was on the phone and he started to speak very fast like he'd been saving it all up and he didn't want me to interrupt or persuade him to do anything else and so it all came out in a rush.

He said: 'You know I love you. I've always loved you. But I can't do this any more. I can't go on. I wish I could love you both but I can't . . .'

'What are you saying?'

'I'm sorry.'

'What?'

'I can't. I love you. But I can't.'

Masood was shutting up shop and his children had been sent to hurry him home before his dinner was cold. I wanted to tell Martin to stop. I wanted to say: 'No, you can't say these things. Don't speak to me again until you can say that you love me and that you will always love me. Don't think of seeing me again until the day that you can do that.'

But what I actually said was: 'Oh.'

Then he said: 'I'm sorry. I feel terrible.'

You feel terrible.

'I know I've behaved badly. I know I've done a dreadful thing and that you thought I would leave . . .'

I said: 'So you're not coming?'

'Not now,' he said.

'Not now?'

'No.'

'When are you coming then?'

'I don't think I can, Linda. I'm sorry.'

'But you love me.'

'I know. I do.'

'You said you did.'

'I did.'

'So you don't now?'

'It's not that. I do.'

'What is it then?'

'It's hard to explain.'

'Is it?'

You put your trust in people and sometimes they don't even know you've done so. From then on, I couldn't hear anything he was saying, only the words 'sorry' and 'no'.

He was still speaking when I put the phone down. He could have been saying anything but I knew that everything was one long farewell and that he would be relieved when it was over.

I had been doing all right before he came along. Admittedly, it wasn't great, but at least I had learnt not to be afraid of the future. I had been at some kind of peace with the world. Now, desire was bleeding out of me and there was nothing I could do to stop it.

EIGHT

Martin

The first time I knew Dad couldn't cope so well was the day we went to the cup final, Tottenham against Nottingham Forest, jostling up Wembley Way in 1991. He was convinced a Forest fan was out to stab him.

'Hold on to me, Dad,' I said. 'Come on.'

'It's all right, son. I can manage. Just let me get a fag out.'

He stopped and the crowds shifted around him. A voice behind called, 'Come on, Granddad, you old fucker,' and I was embarrassed by my father's deliberate slowness: the careful removal of the cigarette from the packet, the search across all his pockets for the lighter, his determination to hold his space.

'Chance'd be a fine thing, mate.'

We found our seats at the Spurs end and chanted how Tottenham always win when the year ends in one, a hundred thousand people waving flags: blue and white at one end of the stadium, red and white at the other. Then the band began to play and we sang 'Abide With Me'.

Dad knew all the words and he sang looking straight ahead, breathlessly and out of tune.

At the end the crowd applauded, relieved that the respectable part of cup final day was over, and I could see a girl below us in the yellow Tottenham away strip, leaning against her man and crying.

Even Dad looked upset. 'Are you all right?' I asked.

'Course I am,' he replied. 'COME ON, YOU SPURS!'

It was a shock to see him so sombre. The only thing that cheered him up was the sight of Princess Diana in the royal box.

'Wouldn't mind giving her a going-over.'

'Dad . . .'

'In my youth, I mean.'

'Don't be ridiculous . . .'

'No, straight up, son. I would have chanced it, bit of posh, you never know, she might have liked a bit of Canvey in her . . .'

'I wouldn't have thought she was your type . . .'

'She is . . .'

'And out of your league . . .'

'Don't bet on it. Some people can score from any position.'

Dad thought that everything could be explained in terms of football. A love affair was a question of patient build-up, making the perfect pass, getting in on goal and scoring. The workplace consisted of honing your talent, working as a team and keeping the opposition out. In family life, you had a game plan, were continually aware of where everyone else was on the pitch and played for each other. Perhaps if I could have explained my relationships with Linda and Claire in footballing terms, Dad would have been a bit more sympathetic.

It was a scrappy game, Gascoigne fired up and going in too hard, Nottingham Forest taking the lead and Tottenham only equalising after Lineker had missed a penalty. I never thought we'd actually win; and even then it was after extra time and a Des Walker own goal.

Dad was unimpressed. 'Two–one. Just scraped home, I suppose.'

'Plenty of incident, Dad.'

'I suppose so.'

We watched Gary Mabbutt hold the cup aloft but then Dad wanted to get home and beat the crowds.

'Not much of a victory.'

'It could have been worse, Dad.'

'Gascoigne was a disgrace. And Lineker missing a penalty! He took it too quick, that was the problem. It was like he wanted to get it over with. He should have taken his time.'

'We won, Dad, that's all that matters.'

'Don't suppose I'll be coming to one of these again. Another thing to tick off . . .'

'You never know, Dad . . .'

'I do know, son. I'm as creaky as the Tottenham defence these days.'

Three years later, I tried to persuade him to move down and stay with us. We could have built an extension or converted the basement, but it was far from his friends and, besides, he told me, 'It's a different coast; I'm Canvey. I don't want to be with dying charlies in the south. I've always hated Eastbourne.'

'Not Eastbourne: Brighton, Dad.'

'Lot of actors and nancy boys . . .'

'It's not like that . . .'

In the end, we found a residential home on the island that claimed to offer every comfort: own furniture if wished, wheelchair access and stair lift, pets by arrangement. It was a well-proportioned building with a glassed-in widows' walk and a conservatory facing the sea, promising 'the peace and tranquillity your loved-ones deserve', which might, I realised, mean silence and despair. But at least it wasn't far from his favourite pub.

The home had once been a hotel that had made the mistake of setting its standards of décor too low for a family holiday and its morals too high for adultery. The two-star wallpaper remained together with the swirling carpet and the linoleum in the hallways. Now it had gained the fustiness of rooms without air, the faint but persistent scent of urine and the bright efficiency of a matronly woman in a blue suit which looked like a uniform but wasn't.

Mrs Harrison was a less fortunate version of Vi, with well-groomed hair, sharp nail varnish and a laugh so loud that I imagined it hid the desperate sadness of a once-lost love. Her bright smile said only one thing: 'Please, please, don't talk to me about the past.'

I walked past the other old boys in the home: those who had made the mistake of never marrying, or of being the youngest child in a family where everyone else had died; of not being rich, or of not having children. One of them was singing a Scottish ballad to companions whose hearts were kept going by surgery, stents and pacemakers. Another was scratching at his scalp, letting the dandruff fall before his eyes.

'Still snowing,' he laughed.

Dad sat in a motorised wheelchair, his herringbone coat on, a tweed cap by his side.

'Hello, son.'

'I'm not late?'

'No. Not late,' Dad echoed, his voice made distant by emphysema. 'But the pub'll be open.'

'Where are we going?' I asked.

'Where do you think? We'll find a corner in the Canute. It's too hot to be outside on a day like this, don't you think?'

'You could take your coat off.'

'I like my coat.'

I looked at the old studio photograph of my family on the wall: Lucy in a gingham dress, Claire and me smiling behind her.

'I booked the chair with Mrs Harrison,' said Dad. 'It was my turn anyway. I won't be able to walk back after a skinful.'

'I hope you'll be careful,' the housekeeper said.

'Well, I've had enough time to get ready. Don't get many visitors round here, son. Only you and Vi. She's still at the house in Cedar Road: you remember?'

'Of course.'

'No Claire?'

'She has to see her parents. And she's working.'

'Doing what?'

'She's training to be a therapist.'

'I thought she was the one that needed the therapy.'

'Don't, Dad.'

'What about Lucy?'

'She's at school. You know that.' I decided not to reveal that she had been sent home after a particularly challenging assembly in which she and a group of friends had turned the Monkees' 'I'm a Believer' into 'I'm a Crack Dealer'.

'Still at least you're here. You've got the time. That's one thing.'

'I've been busy too.'

'Oh, you're not busy. You've never put your arm out straight.'

He wheeled past the conservatory and the men without visitors, residents no longer in control of their lives. They could not choose the meals, or their timing, or the colour of their room. They could not decide what they wanted to watch on the telly, or the volume, or the chair they sat in. *God*, I thought, *they can no longer even decide when to put on their socks and shoes, their pants or their shirts, so dependent are they on the routine of others.*

'Come on, son, what are we waiting for? Open the door.'

Dad revved his wheelchair and sped out through the French doors and into the street. He had decided, long ago, to treat old age as a sick joke which could only be countered with a steady supply of alcohol. He was determined that both its benefits and its disadvantages should outrun any possibility of Alzheimer's. It would be the quicker oblivion.

'I never expected this,' my father called back as I struggled to keep up.

'What do you mean, Dad?'

'Being old, what do you think I mean? It's like they've changed the rules of the game without telling me.'

'You're all right.'

'Sometimes I can feel my own dead body growing inside me.'

He turned down into Long Road and approached a group of schoolboys lighting up. They were blocking his path and didn't look like moving but Dad rang a little bell on his wheelchair and wheezed out, 'Coming through.' He had no intention of stopping and the boys were at first annoyed, and then amused, by the speed at which Dad made his royal progress through the streets.

I wished I could have talked to him as an equal: when he was at his best, as a young man with hope and love before him.

'You never know when the ref's gonna blow the final whistle, son. You can't even tell when it's half time.'

'I'll get you a pint, Dad.'

'Be all right with some beer inside me.'

There was a table free by the door, directly in the draught, but I knew Dad would like the breeze.

I went to the bar and ordered two pints of IPA from a girl in a black-and-white striped top. The pub was scattered with single people sitting at small round tables smoking or silently staring into space, their activity confined to picking up a pint, lighting a cigarette, or turning the page of a newspaper (GERMAN FISH FINGERS ARE BEST, SAY TESCO).

I returned with the drinks and watched Dad survey the scene, his large waterlogged hands resting on the edge of the table. I could not imagine that I would ever think like my father, or be like him; and yet now here I was, with my daughter looking at me in the same way that I looked at my father and Vi: with disbelief, and with a hint of pity and revulsion; how could anyone be so *old*?

'Here you go, Dad.'

How long, I thought, *how long will it be till I am like him?*

Len

I couldn't decide what Martin was up to. I only hoped his visit wasn't an excuse to see Linda again. You could never tell with him.

'Give us a fag,' I said.

Martin produced a packet of ten, bought to con himself that he no longer smoked twenty a day.

'I read in the paper they're going to make the health warning bigger,' I said. 'They think smoking lowers your sperm count.'

'Bit late for that.'

'Oh, I don't know. I don't like to tell tales but one of the boys, Chuckie, gets helped out by the nurses.'

'Not Mrs Harrison?'

'No. Another one. Georgia.'

'The one who's not quite all there?'

'Well, she makes up for it, I can tell you. Ten quid. Extra relief.'

'You're joking.'

'Why would I do that? God's truth. He told me himself. "The lift may not go to the top floor, Lenny boy, but it stops in all the right departments." '

'I don't believe it.'

'Told me I should try it.'

'You're seventy-eight.'

'So? A few years ago one of the boys got the clap. Imagine.'

'That can't be true.'

'Then another. Nurse Georgia was making a fortune. I should think she could get through four in an hour. That's forty quid on top of her wages and no harm done. Wouldn't take her long. Not with those boys.'

'I'd have thought some might have difficulties.'

'Not with Georgia. She's some nurse, I can tell you.'

'Next thing you'll be telling me you're saving yourself for her . . .'

'The lads thought it was Christmas. Then someone read in the paper that regular ejaculation helps stop prostate cancer and they were all at it. Getting your leg over has become a medical necessity. People will start asking for it on the NHS. Do you think I'm making this up?'

'It has been known.'

We looked at the menu: a full English breakfast any time; a ploughman's with Cheddar, Red Leicester or Wensleydale; honey-roast gammon; quiche . . .

'I'll have the widow's comforter,' I said.

'What?'

'The sausage. And another pint.'

I began to assess the clientèle: a woman in a black polo neck with dance instructor written all over her; a thin pale man like the vicar we used to have, the one with the neck rash: 'Call me Terry.' He ran a series of self-defence classes and called them 'Boxing for Jesus'.

A waitress in a low-cut T-shirt that reminded me of Vi in her prime served the food.

'What are you thinking about, Dad?'

'Nothing,' I said.

'Dad . . .'

'What, son?'

'It's about the house.'

'You want to sell it, I suppose? Is that why you've come?'

'Things are a bit tight. I'm the only one that's earning, Claire's training and soon there'll be university for Lucy. I'm sorry but I had to mention it. We don't have to sell it, of course. We could wait . . .'

Until I am dead.

'A lot of memories in that house.'

'I know, Dad.'

'It's all right,' I said, 'I understand.'

'If you could just have a think about it.'

'I'm dying as fast as I can.'

'Don't say that . . .'

'You could always help me out, I suppose: a quick pill, or the pillow over the head.'

'Stop that, Dad.'

'All right. Get me another pint and I'll sign whatever I have to sign. I take it you've brought it?'

'What?'

'The legal document. Power of attorney. We all talk about it. The boys always joke that they can tell from the look on the relatives' faces when they come. They're always after something, trying not to show that what they really want is the money. Sometimes the boys string it out and pretend to be gaga when they're not. Chuckie signed his "Neville Chamberlain". His daughter thought she'd come too late.'

'It's not like that.'

'Will you give me pocket money?'

'Don't be daft.'

'Half a crown a week. Drinking money. Some duty-free fags, perhaps . . .'

'You can still write cheques. And I can too.'

'If there's any money left over it might pay for a few sessions with Georgia.'

'Who?'

'The nurse I was telling you about. I imagine you'd get quite a lot for a hundred grand.'

'Don't, Dad . . .'

'Why not? It's a long time since I've seen any action. Everyone was so much better-behaved in my day. Girls were fast if they caved in too soon. Didn't have the pill. Or the morals. Not like you and Linda.'

'I don't see Linda. I've told you.'

'Yellow card. Lucky it wasn't red.'

'I don't have to be told.'

'Well, I won't then. But I need some air, son. Bit of a wheel about.'

We left the pub and set off down the high street. *This used to be a nice place*, I thought, remembering when the island was full of day-trippers buying jellied eels and Canvey rock. Now it was falling apart: aggressive boys and pregnant teenage girls, all swearing away without any thought to who might be listening.

'I saw her only the other day, you know . . .' I said.

'Linda?'

'She was visiting her old mum in the home next door. She lives in a narrowboat, I think. The creek, you know, up by King's Holiday Park.'

'She married?'

'Didn't say. But you are.'

Martin

The house had been empty for so long that it was impossible to imagine its former life. It smelt of gas, damp and stale cigarettes. Unwanted post had jammed the front door with months of free local newspapers, pizza-delivery fliers and prize draws guaranteeing my father an annual income of half a million pounds for the rest of his life.

I opened the paper to look at house prices but could only find personal columns and trade directories; lawnmower maintenance next to massage services.

Desperate divorcee, forty-eight years with great body, seeks fit males. I'm eager for fun.

Stunning female, forty-four years, still good-looking, in need of thorough service after long boring marriage.

Eager-to-please ex-model, sixty-two years. Fancy meeting me? I'm 100 per cent genuine, better fun than younger women, and won't mess you around.

I wondered what it would be like to phone one of these women instead of Linda.

But why would I do that? I thought. *Why am I even thinking like this? What is wrong with me?*

I looked at the record player in the lounge, a Fidelity GF110. I remembered my father dancing with Vi as she held on to a port and lemon, her husband asleep in an armchair in the corner, his head lolling below the antimacassar. The records looked like they were waiting for a school jumble sale: Ray Conniff's 'Honey', Glen Campbell's Greatest Hits, the Charles Lloyd Quartet, Bobby Darin's 'Inside Out'.

In the bathroom, I found a small greying rectangle of Imperial Leather and a dried-up sponge in the space where the model of a trawler used to be. The showerhead was blocked with limescale and by the time the first trickle of water came through it was a pale and crusted greenish-brown. I tried to work out when my father must have last stood in a shower. Would he have sensed that getting in and out of the bath was too risky, or would the decision have been made after the first fall? How often had Dad realised it would be the last time he would ever go out in his boat, walk briskly or put on his socks unaided?

Outside the kitchen window lapwings were piping over the estuary mud. Two jets roared in tandem overhead, making their way back to Lakenheath, the sound far behind the sight of them, and then, almost in imitation, a marsh harrier hovered in the air, its wings fluttering before the kill.

I remembered my mother sitting at the window when it was too wet to go down to the beach, holding me steady, her arm round the back of the red jumper she'd knitted, and stroking my hair, laughing at the sight of the wind blowing the scarf off Mrs Morrison's head as she scuttled back to the dairy.

I began to clear the rooms, remembering that I needed to make them look large and uncluttered for the estate agent. I would be ruthless, discarding the past, bagging up objects for the dump, the charity shop and for sale. Then the house would need decorating. I phoned Ade.

'Bit short notice, Marty boy . . .'

'I'm sorry . . .'

'It being summer. Lot of people away. You can do cash, can't you?'

'How much would it be?'

'Eighty a day for each of us; then the materials. Do you want us to do weekends?'

'Does that cost more?'

'Not for you, but you might have to tip the boys a few quid extra: drinking money. Say twenty quid?'

'Each?' That would make it a hundred.

'No, don't be daft, for all of us. We're not taking you for a ride or nothing.'

I would have to raise some money and talk to the bank. At least I had arranged to sell some of my father's things: the furniture, the clocks and the bookcases. We should have kept the stuff we had from the fifties instead of chucking it away in the sixties and seventies.

I started to clear cupboards of crockery, trinkets and faulty kitchen machinery that my father had been given and never mastered: an electric mixer, a liquidiser, a juicer, which even Dad had thought optimistic when Claire had presented it at a birthday ten years ago.

In my mother's old desk in the bedroom, I found a set of keys that had not been used for years, the stubs of old chequebooks and discarded perfume bottles. It was an Edwardian bureau with lockable drawers. I remembered my mother waxing the drawers with the base of a candle to make them glide.

I pulled down the foldaway metal ladder to the loft and climbed up. I could see the dust circling in the light of the Velux window above boxes of memorabilia, papers and magazines. Tins of paint had been stacked under the eaves, their colour dribbled down the side: magnolia, duck-egg blue and dusty pink. Rolls of wallpaper samples leant against a Black & Decker workstation.

Starting with a tea chest from Ceylon, I found my old fossil collection wrapped in faded copies of the *Evening News* (*SUEZ SITUATION GRAVE, SAYS EDEN; LOVE DIARY NEAR SWEETHEARTS DEAD IN CAR*). All the objects I had discovered in the petrified mud of the coastline, the survivors of the brittle cliff strata, were here; the silicified trunk of a willow tree, seed-fern fronds, a shark's tooth, ammonites with curling French pleated shells and serrated chambers. At the bottom of a Start-Rite shoebox was an essay I had written on the Swiss naturalist Jakob Scheuchzer. I could see my teacher's marks in red. 'Very good, Martin. Excellent work.'

Scheuchzer was a name I had forgotten, but I saw my own childish hand telling of the book *Complaints and Claims of the Fishes* in which fossil fish complain about the flood being brought about by the sins of humankind and how they had suffered as a result. The great palaeontologist had produced a skeleton from the time of Noah, proof that a man had witnessed the Universal Deluge and seen the face of God.

I put the essay and the fossils back in the tea chest. An orange crate with MARTIN written in black on the side contained a folder of school reports and I remembered Vi reading the bad comments aloud, never praising me, concentrating only on those areas in which I should do better.

There was a school photo that must have been taken around the time of my eleven-plus. I saw myself standing with my arms behind my back in the third row, looking abnormally thin, my hair parted to the right. I tried to remember the names of my friends: Terry Osborne, Johnny Milner and Ade, of course, Adrian Burrows, already looking like he might do someone in if ever they crossed him.

Underneath was a picture of the football team and a beach photograph of me holding hands with Vi and my father and all of us laughing. I couldn't ever remember being happy in her presence.

I had hoped to find some memories of Linda but there was nothing; not even a Christmas card. I put the photographs back in the crate and picked out a manila envelope. Inside was a tinted colour studio portrait of my parents' wedding: Dad with his chest pushed forward, dressed in a three-piece civilian suit; Mum in a white satin dress and veil carrying a bunch of dahlias wrapped in white lace. A silver horseshoe hung from her waist.

Then there was a photograph of my mother under a parasol with George and a baby. They were arm in arm with the child between them, looking proud as they stood together under a striped awning with the sea behind. The baby must have been me.

I tried to imagine the lifetime of my parents when they were hopeful and the world was all before them, dancing the Gay Gordons and the Paul Jones.

I went downstairs and drank a can of lager I found in the kitchen. Then I put on one of my father's records. Frankie Lane singing 'That's My Desire'.

I thought I should phone Claire, go for a walk, get out of the house.

I packed the car with the rubbish sacks and drove on to the dump, past the Haystack pub where 'the fun never stops', the tattoo studio and chiropody clinic, and took my place in a queue of people listening to the sounds of summer. Nirvana's 'Nevermind'. REM's 'Nightswimming'. The Lemonheads singing 'It's a Shame About Ray'. Fans were phoning in with their stories of Glastonbury or of Guns n' Roses at the Milton Keynes Bowl.

At the dump, everything was being thrown away: beer cans and wine bottles from summer barbecues, white plastic patio furniture, branches of trees and stretches of wisteria from garden clearances. A ripped leather three-piece suite waited forlornly for collection. I imagined Claire's voice: 'Only men buy white leather sofas.'

People in shorts, socks and sandals struggled with heavy black bags between saloons and estates, fearful of car alarms or scratching the edge of the nearest Mitsubishi. They lurched up steps and catapulted their past into the compressor as Blur sang about 'Parklife' from a radio in the council Portakabin.

I imagined old computers, dead rechargeable batteries, ordnance and pacemakers, lying under the landfill golf courses of the future.

When I got back to the house the phone was ringing.

'I thought you wanted to make some money?'

'I do, Dad, I do.'

'Well, hurry up and make it. The bank's been on to me. Want to work out how much I'm giving away. Wanted to know if I could trust you.'

'And what did you say?'

'I said you were a lying deceitful little bastard. What did you expect me to say?'

'Thanks, Dad.'

'Found anything interesting?'

'Some old photographs . . .'

'I'd like to have a look at them.'

The following day Ade came with Nigel, Jason and Al to sort out the house. They began to steam off layers of wallpaper in the hall, some of it sticking and refusing to peel so that faded regency stripes bumped up against the brown and orange roses from the seventies, then a grey and pink skylark design, and finally the original blue thread was revealed. It fell away with the flaking plaster, taking whole sections of wall with it.

'Big job here, mate. Sure you don't want Anaglypta? Cover all this up?'

I could smell the paint at the back of my throat and on the front of my tongue. I even began to taste it. I kept brushing the tips of my fingers, rubbing off the thin film of white powder that had fallen like silent snow. Al and Ade, Nigel and Jason were laughing and whistling as they worked, singing fragments of songs while listening to *Sports Talk*, discussing Tottenham's chances, the purchase of Klinsmann and Dumitrescu and if Ardiles, the manager, was going to last the season.

They had found a wasp nest in one of the air bricks and were busy spraying the space before returning to steam off the paper, burning off layers of the past and replacing it with bare white walls and wooden flooring.

Ade was installing new sockets in the front room. 'You can never have enough these days, Martin.' He began to whistle, then stopped and looked up. 'I forgot to say, I saw that Linda of yours the other day.'

'She's not my Linda.'

'No, but you know what I mean. Told her I was doing a little job for you.'

'What did she say?'

'She said to say hello.'

'Is that all?'

'She wasn't that interested, to tell the truth. Still, I suppose it was a long time ago.'

'What's she up to?'

'Works at Spar, I think. Married to Dave, you remember, in the band . . .'

He returned to his work, adding another socket by the window, and I stood in the centre of the room.

She wasn't that interested, to tell the truth.

That night I cooked a fish pie. I had bought mussels, haddock, bay leaves, parsley and potatoes together with two bottles of white wine. I put the smoked haddock in the saucepan with the bay leaves and added the milk, letting it simmer for a few minutes. I opened the wine and looked out of the window as I had done every night as a child.

Don't let the giraffe in, Mummy.

What do you mean?

The giraffe. You said close the door to keep out the giraffe.
A draught. Not a giraffe, silly.

I began to rinse the mussel pan and melted some butter. I remembered my mother scaling, gutting and filleting fish with her strong hands, cutting off the fins with scissors, running the back of a knife against the scales from the tail to the head, slitting the stomach without sentiment, removing the gall bladder, then sliding the knife under the backbone from the head to the tail so the fillet came neatly off the bone.

I tried to think what it would be like if I'd had a different life, if my mother had lived, if I'd never met Linda, and if I'd never married. I wondered what it would be like if I rented some other place, told no one and never went home. Perhaps I could even disappear, like Linda's father. He had walked out when she was eight. The next time she saw him was fifteen years later when she had to identify his body. People did it all the time. Missing. I began to like the sound of the word.

I wondered what it would mean to go back and begin again, shrinking away from the second half of a life, the unknown approach of age and strain, and return to childhood where I once, despite my memories and misgivings, might well have been happy.

Linda would tell me, of course. She would know.

And why, pray? I heard Claire ask in my head. *Aren't I enough for you? What is wrong with what we have?*

Nothing.

So why return? Why can't you leave the past alone?

I want to see her again, I thought. *I can't discard it all as if it never happened, as if Linda was never part of me.*

You can't?

No. But this is why we don't have these conversations, I thought. *I can't describe it to you because if I do then it will hurt you and we will not be as you want us to be.*

I want you to be honest.

I know you, I thought. *I cannot talk about her at all, however much you say you want me to tell you everything. And I need to do this.*

Oh, you 'need' to, do you? And why is that?

Because I can't stop thinking about her . . .

265

You can't stop. Or you don't want to stop?

I can't stop . . .

Then you have to make a choice, Martin.

And it's because seeing her is forbidden, I thought. *Because it is the one thing I must not do. And so I cannot stop wanting to do it.*

NINE

Martin

It was a damp evening and mist hovered over the estuary. I could see the steam from the power station in the distance merging into the low rain clouds. I walked through shacks, shanties and allotments, listening for the chiming of ships' rigging. *If clouds be bright, 'twill clear tonight. If clouds be dark, 'twill rain – d'ye hark.* The outlying waters of Smallgains Creek lay in the distance and with it came the memory of looking for Saxon fish-traps and learning the Battle of Benfleet at school; an heroic defeated nation caught in the fog of war.

I was wearing my smarter work clothes, a fleece and a white polo shirt, jeans and Timberland's, but even this felt overdressed as I approached the edge of the island, a ramshackle world of roofing felt piled outside sheds, goose huts and chicken coops. The only businesses left were pubs, bookies and newsagents. I reached the creek where the boats were moored and headed across a narrow walkway, following the loops and swirls of the water as the waves retreated from the banks.

Linda's narrowboat was about fifty feet long, and it was decorated in traditional green and red with faded paintings in the picture panels. It was low tide and Dave was waxing the hull of the cockpit.

'Martin . . .'

'Dave . . .'

'We heard you might be coming.'

'I didn't want to trouble you.'

'Why would you do that?'

Dave scooped the marine wax from the tin on to his cloth, rubbing in the finish. 'It's been so hot I don't want the paint to blister or the wood to crack. It's a good day for it.'

'It's a fine boat.'

'We get by.'

Dave had the look of a man who had left his hopes in a pub a few winters ago and had forgotten which one. The eyes that had once possessed a bulging, thyroidal energy seemed afraid; the hair that had once been glossy and slicked was grey and cut close to the scalp.

'You all right?' I asked.

'Can't complain. It's a life.'

He'd never made it in the music business. Ade told me how he'd also been made redundant from the docks. He had tried a bit of chef work and earned money part-time in a friend's second-hand shop, but now he spent most of his time knocking about with boats: caulking leaks, doing a bit of stripping and repainting, repairing old sextants.

'Is Linda here?'

'She'll be back soon enough.'

I looked at his smoker's fingers, yellowed like my father's. His eyes carried a faint air of accusation: *if I'd had your privileges I wouldn't be in this mess.*

I didn't notice Linda arrive with the shopping. I only heard her soft voice and its cigarette rasp.

'Hello, love, I'm home.'

It could have been me, I thought, *it could have been me that she was calling.*

'We've got a visitor. A surprise. Like Ade said.'

At first I thought I had made a mistake, that Linda was somebody who had come to collect something. Her hair was longer and thicker, shoulder-length with grey curls. The shadows were deeper in the cheeks and her eyes weren't as vibrant as I had remembered. She was wearing a sky-blue cotton dress and espadrilles which made her shuffle slightly as she walked.

'Didn't expect to see you.'

'He popped round,' Dave explained. 'Been seeing his dad.'

'How is he?'

'He's fine.'

'That's good then.'

'I'm sorry, if it's a bad time . . .'

'No, no,' said Dave, 'you're all right.' He picked up a T-shirt. 'I'll have a quick wash and change.'

'What brings you here?' Linda asked.

'I just thought . . .'

'Tea?'

'If you're having some.'

I followed her through a pair of doors in the rear deck and down through the boatman's cabin. The walls had been decorated with roses and castles and the floor and coal box were painted with diamonds, hearts and circles. Deep pelmets of white crocheted lace hung from each shelf; pierced-edge china plates had been stuck to the walls.

'You'll have to take us as you find us, I'm afraid.'

I noticed how small the double bed was.

I watched as she packed away her shopping. Linda had never worn jewellery. Now there was a silver bangle and a wedding ring. Her lipstick was raised above her lips, and she wore pale-blue eye shadow that didn't quite match her dress.

She put the kettle on the stove. 'Here we go again, I suppose.'

'No,' I said. 'It's not like the last time.'

'I should hope not.'

'I'm sorry.'

'I didn't think you were interested in me any more . . .'

'Well . . .'

'I thought you made your position pretty clear.'

'I wanted to see how you were.'

'If I was alive, you mean.'

'I wanted to explain.'

'After ten years? Bit late for that, don't you think? A postcard would have done.'

'I sent one.'

'Oh yes. "Sorry. I'm so sorry. Things are difficult." Very good. Nice and concise, that. And then the end, "All my love, M xxx." All my love? I don't think so.'

'I meant it.'

'All my love. Well, let's see: there's the love for your daughter, the love for your wife, and the love for your father, your friends and your job. I'd have been lucky with five per cent. Come to think of it, that's about what I got.'

'It's a means of expression.'

Dave emerged from the shower and changed back into his jeans. 'I'd better be going . . .' he said.

'No, no, you don't have to . . .' I almost wanted him to stay.

'It's all right. I'm off.'

'You got money?' Linda asked.

'Enough . . .'

As soon as Dave left Linda turned to me and said, 'Do you want this cup of tea then?'

'Do you have anything stronger?'

'I've got vodka.'

'Wouldn't mind.'

'We can drink it upstairs. It's too hot and cramped down here. I'll get a tray.'

We went back up on deck and on to the roof. There were people in the other boats getting ready for Saturday night: young couples without children, miming telephone calls after they had turned to part, smiling and laughing, confident their love had a future and that nothing bad would ever happen to them. A passing dog-walker called out: 'You've got the right idea.'

Linda mixed the vodka with orange. 'What are you doing here?'

'I thought it would be nice.'

'Nice?'

'Well, I suppose that isn't the right word.'

'I don't know why I let you stay so long the last time. I told myself I wouldn't.'

'I'm sorry it got so out of hand.'

'Out of hand? For God's sake, Martin. You can't come into a woman's life and say that you have never loved anyone as much as her and think that it will have no impact.'

'It was true.'

'But did you mean what you said?'

'It was the truth.'

'Sometimes the memory of you fills my head and there's nothing else. It's

272

*you and only you and I feel this pain behind my eyes like I'm about to cry but
there are no tears left.'*

'I'm sorry.'

'No. I don't think that. You said that. To me.'

'I can't remember everything.'

'Oh, very good . . .'

'I just tried to tell you the truth.'

'The problem is, Martin, that a man's truth changes all the time.
Women go over and over what you say even when it's ridiculous. I
was once with a friend in the toilets as she was crying her eyes out
because her boyfriend had chucked her. He had told her, "I never
want to see you again," and she asked me, "What do you think he
means by that?"'

'You're exaggerating.'

'I'm not. That's what women are like. We listen. We call our
friends. Men say what the hell they like. They get it out of their
system, move on and watch the football.'

'I hadn't expected you to be angry.'

'Oh. And what *had* you expected?'

'I just wanted to talk to you.'

'What about?'

'I don't know. I couldn't imagine the conversation. I just wanted
to remember us being together.'

'Oh please, Martin. Don't give me that crap.'

'I'm sorry,' I said. 'I didn't know what I was doing. It was selfish of
me. But I missed you. I couldn't stop thinking about you.'

'You couldn't stop thinking about me?'

'Yes, that's right.'

'But you shouldn't have thought about me at all. You had a wife.'

'I know.'

'And then you left. Without a backward glance.'

'If I had looked back I'd have gone mad.'

'Well, if you had happened to have glanced backwards you
would have seen a pregnant woman of thirty-six wondering what
the fuck to do with her life.'

'What?'

'You heard.'

'But you didn't tell me.'

273

'No,' Linda said. 'I didn't.'

'Why not?'

'I don't know. Perhaps it was because I didn't think it would make much of a difference.'

'It would have changed everything.'

'No, Martin, I don't think it would have done. You'd still have gone back.'

'You don't know that.'

'No, I don't. But I didn't want you taking over or thinking that I had got pregnant deliberately to blackmail you into leaving your wife. I wanted some dignity.'

'Tell me,' I said. 'Please, tell me what happened.'

'God, I didn't want to get into all this. You've upset me now. You've upset me all over again. I can't believe how you keep doing this to me.'

Linda

'I knew I couldn't go through with it. I spent hours staring out of the window and playing the same record over and over. It was Billie Holiday singing "You're My Thrill". Then one day I'd had enough and I smashed it. I threw it on the floor and it broke into two. But that didn't do it for me, it just felt a bit pathetic, so I got a hammer and bashed it about until it was all in tiny pieces all over the floor. I almost sent it to you in a big brown envelope but then I thought no, you wouldn't understand, and besides, what would your wife say?'

'Why didn't you tell me?'

'It was too difficult,' I said, 'and in the end I didn't want the child to be yours, reminding me of the mess I'd made of my life. Once you'd left, it wasn't to do with you any more. It was about me. And I decided that in some way I deserved it for being so stupid. A mistake. And I was too tired and too upset and too scared to do it on my own. I ran out of confidence. And hope. And love.'

'You could have said. At any time you could have said something.'

'And you would have come running? I don't think so.'

'It would have been different if you'd told me, completely different.'

'Did you tell her about us?'

'It doesn't matter.'

'That means you did. So there's nothing special between us anyway.'

'There is, Linda.'

'No, Martin, Claire has everything. She has all the knowledge. I don't have anything.'

'I don't think it's like that.'

'Married men don't talk about their wives, of course. Not if they want something. And we, the other women, don't ask. But Claire's been fortunate. And lucky with me. You both have. I almost wondered if you worked that out – that I'd be safer for you than having an affair with someone else, someone you didn't know so well who might have cut up rough. Was that part of your thinking?'

'No.'

'Liar.'

'I'm sorry . . .'

'And now every time I pass a ten-year-old boy, I think: "That could have been mine if I'd kept him." '

'It was a boy?'

'Yes. Funny that, isn't it? I asked especially. You could have had a son.'

'I can't think about it.'

'You don't have to. But I do. Every day I think about it. I learn to look so that I can tell the difference between nine and eleven. I've done it for years, but I never say anything. I never told your father he could have had a grandson. Perhaps he would have liked that. But he's a decent bloke and I didn't want to upset him. He gave me some money. Helped Dave. Saw we were OK. I don't know, perhaps he guessed. But he did right by me. I like your dad.'

'Does Dave know?'

'Of course he does. I tell him everything. Isn't that the point?'

'He's a good man.'

'We survive. Unless you want to make us picturesque and romantic; salt-of-the-earth types who live by the sea and it's *Great Expectations* and Pip comes to visit and he's a bit too grand for them but somehow their lives are a bit richer and they've got something he hasn't. Why are you here again? Remind me.'

'My dad.'

'No, I mean here on this boat.'

'It doesn't seem right now.'

'I bet it doesn't.'

'Don't be hard on me.'

'Oh God, I'm not your mother.'

'I never asked you to be.'

'It's as well you found one in the end then.'

'Don't.'

'I'm sorry, Martin, I don't know what to say. I was never good at all this talking.'

'No, I'm sorry. I should go . . .'

'Have you got a cigarette?' I asked. 'That vodka's taken a hit.'

I couldn't quite understand how I had ever loved him, this strange middle-aged man on my boat dressed like something out of the Rohan catalogue. I wanted Dave to come home.

'It is irritating, you know, Martin: men wanting to be forgiven, men wanting to be told it's OK.'

'And so what should I do?'

'Not everyone can like you, Martin. That's what you have to learn in life.'

'But are you all right?'

'Yes, I'm all right. Of course I am. I get by. I've learnt not to expect too much. Nothing surprises me any more.'

'I should go,' he said. 'I suppose I just wanted to see if you were happy.'

'Happy?' I said. 'Do you know, Martin? I don't know what happy is.'

Claire

Lucy kept asking about her father and when he was coming back. What was he doing and why was he at home so little? She had that adolescent trick of always being one meal behind, eating her breakfast at lunchtime, wanting proper food at eleven at night. She always wanted to ask questions before I was about to go to bed. She stood in the centre of the room expecting me to entertain her; too old to be a child and too young to be a friend.

The questions were a mixture of homework, social history and personal interest. 'When did Kennedy die? What did the Mamas and the Papas look like? Did you ever go to a Who concert?'

I could see where it was going and tried to stop the follow-up: 'Did you ever do free love? Did you ever have an abortion? How many people did you sleep with before Dad?'

'How much do you really want to know?' I wanted to ask.

I took out my earrings and put them on the bedside table. I realised I could tell the story of my life through my jewellery: the hand-painted cameo left by my grandmother; the brooch given by my sister; amber earrings from Lucy; the emerald engagement ring and the gold wedding ring. I still had the silver bangle Sandro, my first boyfriend, had given me in Florence. Everything was perfectly agreeable; *I could have no complaints*, I thought, *but no one will ever undress me in passion again.*

I still wasn't sure Martin had got the longing out of his system. It certainly didn't help when he phoned and told me he'd seen Linda again. He kept saying I shouldn't worry and that his feelings were under control and that he loved only me and always had. He apologised so much that I thought it was going to be far worse than it was: not that it was good, but when he got to the end I had to stop myself from saying: 'Is that all?'

'Are you still there?' he asked.

'I am.'

'Aren't you going to say anything?'

I certainly wasn't going to make it easy for him.

'So,' I said at last. 'You saw her. Without telling me.'

'I'm telling you now. If I'd asked, you would have said no.'

'Too right I would. And how was she?'

'I didn't feel anything. I felt that nothing had ever happened between us. It was like we were strangers to each other.'

'And were you disappointed in that?'

'A little. I don't know.'

'What were you hoping for?'

'I'm not sure. Some kind of end.'

'And did you get it?'

'Yes.'

'Then I'm glad for you.'

'Don't sound so frosty,' he said.

Here we go, I thought, *when in doubt go on the attack.*

'You expect me to be calm about it?' I asked.

'Nothing happened, for God's sake. I didn't have to tell you.'

'I think you'll find that it's always easier if you do.'

'It's all right,' he said. 'I love you.'

'And is she married?' I asked.

'There was a man there. Dave. He was at our wedding.'

'And did you try to imagine what it would have been like if that man had been you?'

'God, you ask all the right questions, don't you?'

'Well, I've had plenty of practice. You haven't answered the last one.'

'I did,' Martin said.

'And what did you think?'

'I didn't like it. It made me think of you and how lucky we've been.'

'That's the right answer, Martin,' I said.

'I'm just glad it's over,' he said.

I didn't know whether he was talking about his confession or the relationship with Linda.

'So are you coming home then?' I asked.

'If I'm allowed.'

'Is that why you phoned?'

'Well, I thought I'd better check. And also I rang to see how you were.'

'Oh, I'm very feisty,' I said. 'On fighting form.'

I remembered the Bible my father had given us when we were married, his large confident handwriting on the inside: *Love never faileth.*

TEN

Violet

The whole family spent Christmas at my house in Canvey. That made Len happy but no one in their right mind would have said it went swimmingly. Most of the time it was easiest just to keep our mouths shut and watch the telly. *'Allo, 'Allo* was Len's favourite. He never stopped thinking the word 'sausage' was funny. Claire had that patient look on her face, which meant she wanted to leave but knew she couldn't, and Lucy kept reading the whole time; she was such a serious child. At least Martin had brought plenty of alcohol, catering for both sides as it were: wine for his family and beer for the rest of us.

Sometimes I thought Len and I were getting on a bit for Christmas. We had most of the things we wanted and never liked to be reminded of another year passing. We tried to avoid the kind of presents old people give each other: jar openers and padded trays for TV dinners, folding canes, extra-long shoe-horns and magnifying nail clippers. Len presented me with a black leather handbag and gloves to match and I gave him a couple of shirts and a pair of braces. I couldn't abide his worn-out old Tattersalls and never liked to look when his trousers started to sag. Age was no excuse for letting go, I told him, and I kept nagging him to hold his stomach in even when it was full of turkey.

I laid on some quiche, a cheese selection and a couple of salads for Martin's family; vegetarians never get any easier, I must say, and that lot didn't even like Christmas pudding. Luckily Claire brought over extra supplies and busied herself making cucumber dip and toasting sesame seeds before we had even opened our presents. Sometimes I wondered why I bothered.

Still, it was good of them to come, especially since Martin didn't visit as much as he should have done. I knew that Claire kept him on a tight leash after all the Linda business but I don't think any of them realised how few of these special times there were left or how much Len was beginning to fail. He was forever running out of puff, and sometimes he had this dreadful colour to him. It amazed me when people came up and said: 'You're looking well, Len.'

Looking well? I thought. *He's half-dead. Can't you see that?*

Perhaps it was all part of the great pretence of ageing. If nobody said too much out loud then everything was hunky-dory. But in his heart Len knew, I could tell that much, and when we were alone or he'd had a few drinks he came over all depressed and it was a devil to shake him out of it. One day we were driving past an old bungalow, and Len gave a little nod in recognition. He didn't have to say anything to me because I knew. He was remembering how the last resident had asked for his ashes to be mixed into the pebbledash when it was renovated.

'Me next, I suppose . . .'

'Don't be silly . . .'

'We both know it's true.'

'Well, don't go on about it, love. I don't like to see you upset.'

'Go on about it? I've hardly started . . .'

It was a Saturday night when he had the setback. We were in his room enjoying a nightcap before I went home. We'd had our tea but it wasn't late. The other boys were in the lounge, either playing cards or watching *Wheel of Fortune* with Nicky Campbell and that annoying Carol Smillie woman.

Len was telling me the latest about one of the nurses in the home, Georgia, who'd been giving one of the boys what they called 'a special' and it had all got a bit too exciting. He was so involved in thinking about the end of the story that he couldn't stop laughing, chortling and then coughing so that he could hardly breathe, and then there was this choking sound from his throat. I'd seen him laugh that way before, but it turned into a shaking thing like George used to get and he couldn't stop.

'Come on, Len, that's enough; just tell me what happened . . .'

He put out his arm, telling me not to interrupt. Then he looked round for a glass of water but there wasn't one to hand. I told him to lean forward so that I could give him a good bang on his back to get rid of the obstruction but he kept pointing at the sink for the water. He couldn't control his breathing, his face started to purple up, and I began to panic.

I went over to the sink as quickly as I could and he started to bend forward properly, taking it seriously at last, and I didn't know which to do first: call a nurse, bring back the water or give him a good sharp thwack.

'Len, stop that,' I said but he slid out of the chair and on to the floor. I think he was trying to crawl to the window to get air because he couldn't breathe. I knelt down beside him and tried to make him drink the water but he was gasping. I gave him a bang on the back because I still thought he might be choking, perhaps it was a bit of cake or something, but then there was this strange rasping sound, it was like he was drowning, and I knew I had to get the nurse. I prayed it wasn't going to be Georgia because even then I could tell that would set him off even more.

I got up, pressed the panic button by the bed, opened the door and shouted out down the hall. I'd heard people in the home calling out before, frightened voices saying, 'Somebody help me,' and they were ignored because everyone knew it was something they said out of loneliness. But this was an emergency. I pressed the panic button again and then returned to Len on the floor. I thought that if I could just get him sitting upright then I might have a chance of helping him breathe more easily, but he was like a dead weight and I couldn't hold him.

The nurse came in and told me to call an ambulance. I thought that was her job and I wanted to stay with Len but she was checking his breathing and then his mouth for any obstruction. Then she took out his false teeth.

'Go on, Vi,' she shouted and began to give Len mouth-to-mouth respiration. *I should be doing that,* I thought.

I went outside but then, in my confusion, I couldn't remember the way to reception. One of the boys playing cards asked me what the hurry was and I remembered Len telling me that sometimes they took bets on who was likely to go next. He said that recently his odds had shortened to 9–2.

I couldn't concentrate on anything, my head was a spin-drier, and all those men kept playing cards, but luckily I saw Mrs Harrison and she said she'd phone the ambulance for me. I was best staying with Len, she said.

'That's what I wanted to do all along,' I said.

When I returned to the room I saw that the nurse had put Len on to his side. It was such a shock to see him on the floor. I think part of me had hoped that when I came back everything would be like before, and Len would be sitting there with a rug over his legs wondering what all the fuss was about.

'He's still breathing,' the nurse said, 'but it's very faint.'

'What is it?' I asked.

She looked up at me. 'Cardiac arrest, I think.'

'But he was laughing,' I said, and even as the words came out I knew it was the wrong thing to say.

The ambulance came quick enough and I only hoped the traffic was going to be all right because the island had always been too small to have its own hospital. We had to go to Southend.

One of the ambulance men was a big black man, very strong; the other was a wiry little Scot, quite old he was, and a drinker, I could smell it. I couldn't imagine what they talked to each other about. They gave Len oxygen, lifted him on to a trolley and wheeled him out. I held his hand the whole time. I wasn't going to let him out of my sight.

He couldn't speak, of course, and I just sat with him in the back as we bumped our way out of Canvey, up through Benfleet to Southend. I think I wondered even then if Len would ever return, if he was perhaps leaving the island for ever and that this wasn't the way either of us had imagined it. Everything was coming at us and we couldn't make any decisions for ourselves.

'Don't die on me, Len,' I said. 'That's all I ask.'

Martin

For the first time in my life I ignored the turn for Canvey and drove on towards the hospital in Southend, passing the Avenue of Remembrance, with its tributes to road-accident victims, the dead flowers and wisps of cellophane tied tight round the trees. I remembered walking in the cemetery after my mother had died, the grass waves tilting back against the gravestones, and thinking of the way sailors sometimes saw the sea as fields in the height of their fever: calenture, it was called. I had even been there with Linda, imagining the grass was the sea, the reverse of the sailors' fever, kissing under the yew tree as night fell, reading the inscriptions, imagining lives that once had been: Charlie Pym, Stephen Pugh, Frankie Bailey.

I remembered my father showing me the graves of those who had drowned. Jimmy Fingleton, Malcolm 'devil by' Knight and Marty Pritchard. That's why I had been called Martin.

I remembered counting the ages, making lists of lives once led, so the numbers totalled hundreds and then thousands.

Sixty-seven years, sixty-two years, forty-six years, thirty-seven years, seventeen years, two years, one year and nine months, five days.

Beloved son, only daughter, devoted mother.

In affectionate remembrance, after a long and painful illness, rest at eventide.

The left side of Dad's heart wasn't pumping properly; there wasn't enough oxygenated blood going through his system. The pressure had risen in the veins and his lungs were swollen. It was pulmonary oedema.

He lay in a small room off the geriatric ward with a wan and frightened face, a cannula in his arm.

'I've brought you a bottle of whisky, Dad. In case things get desperate.'

'For God's sake,' he whispered, 'keep your voice down or they'll take it away.'

'Vi told me you were telling a joke . . .'

'Can't even have a sense of humour these days. Doctor already told me I had to give up the fags and the drink. Now I suppose it's jokes as well.'

He started to cough.

'Are you all right?'

He raised his hand, asking me to wait until he had finished. I passed him a glass of water and tilted his head so he could drink. Dad's hair was wet with either sweat or hair oil, but the rest of his face was dry; the skin slack and papery.

'Thanks, son. Next time make it a bit stronger.' Then he stopped. The geriatrician was making his rounds. He looked at my father and smiled.

'Bit more colour to you today, Mr Turner . . .'

'I'm doing my best,' said Dad and then whispered to me, 'It's all right for some.'

I didn't believe my father could look any paler. The doctor checked the chart at the end of the bed. 'We could be letting you home soon.'

'Dead or alive?'

'No, no. Once everything's back to normal.'

'I don't know what normal is any more.'

The doctor smiled again and moved away. Immediately Dad started grumbling. 'Don't know why I have to have one of them.'

'What do you mean?'

'You know . . .'

'Dad, he's probably very well qualified.'

'Oh, for an Indian gentleman, he knows his stuff. I'll give him that.'

'Then what is the problem?'

'It doesn't feel right, that's the problem.'

Dad knew he couldn't be rude about someone upon whom his life depended but he was determined to have the last word.

'Here, son, you know why Asians are no good at football?'

'Yes, Dad, I do.'

'Every time they get a corner they open a shop . . .'

He had never accepted the pace of social change: that it wasn't funny to bite the heads off black jelly babies or to say 'ten points' while accelerating towards an Asian on a zebra crossing. He still thought it acceptable to call West Indians 'one swing from the jungle', just as Claire's mother had shut her cat away when black missionaries had come to visit: *We don't want them eating Mittens, do we?*

'I know what I think, son. I'm too old to change now.'

'That's just an excuse.'

'I've seen what I've seen.'

Apart from the war Dad had only been as far as London. He didn't even have a passport.

I was afraid for him and fearful of everything that lay before us: not only my father's decline and eventual death, but also the future lives of my wife and child. Even on our wedding day I had looked at our surviving parents and thought, *Well, that's at least three deaths we have to get through.*

Out of the hospital window the sky was dull silver, like the back of a herring too late to sell.

Violet

Len made a bit of a recovery and we got him back home after ten days, which was a bonus because I couldn't abide the nurses in the hospital all calling him by his Christian name.

'It's Mr Turner to you,' I said. Coming over all familiar took away his dignity, if you ask me.

Len never did tell me what the joke was that had set him off and I didn't want him to start now. He smiled and told me how one of the boys in the home had died in Georgia's arms. 'Going out with a bang,' he called it and started to chortle but it was a much sadder laugh now, and all the energy had gone.

He started to have relapses, coughing up stuff that looked like candyfloss with blood on it, and I could tell his lungs were filling up, no matter how much they tried to drain them.

'I'm turning into a balloon, Vi,' he said. ' "Up, up and away in my beautiful balloon". I never liked that song . . .'

'Well, don't sing it then.'

'Can't sing anything any more. Nothing to sing about.'

'Now, now. Don't get maudlin.'

We could never get Len comfortable; that was another thing. Every time he lay flat he felt he couldn't breathe and we had to keep propping him up with pillows.

It took me a while to realise that rather than releasing Len home from the hospital to make him better they had actually sent him home to die. You could tell there wasn't enough blood going round his body and his chest was as white as lard. I'd never seen so much of it, it just kept swelling.

It was a Tuesday when it all happened and Martin was with me. I could tell something was up as soon as Len's breathing changed. It had a low rasping sound and his lips had gone a bit blue; cyanosis, the doctor called it.

He looked frightened and a bit anxious, like he thought I was going to leave, but I'd taken my jacket off so I don't know what gave him that idea.

'I'm not going anywhere,' I said, stroking his face. 'Don't you worry, Len. I'll always be with you.' It was hard to speak without a tear in my voice. He looked so frail.

Then he smiled, as if he'd thought of a joke.

I'll never be rid of you then. The only way I can get a bit of peace and quiet is to die.

He gave a little chuckle and I could see his eyes gleam for an instant, like something had lit up in his mind, and then he was gone. It was so quick that I thought I'd missed it. Martin did too.

'Is that it?' he said.

Len's face had stopped like it was frozen. Even though I'd been trying to anticipate it, the end came too early. It was like the end of a dance when you want to keep on going.

I didn't think I would know the moment but I did.

'Oh Len . . .' I said.

Martin didn't want to look. I couldn't comfort him because he was on the far side and Len was between us. I don't think he was crying but I didn't want to stare. Then I stood up, opened the door and let the world in.

The nurse came, leant over and listened against Len's chest and mouth. Then she tried to take his pulse.

'Just,' she said. Perhaps she didn't want to say the word 'dead'.

'He was such a lovely man,' I said.

'Dad,' said Martin.

Martin

I had to see to the undertakers, the death would have to be registered, and there'd be a notice in the papers, but I didn't know what to do first.

'Would you like to be on your own with him?' I asked Vi.

'Do you want to go, dear?'

'Just a bit of air.'

I walked out to the King Canute. It was about four in the afternoon and the pub was empty apart from three or four boys playing snooker and a couple of decorators who had knocked off early. I could already imagine my father greeting them. *Plastered already?*

The barmaid asked, 'How's your dad keeping then?'

'Very well.' I didn't know whether I wanted to spare her embarrassment or prevent her pity. I ordered a large whisky for the grief and a pint of lager for the heat.

'As long as he stays out of mischief. He's a good bloke, your dad. Very popular round here.'

I avoided the table where we'd sat before and watched the boys playing pool. It seemed too early to tell Claire.

When I got back Vi was busying herself around the corpse. She was wearing an apron over her blouse and skirt.

'Here, Martin,' she said, 'put these on.'

She handed me a pair of disposable gloves and closed the windows. 'I know it smells musty but we don't want him getting too cold too quickly. You fetch his clothes. We can't have him going into his coffin in his pyjamas.'

'What are you doing?'

'We're going to wash and dress him. It won't take long.'

'Don't the nurses look after that?'

'We're going to do it. It's only right.'

'But I don't know how . . .'

'Oh, Martin, don't be a baby. We'll do it together. We want him to look nice, don't we?'

She began to unbutton my father's pyjama top, exposing the white mound of his chest, the nipples indented and faded, the hair still matted with the sweat of death. She wrapped a strip of cloth tightly round Dad's jaw so that it wouldn't slump forward. Then she lifted his head and placed a towel underneath.

I went to the wardrobe and opened it to see my father's clothes. Vi had already sorted them in readiness for the charity shop: his donkey jacket and tweed cap; an Aran-knit cream cardigan with leather buttons; the grey shoes with a Velcro strap that he always hated but wore for comfort; the dinner suit and dancing shoes.

'There are some good clothes in there,' said Vi. 'You might find them useful. We don't want them going to waste.'

He's not my size, I thought.

'I've had a word with the nurse,' Vi said. 'Told her we didn't need any help. After all, we don't want strangers, do we?'

'Shall I bring his suit?'

'That would be best. And a nice white shirt. Don't forget the pants and socks.'

Pants.

Vi had laid out towels round the bed and was filling a bowl of water. 'Come on, Martin, don't dilly-dally.'

I hung the suit and shirt on the back of the door and laid the socks and underwear on the chair.

'We'll start with the eyes. It's best to do them first, when everything is clean. We don't want him getting an infection.'

I realised the only way to get through it was to pretend that Dad was still alive. His eyes had opened as the muscles relaxed and I only wished the undertaker would come and put in the caps so they would stay shut. I didn't want to look into their milky vacancy.

Vi wrung out the washcloth and handed it to me.

'Go gently,' she said. 'Wipe from the inner corner of the eye to the outer corner. Then dry the eyelid.'

I felt the soft pressure of my father's eyes under the towel.

'Don't be scared. It may be the first time, but it's also the last.'

Until she said the words it never occurred to me that I might ever have to do this again. But then I thought: *What about Claire, or Lucy?*

'Good,' said Vi. 'Now let's do the face, neck and ears. You wash, I'll rinse and dry. We want steady, even movements.'

'I don't know how to do this.'

'Don't worry. He's hardly going to complain. And I'll clean up if you do anything wrong.'

She began to pat my father's face. The eyes, temples and cheeks were hollow; the corneas were filmy and flat.

'We'd best take his pyjama top off now. It will make things easier. Here, Martin, get behind him and help me lift him up. I'll hold on to his forehead so his face doesn't fall forward.'

I put my hand in the middle of my father's chest, the other under his back, and lifted the dead weight of his torso. Vi eased off his right sleeve and folded the pyjama top across his back.

'I've got him. Let go and take the rest of the pyjamas.'

'Are you all right?'

'Just get on with it, Martin. I can't hold him for long.'

I pulled the pyjama top away and eased Dad's arm out through the sleeve. The flesh had yellow-brown pigmented patches and tiny blood vessels breaking through the surface.

'Shouldn't we do his back now?' I asked. 'While he's up.'

'That's not the order.'

Vi lowered Dad gently back, supporting his head as she did so, but it lolled over towards me, resting on its side. I was glad she had bound the chin. I could already imagine what it would be like if the jaw fell further, the open mouth like the last gulp of air before death.

We each took a hand. The thumbs had curled inwards, approaching the root of the little fingers. I wondered what would happen if my father's hand suddenly tightened around mine, as if we were in a horror film and he had come back into momentary life, and I remembered how, in my own bed at night, Claire squeezed her hand in mine as a final farewell before turning away into sleep.

Night night, darling.

I washed between my father's fingers, taking each one in turn. I wondered whether I should find a brush and scrub the cracked nails. They had already yellowed but the shrinkage of the skin made them appear to grow after death. The hair on the back of the hands might still yet. His breathing had stopped, but Dad was warm and there were marks of sweat on his face. They renewed themselves even after Vi had dabbed them away. I could sense the blood beneath the skin, the motions of fluids continuing in the minute vessels as if the body was alive even in its degeneration.

It didn't feel right to be wearing gloves. I looked at the water bubble on his fading skin, the veins more prominent than I had remembered, raised but already losing their colour. Then I washed over one of Dad's tattoos, the mermaid's tail with the word 'Lily', and I tried to imagine how proud he must have been when he'd had it done; with the future before him and love secured.

Vi folded down the blanket to wash Dad's chest and stomach. I couldn't decide if his abdomen had already taken on the greenish tinge of death or whether it was a trick of the light. I went over to the sink and changed the water, grateful for something simple and necessary. As I did so I looked at myself in the mirror and saw a tired hot face and three days' stubble. I wondered how Claire had ever agreed to marry me.

Vi patted my father's chest dry. 'Now let's turn him on his side. Towards me, Martin. Put one arm round his head and shoulders, the other underneath his waist and lift him across. I'll come round and take the legs.'

It was a single bed and I could see that we had to be careful not to tip Dad off the other side and on to the floor. I reached right over underneath him and pulled him towards us.

'What are you doing?'

'Making room. Now we roll him, Vi. You stop him so he stays on his side.'

As I lifted and turned I had a sudden memory of childhood – roly-poly down the hill. I remembered a slope, newly cut grass, lying at the top, closing my eyes and rolling as far as I could, opening my eyes to a circling, dizzy world. I had even shown Linda how to do it.

Roly-poly? At our age? Don't be daft.

'All right, Martin. Now we have to take his pyjama bottoms off. You lift and I'll pull.'

Vi took the elasticated waist and eased the trousers away. I saw my father's heavy white thighs and hoped he was wearing pants but he wasn't. His pubic hair was coiled and grey, but it was also sparse, almost downy, like baby hair; the penis limp and shrunken, the circumcised head overwhelming the stump. Below, the scrotum and testicles had swollen in death, resting heavily between the thighs.

I do not want to be here, I thought. *I did not ever think that my life would be like this.*

'Come on, Martin, don't be squeamish. I'll just finish up round here. Give him a good clean round the back. The nurse gave me one of these plugs to stop him up. I don't mind what happens after we get to the crematorium, but we don't want him soiling himself after all our hard work, do we?'

Vi soaped Dad's legs and feet, then lifted his penis and washed around as if she was cleaning the edge of the bath.

'Fetch his pants, Martin, there's a good boy.' She began to towel him dry. I put each foot through the holes in Dad's pants and then lifted him from the waist so that Vi could ease them on. We repeated the action with his suit trousers.

'Do you think we need his braces?' Vi asked.

'Well, he's not going anywhere,' I said. 'But you'll know, won't you?'

'Let's put his shirt on first. You can do the tie for me, can't you?'

I fetched the shirt from the chair. Although it had been laundered it still smelt of tobacco. The collar had worn and I wondered for a moment if we should buy a new one. Perhaps we should have bought everything new and clothed Dad especially for death.

'Lift again, Martin, nearly done.'

I was sweating from the heat of the room and from the exertion of moving my father. My breathlessness was just as his had been.

Vi put on the left sleeve, passed the shirt round the back and I put on the right. 'Let's button him up while he's still upright otherwise we'll have to keep pulling it out from the back. Hold on, Martin.'

She began to do up the buttons and fetched the braces, clipping them to the front and back of his trousers.

'Len never did like a belt. He thought it spoilt the look of the suit.'

Then she lifted the collar ready for the tie.

This is ridiculous, I thought. I had to climb on to the bed and kneel behind my father with his head supported against my chest so that I could put on the tie as if I was doing it for myself. A black tie for Dad's own funeral. I kept the knot loose, Vi fastened the top button, and I tightened the tie to the neck. Then, while Dad was still upright, we put on his suit jacket.

'You put on his cuff-links, Martin, and I'll find a handkerchief for his breast pocket.'

'What about socks and shoes?' I asked.

'His feet are too swollen for that. It's the top half that's important. Then I must do his hair. The oil's over here somewhere.'

I looked at my father's bare swollen feet, the trousers raised around his shins. It was as if he was about to do a spot of paddling in the sea. I pulled the blanket back over him and folded it down over his waist. I wondered whether we were going to have to clean Dad's teeth. Perhaps we were even going to photograph him like the Victorians did.

Vi lifted Dad's head and began to shake the oil into his hair, letting her fingers run through the grey-black strands. I noticed that she had taken her gloves off.

'There you go, my darling.'

It was as if Dad was alive but a child again and she was soothing him to sleep. She fetched a comb, parted his hair and began to brush it back. Then she reached into her handbag and took out her compact and blusher.

'He looks a bit pale, doesn't he? I'll just put some colour back in his cheeks. I know it's silly but I'd like him with us a bit longer.'

I took off my gloves and washed my hands. I didn't want the smell of death to remain: gases, ammonia, carbonic acid, nitrogen.

I wanted to phone Claire. I wanted to be anywhere other than in that room.

'I feel we should pray,' Vi said, 'even though your father said he never believed.'

What? I thought. *Just in case we can get him in at the last minute?*

'We might find it a comfort. We don't have to say anything out loud.'

She sat beside my father and took his hand once more. I stared out of the window because I did not think I could continue to take in the sight of my dead father, dressed in his Sunday best, waiting for his funeral without his socks and shoes.

Outside an elderly couple were standing at the bus stop. Perhaps they had just finished visiting a friend and were wondering how long it might be until they too ended up in the home. Perhaps they were thinking which of them might die first. As I watched them I thought of my own marriage, and Claire's words to me on our honeymoon. She had turned to me and said: 'I hope I never see you dead.'

I opened the window. For a moment I did not want to turn round. If I did so then everything that had just happened would be true.

'It's all right, Martin,' Vi said. 'I think I'm ready now.' She stood up, took off her apron and put on her jacket. 'The undertakers will be here soon.'

I looked at my father and could hardly remember him being alive: sitting at the kitchen table with a mug of tea and a plate of shrimps before it was light; tapping the packet of fags to release a cigarette; shifting in his chair before the look of surprise came to his face when he remembered a joke.

Now he lay waxen and still before me. There was nothing between me and my own death, no protecting grace.

Despite the drained pallor of the features. Dad's face began to glow in the diffused light of death. I thought that I should probably kiss him but I didn't want to say goodbye. I remembered the last joke he had told me, of a wife moaning to her husband, 'I think you love Tottenham more than you love me,' and the man replying, 'Don't be daft, I love Hartlepool United more than I love you.'

The undertakers came to zip him in a bag and take him away.

Mrs Harrison arrived with some of his possessions. 'These are his things: a few photographs; his watch and dentures. You can wait in the conservatory. I'll make sure you're not disturbed.'

'Is that what people do?' I asked.

'It's best if the undertakers get on with it themselves.'

I sat with Vi in the Lloyd Loom chairs and looked out at the sea view. In the distance, a man in a rugby shirt was skimming stones, teaching his boys to do the same, ignoring the black Labrador who was still waiting to chase a stick they had forgotten.

'You should have his stuff, Vi,' I said.

> *A coffee-pot without a spout*
> *A cup without a handle,*
> *A tobacco pipe without a lid,*
> *And half a farthing candle.*

'What's that?'

'Something I used to sing with your mother. About our dad:

> *My father died a month ago*
> *And left me all his riches;*
> *A feather bed, a wooden leg,*
> *And a pair of leather breeches.*

'I should give you these while you're here . . .'

'What are they?'

'They're just photographs. From the attic in the old house. I gave them to Dad.'

I handed her the envelope but she didn't want to look.

'Oh,' she said. 'George and Lily.'

'Did you take that?'

'I've never seen this one before.'

'And the baby is me?'

'I suppose it must be.' She was still hesitant. 'Lily must have kept it. You with the two of them. I thought all these had gone in the flood.'

She started to put them back in the envelope but stopped. 'And, look, here's one of me when I was young . . . and my wedding . . .

George . . . and one of Len too. He always was a looker. And he could dance; for a small man he could dance so well. All those nights upstairs at the Casino or over at the Kursaal. On a clear night they didn't close the curtains and you could see the stars over the sea. We were almost the same height and that helps when you're dancing, you can keep close, cheek to cheek rather than cheek to chest; a man doesn't have to lean down so much.'

She gave me back the photographs. 'You keep them. I don't need them.'

'Are you sure?'

'I like to think of the last time we danced together. We'd had such a happy time with the champagne and the memories and we just danced into and away from each other. He was so proud of me. He even laughed when I swapped my high heels for dancing shoes. "Still going strong then, Vi . . ." he said.

'I told him I was the last of our generation to wear them. I've always had good legs. They're the last things to go south. I even told your Claire that.

'Len laughed when he saw my shoes but I knew he was proud. "Amazing you don't fall over."

' "I can keep my balance," I said. "And I still find them comfortable."

' "I love a girl in high heels," he said and I shivered. I was still a girl to him. Always a girl. I'm going to keep remembering that.'

'You loved my father, didn't you?'

Vi waited. 'Oh no, I didn't love him,' she said. 'I adored him.'

Linda

I heard about Martin's dad. Dave and I even went to the funeral because we knew there wouldn't be that many people there. It was the kind of event the word 'smattering' had been invented for. A tape recorder on the back pew was playing old ENSA hits when we walked in: 'I Cover the Waterfront', 'Hey, Good Lookin'' and 'She Does It All For Me'. We sat halfway back on the left behind an old couple who weren't sure they had come to the right service. They kept looking round every time anyone came, in the hope of recognising someone, anyone, and finally decided that it would be easier just to ask us. We tried to be discreet because I didn't want Martin's wife seeing us. Ade turned up, which was good of him, and someone from the Navy, and Vi sat in the front on the right in her black hat and veil, the smartest person in the crematorium, a new leather handbag matching her shoes, her lace handkerchief at the ready.

Martin read from the Book of Revelation.

I saw a new heaven and a new earth: for the first heaven and the first earth were passed away; and there was no more sea.

God, I thought, *I bet it didn't take you long to choose that.*

Then he gave a tribute to his father, talking about the times when they'd gone out fishing when he was a boy and how they were more friends than father and son. He talked about how Len was amused by his granddaughter, and how supportive he had been to Claire when she'd had post-natal depression, and I wondered whether any of us really needed to know all that. Then one of the old boys' hearing aids kept going off and he couldn't stop it so anything Martin said was accompanied by high-pitched whistling.

The priest stood up and said that Len was 'one of life's great characters', which meant that he didn't know that much about him, and that 'the genial fisherman we all knew and loved' would live on in our hearts and prayers.

He told us that the people from the home had set out refreshments and that we would all be welcome to join them afterwards. Dave said he'd rather give it a miss. I didn't know whether it was the thought of the old people's home or the presence of Martin but I wasn't going to disagree. It was good enough of him to come as it was.

We both found it depressing, not just because it was a funeral and the end of an era, Len being the last of our parents to die, but because the service was all so matter of fact, not like the funerals we'd known after the flood. We were only in there for about twenty minutes and the next mourners were already queuing up when we came out. It didn't seem right.

Dave was still a bit distracted when we got back to the boat and I could tell it was because we had seen Martin.

'Do you miss him?' he asked.

'Of course not.'

'And do you still love him?'

'No, Dave, I love you. You don't have to ask.'

'Then I won't any more. It was seeing him again . . .'

'He won't be back,' I said.

'And you?'

'Oh, don't you worry about me. I'm quite strong. You know that.'

'Strongest girl in the world, you are.'

Ours wasn't a complicated relationship. We didn't have any great hopes or dreams any more. 'Life when the lust goes,' Dave called it. Once he was going to be the next Pete Townshend and I was going to be a great painter, but after all the drink and the setbacks and the failed ambition we had decided to live a simpler life, messing around in boats, earning money hand to mouth, surviving however we could. Sometimes friendship can last longer than love.

It was one of those rare days when even the weather was hopeful.

The tide was going out, water fizzing through the channels, the sea curling away from the land.

'Let's take the boat,' Dave said. 'Get out of Canvey for a while.'

'Where shall we go?' I asked.

'It doesn't matter, petal: canals, rivers, a bit of sea, who knows? We could even do the waterways, just the two of us.'

'You mean now?'

'What do you say?'

He started to untie the boat and threw the rope on the deck. Then he jumped back on board. 'Do you want to take the tiller?'

'We'll take it together,' I said. 'Is that all right?'

'Then let's see where the water leads us. I don't care where we go provided we have each other.'

A swift darted up in front of the boat and circled away. I stopped for a moment, taking everything in, knowing that I was happier than I had been for a long time. I listened to the knocking and the ringing of ships' rigging, to distant traffic, and to the last cries of the oystercatchers, singing on the wing. I could hear a radio playing in the caravan site, I think it was Youssou N'Dour and Neneh Cherry singing 'Seven Seconds', and I stood there with a light breeze on my face, listening to the music, letting time come to me.

Dave started up the engine.

'Straight on till morning?' I asked.

Once we were away from Canvey and all that was past, I would start painting again. I didn't know what. I didn't care. But I knew I would reduce my life right down into what could be trusted and known, and that I would be free, guided, as I had always wanted to be, by currents and tide, moon and stars.

'Are you all right, treasure?' Dave called as we headed out into the estuary.

'As long as you keep calling me that,' I said.

Violet

Nobody asks me for my opinion any more. That's another thing no one tells you about old age. People talk about the weather or the telly, and sometimes they ask a little bit about how you are keeping, but they don't stay long for an answer. Everything has to go on in your head because there's so little life left in the world outside. I think that's why so many old people go crackers. If the dementia doesn't get you then the loneliness will.

When I look back over my life, it's not always the big events that I can remember. It's mostly silly little things: a laugh at a party, Len taking my hand or George flying a kite that Christmas after the flood. Sometimes I'm not so sure that any of them happened at all. *Was I actually there?* I wonder. It's like I'm looking at a photograph of myself and thinking that the woman in it could be almost anyone. It certainly never seems to be me.

Of course I can't acknowledge how much of my life has gone and that there's so little of it left. I can't accept that Martin is no longer a child, that the men who mattered to me are dead, or that I am old. How many springtimes will I see? How many birthdays? And who will be with me to celebrate them?

Celebrate: well, there's a funny word for it.

I was a different person in the past, always up for a bit of larking. Now I'm more serious. I suppose it's because there's so much less to be larky about. And it's all gone so fast; that's what Mother always said: *gone so quick.* I never believed her when she told me. I thought I had ages and that she'd just wasted her life. I even thought that she was somehow to blame for her old age, and that perhaps if she'd lived differently and appreciated everything more then she wouldn't have found herself in such a state at the end. I thought it was all her fault. And yet, of course it wasn't. I know that now.

When you're old and alone you sometimes have to stop yourself thinking too much. You have to give yourself a good talking to, or have a chat with an old photograph. Imagine he's there with you for a cup of tea and a bit of a laugh. People might think it a bit mad but sometimes it's the sanest thing you can do. If you can't do that then you have to find things to look forward to and get on with it. No one likes a moaner.

Sometimes I think, *Oh, why bother? Can't I take a pill or something?* but then I hear Len's voice coming back to me all over again: *Come on, old girl. The last battle.*

And that's what it is. And I'm fighting it in every way I can. Mostly it's the small things, having nice soap and making myself presentable, but they all add up. I can still cook and I like to keep everything clean. It may be a bit vain but I think it's only common courtesy. You don't want other people seeing you when you're not at your best or without your make-up.

I do think about dying, of course I do, but I can't ever quite imagine it happening to me. George had the right idea. He must have known, walking off the jetty like that. And for Len to die with a chuckle thinking the whole thing was a joke, well, you have to hand it to him. Both of them knew how to go, whereas I haven't the foggiest.

When I do get scared I think of all the things my friends have said to me in the past. I hear their voices. I see their smiles. I remember the way they laughed and I try to imagine they're still with me.

It's the voices that matter most because when I hear them I can make myself believe that they haven't died at all. They keep talking, and laughing, and dancing, and they won't fall silent, I know they won't, because I am keeping their memory safe for them and they're always close by.

And in the end it doesn't really matter whether they are alive or dead because they are still with me and with all who remember them.

And then I think of the things I've learnt in life, and how you have to keep living through it as best you can, and that death is simply the last thing you have to get through.

I try to picture myself dancing towards it with everyone I've ever known in an endless reel, all of us changing hands, one and then another, each in turn, past all our memories and our fears towards a future we cannot ever quite grasp. The orchestra is playing and we have forgiven each other everything and we keep moving, dancing towards the light, and I can't ever imagine it ending because we are together at last and for ever, it's as simple as that, and no one is ever going to ask us to stop.

Martin

I tried to imagine Dad was still with me. *You're never bored by the sea*, I remembered him saying as Mum waved to us from a distance. I was a child then and her arm was raised high above her head. Her gesture swept across the sky, a rainbow arc touching the horizon to her right, the cliffs to her left. She was describing the world, waving hello and goodbye at the same time.

I walked along the coast to Holehaven. The pebbles underfoot were mottled like birds' eggs: pink-white, blue-black, dove-grey. I remembered my childish curiosity about such stones; how they could be sharpened by the tide to flint axe-heads, or used to light fires or become counters in a children's game:

> *One-ery, two-ery, tickery, seven*
> *Hallibo, crackibo, ten and eleven,*
> *Spin, span, muskidan,*
> *Twiddle-um, twaddle-um, twenty-one.*

A ship's horn sounded in the distance. There would be a summer storm tonight: violent thunder, cracked shards of lightning cutting through the sky. I thought of the walks I had known along the strandline, watching the sand turn to mud, the visitors departing, the end of the season.

I imagined my father's voice. 'Things keep coming at you and then one day it's all gone from you, son. The tide stays out and you know that you won't ever see it back.'

I remembered my mother still alive, and the house filled with laundry and baking, and how the shirts left to dry on the rack above the stove sometimes smelt of bacon when you put them on. She was always busy, my mother, washing, cooking and cleaning, never still. Nothing was ever wasted: not food, not time, not life.

I remembered her dusting the flour from her hands and coming in to sing me a bedtime song: *I'm a little butterfly born in a bower, christened in a teapot, died in half an hour.* I could still see her smiling down upon me, her hair falling across her eyes and her brushing it back, turning away, bidding me goodnight from the doorway.

I could hear her singing. *Ickle ockle, blue bockle, fishes in the sea, if you want a pretty maid, please choose me.*

Then I heard my father's voice. *Don't you worry, son. We'll be watching you.*

But you can't, I thought.

I can, son. I'm here. Always will be.

And I heard Claire's voice and the sound of Lucy calling: *Come back, come back.*

I walked away from the jetty, up on to the sea wall, and looked out over the sweep of the island. There, amidst the coastguard cottages and mobile homes, the gas cylinders and the oil refineries, were new buildings and new futures; homes as ours had been fifty years ago.

I tried to imagine what the island had been like when the Dutch had first reclaimed it: a meeting of river and land, the mist lifting from patches of earth, rock and inlet; water draining away through the sluices and creeks.

'We're special, Canvey people,' Dad said to me, 'and don't you forget it. We're islanders. We look out for each other.'

'We like simple things,' said Mum. 'A little bit of love and a little bit of family.'

I walked back along the seafront and watched the last of the swallows gather over the swing of the sea. The smell of the island hit me once more, of sugar and sewage, petrol and salt winds. River barges carried the detritus of the city on the ebbing Thames tide, out into the estuary where my life had begun. I waited for the silvered surface of the sea to darken with the last of the light; its turbulence calmed, the moon rising.

ACKNOWLEDGEMENTS

For a documentary account of the floods of 1953 I have drawn on Hilda Grieve's survey written in the aftermath of the event for Essex County Council and published in her book *The Great Tide.* I am also indebted to Geoff Barsby for his book *1953 Remembered – Canvey Floods* and for his photographic collection and advice. Patrick Wright took me, memorably, to Canvey for the first time and I am particularly grateful to him.

The water experiment in Chapter Three is taken, in part, from Fiona Dow, Gilson Gaston, Ling Li and Gerhard Masselink's *Variations of Hydraulic Conductivity in the Intertidal Zone of a Sandy Beach.* I am also indebted to Andrew D. Short's *Handbook of Beach and Shoreface Morphodynamics* (Chichester, 1999).

For the sections on Greenham Common I have been aided by Barbara Harford and Sarah Hopkins's important book *Greenham Common: Women at the Wire* (The Women's Press, 1984), by the film *Carry Greenham Home,* directed by Beeban Kidron and Amanda Richardson, and by Julia Foot's Timeshift Programme for BBC Four.

I am grateful for the stories, advice, ideas, anecdotes and opinions of Diane Atkinson, Georgina Brown, Nici Dahrendorf, Brenda and Gerald Davies, Louise Dew, Fiona Dow, Sarah-Jane Forder, Rachel Foster, Gaby Hornsby, Anne-Louise Jennings, Rosie Kellagher, Ian Kennedy, Mary Loudon, Joanna MacGregor, Juliette Mead, Susan Meiklejohn, Jamie Muir, Marion Nancarrow, Siobhàn Redmond, Lady Runcie, Charlotte Runcie, Lareine Shea, Mary Taylor and to Pip Torrens – early reader and true friend.

Special thanks to Alexandra Pringle at Bloomsbury, to Anna Ledgard, and to David Godwin – for faith.

A NOTE ON THE AUTHOR

James Runcie is the author of two novels, *The Discovery of Chocolate* and *The Colour of Heaven*. He is also an award-winning filmmaker and theatre director and has scripted several films for BBC Television. James Runcie lives in St Albans with his wife and two daughters.

A NOTE ON THE TYPE

The text of this book is set in New Baskerville, which is based
on the original Baskerville font designed by John Baskerville
of Birmingham (1706–1775). The original punches he cut
for Baskerville still exist. His widow sold them to Beaumarchais,
from where they passed through several French foundries
to Deberney & Peignot in Paris, before finding their way
to Cambridge University Press.

Baskerville was the first of the 'transitional romans' between
the softer and rounder calligraphic Old Face and the 'Modern'
sharp-tooled Bodoni. It does not look very different from the
Old Face, but there's a crisper differentiation between
thick and thin strokes, and the serifs on lower-case letters
are closer to the horizontal with the stress nearer the vertical.
The R in some sizes has the eighteenth-century curled tail,
the lower-case w has no middle serif, and the lower-case g
has an open tail and a curled ear.